PASSION'S JEALOUS CAPTIVE

Clint moved his hands over her, unable to get close enough. His lips moved from her mouth to press kisses down the smooth column of her throat. She moaned and opened to him. Her arms went around his neck, her fingers in his hair.

Suddenly, he stopped. Lacey had tended soldiers, lots of soldiers throughout the war. And they would have been putty in her hands — alone, wounded, doctored by a beautiful woman. Jealousy flooded him, and he saw red. He jerked away.

"I guess you've known a lot of soldiers, haven't you?"

Startled, she could only stare at him in shock. "I beg your pardon?"

"Soldiers! How many men have you led down the garden path, little miss prim and proper?"

"You, sir, are insulting." She turned.

"Not so fast." Unwilling to let her go, he grabbed her arm, swung her close, and crushed her against him. Then he lowered her to the ground and anchored her with his body. Finally, he had her where he wanted her. . . .

REBEL SEDUCTION

JANE ARCHER

ZEBRA BOOKS
KENSINGTON PUBLISHING CORP.

*To the readers who've been with me
since* Tender Torment
*or joined me later,
here's another romance just for you.*

ZEBRA BOOKS

are published by

Kensington Publishing Corp.
475 Park Avenue South
New York, NY 10016

First printing: December, 1990

Printed in the United States of America

Part One

Days of Fire

Chapter One

"Stop that train," Lacey Whitmore cried as the rain beat down, molding her clothes to her body. Lightning pierced the sky and thunder rumbled, shaking the ground around her.

A soldier in a tattered Confederate uniform held her back.

"Let me go." She struggled to get free, for through the rain she could see the single pale light of the train as it made its way down the lone track that snaked through the dark green forest of northern Georgia.

"Can't." The soldier held on to her. "We've got wounded on that train. It's our last chance to get them out alive. Randolph's Raiders are right behind us."

Lacey gritted her teeth. Three months after the end of the War Between the States, the renegade Yankee soldiers called Randolph's Raiders were more feared than almost anything Southerners had seen in the war.

"It's a trap!" She clutched the front of the man's shirt, desperate to make him believe her. "You've got to get everybody off that train or it's going to—"

A sudden loud explosion split the air as the train went up in fire and smoke, its three cars tilting precariously as it came to a stop.

Shocked, the soldier reflexively dropped to the ground, pulling Lacey with him. Instincts honed to a fine edge from four years of war, he glanced around the area, decided there was no instant threat from nearby, and pushed Lacey toward the cover of the trees.

"Stay there," he ordered, and started for the train.

But Lacey was right behind him. As she hurried to the wreck she heard the cries of dying and wounded men, slightly muffled by the falling rain as it began to put out the fire. Even though she was used to the sound of men in pain, experience didn't make it any easier.

Passing the soldier, she saw him helping two men from the first car. She didn't recognize either of them and saw no one else alive. Hurrying on to the second car, she heard the soldier call after her. She ignored him, nodding in approval when she saw a wounded man helping another from the second car. But she didn't recognize them, either.

She hardly noticed the tears rolling down her cheeks or her labored breathing as she stepped over burning wood quickly being extinguished by the rain. She stopped briefly at several bodies, then went on. She was relentless, searching until she came to the last car. A man hung half out of it, blood glistening on his face in the fire and lightning.

"Papa!" She ran to his side, then gently lowered him to the ground. Pulling a cotton handkerchief from her pocket, she wiped the blood from his face.

"Lacey?" His eyes fluttered open, then closed.

"Yes, it's me."

He attempted to smile, but the movement caused blood to trickle from the corner of his mouth.

She put a hand to his chest, felt the wound, and knew he hadn't long. Tears mixed with the rain on her face. "It's all right, Papa."

From around her neck she took a slender gold chain. Half a gold heart hung from it, glinting in the light of the fire. Pulling his pocket watch free, she found the watch fob with the other half of the golden heart. Slipping his half of the heart off the watch fob, she transferred it to the long chain and pressed the two halves together, creating one whole heart.

"Mama sent you her half of the heart." She opened his hand, placed the golden heart in his palm, wrapped the chain around his fingers, then closed his hand.

"Then . . . she's gone." His breath wheezed in and out as he struggled to stay alive.

"Yes. She died two days ago. From a sudden fever. One of the wounded brought it." Lacey clung to her father's hand, pushing aside her emotions so she could continue. "But she saw the train wreck in a vision just before she passed away. She said she'd be waiting for you on the other side of life if I didn't get here in time."

Gripping the heart, he smiled.

"Don't worry. I'll get you back to her." She felt his hand go slack. Suddenly, tears blurred her vision and she blinked. "Papa?"

He didn't respond.

"Oh, Papa!" She laid her cheek against his. There was no pulse, no shallow breaths. Dead. She swallowed hard. At least she had made it before he died. She had done the best she could. Her parents would be together now for all eternity. And it was only right. She had never seen such a love between any other two people. A lot of times she had felt left out, as if their love were so great there was no place for anyone else in their lives. And yet they had loved her. She had always known that.

Her mother had explained that when Lacey met her soul mate she would recognize him because she would always know when he was in danger. It was the legacy passed down by the women of their family from generation to generation. But in Lacey's twenty-one years she had never felt such a thing or seen such a vision. And she remained alone. She also thought it was for the best, since she had seen the loss and heartbreak of the war and she wanted none of it herself.

A hand on her shoulder made her glance up. The

soldier had followed her. He was tall, lean, and there was a pinched look to his face that meant he hadn't eaten or slept well in a long time. Firelight flickered over his face, revealing a mane of dark hair, several days beard stubble, and steely gray eyes. Rain soaked his clothes, revealing a hard-muscled body. Probably in his mid-twenties, but his eyes looked older.

He might have been considered handsome except for the narrow white scar running from his temple to the prominent cheekbone on the left side of his face. It gave him a dangerous, deadly look. Standing in the misty rain, he could almost have been the specter of death come to take more people.

Lacey narrowed her eyes. Death had already taken too many. If it were within her power, she would keep those around her safe from now on. She glanced down at her father. It was too late for him, but death had to realize that his time was done. The war was over.

"We've got to go. The Raiders are on our trail." He glanced north, frowning.

A sudden, unreasonable fury washed over her. If not for this man, this death specter, she could have stopped the train, then gotten her father and the wounded off safely. This man was responsible for the death of the last member of her family. White hot hate seized her and she jumped to her feet, lashing out at him.

"Murderer!" She beat at him with her fists. "If you'd listened to me, they'd all be alive now."

He didn't try to avoid the blows she rained against his chest. "There wasn't time."

"Yes, there was!" Suddenly, she stopped, clenched her fists, and stepped back, reminding herself that there'd already been too much violence during the war. Taking a deep breath, she briefly closed her eyes, controlling herself with effort.

"Was he a friend of yours?"

"My father." She glared at him.

10

"I lost mine in the war, too."

"But we could have saved mine."

"No time." He glanced around. "You can hate me later. Take revenge. Whatever. But right now you're going to help me get the men still alive to safety. We're headed for—"

"Whitmore cottage."

Surprised, his eyes narrowed. "How'd you know?"

"I'm Lacey Whitmore. I'll take you in."

"But the end of the line's not for several miles, and how did you know about the dynamite?"

"Later." She saw no point in telling him about her mother's vision, since most likely he wouldn't believe her. But her mother had recognized the track and known her husband was on it, finally coming home from the war. After her mother had died, Lacey had loaded a wagon and started out, hoping against hope she would be in time. But she hadn't. "Come on, I've got a wagon back in the trees. Let's get the men loaded up, Mr.—"

"Clint McCullough. But using the Whitmore name isn't good enough. You could be spying for Randolph."

"With my accent?"

"Accents can be changed. Let me see your left hand."

She was irritated at the wasted time but glad he knew to ask for what substituted as a password. She thrust her hand toward him, and when he took it gently in his own, a sudden heat leaped between them. Surprised, she wanted to pull away but made herself stand still.

Holding her hand up to the firelight, he nodded in satisfaction. A spidery-shaped birthmark the color of amber stood out against the paleness of the palm of her hand. He'd been warned to trust nobody but the Whitmore women with the special birthmarks. He rubbed a thumb hard across the mark, the rain making her skin slick. The birthmark didn't budge, and he hoped like hell he wasn't making a mistake trusting her.

"Thanks." He reluctantly released her hand, for she was making him well aware he'd been too long without a woman.

But he also realized that right now it wasn't just any woman he wanted. He wanted Lacey Whitmore. She wore a simple cotton dress, but it was soaked with rain and clung to a body well worth remembering. He wanted to hold her, but he also wanted to release her dark blond hair from the neat chignon that held it back from her face. Her dark blue eyes watched him cautiously. Her emotions were obviously under tight control, and he wanted those released, too. But he wanted to be the one who set them free.

Then he cursed himself for a fool. He didn't have time for a woman, any woman.

"Now, Mr. McCullough, why weren't you on that train?"

He brought his mind back to the problems at hand. "Call me Clint. I was scouting. That's why I know the Raiders are closing in."

She nodded, wishing she could trust him. But he made sense, and that was the best for which she could hope since there wasn't time for anything else. "If you'll carry my father, I'll show you the way to the wagon."

"We can't take a dead man. Wounded come first."

"You either load up my father, or you and your men will be here to greet Randolph."

Clint gave her a hard stare, judging her, then decided she meant it. There was no time to argue. He needed her help, and he didn't want to force her. Giving Lacey a curt nod, he picked up her father and started after her. The war had changed women, too. This was no fluttering soft-spoken Southern Belle. This woman was used to giving orders and having them obeyed without question. Just like he was.

12

He was well aware Whitmore cottage had been aiding wounded men and women through the war and during the months afterward, for it'd gained a golden reputation throughout Rebel forces. Somehow Whitmore women had managed to keep food and medicine available to those who were in need. And even more amazing was the fact that Union soldiers hadn't found them. Their home had to be well off any main road and a Confederate secret.

He was anxious to reach Lacey Whitmore's haven of peace and quiet. In fact, he wanted it so bad he could almost taste it, because he'd slept little in days and he didn't know how long he could keep going. But he couldn't stop now, not when so much and so many depended on him.

Lacey led them into the woods and stopped beside a large, sturdy wagon. Clint laid her father carefully in back, and she unfolded a blanket and covered his body with it. She stood for a moment with her head bowed, then glanced at Clint. He saw the hurt in her eyes, then she blinked and was in control again.

Trees kept the rain from hitting them very hard, and he was able to see her better. She was an attractive woman, although not beautiful in the usual Southern sense of the word. Instead, she looked cool, regal, almost untouchable, as if her passions and emotions had been long buried. Suddenly, he wanted to see the ice queen melt. Just for him.

He started to help her onto the seat of the wagon, but she avoided him and stepped up herself. Cursing under his breath, Clint grabbed the lead mule by its harness and led them out of the trees toward the train. He knew it was an unnecessary action and one that would probably inflame her, but he wanted her inflamed. Then he cursed himself for it.

As he led the mules up to the train, he could see the rain was finally extinguishing the fire. A black husk was all that would be left.

13

"We can't take time to bury the dead." He glanced back at her.

"They can't be left."

"If the Raiders find the train and dead bodies, they'll think they got us all. I hope. It could give us the extra time we need to escape."

"But—"

"There's no other way. We've got to think of the living."

Lacey hesitated, hating the thought of leaving the dead, but Clint was right. She nodded in agreement.

Five men waited. Three were lying on the sodden ground while two crouched nearby, watching over their unmoving friends. Clint stopped the mules, and Lacey stepped down from the wagon and hurried to the wounded.

"I'd better have a look at the worst of them now." She started to kneel.

Following her, Clint caught her arm. "No. There's not time."

"But we don't know how badly they're injured." She jerked her arm out of his grasp.

"It'll have to wait. I'll get them loaded, then you can tend them." He picked up one man and started for the back of the wagon.

Lacey frowned, unused to taking orders, but once more she agreed with his opinion. She glanced at the other men. "Aren't there any more alive?"

Two of them stood up, rain mixed with the blood soaking their clothes. "We're all there is," one replied.

Nodding, Lacey could think of nothing to say. She had seen too much of death during the war, and to have it continue here was almost more than she could stand. But she had to be strong . . . now more than ever.

While Clint continued to load the wounded, she smiled at the two men in encouragement. "Let's go ahead and get in the back of the wagon. I'll take care of

14

your wounds as soon as we get started."

Lacey assisted them to their feet and let them lean on her as they limped to the wagon. She helped them up, then watched Clint as he brought the last one. When all five were settled, Clint turned to her and extended a hand.

"Thank you, but I don't need your help." She wouldn't soon forget he hadn't help her save her father and the other soldiers. As she stepped up, he put his hands around her waist and lifted her to the back of the wagon.

When she turned a cold look on him, he shrugged. "Might as well save your strength." He'd enjoyed touching her . . . first woman in a long time . . . and it'd been worth a frown.

She stepped away from him, feeling as if his hands had burned into her flesh but giving no indication he'd touched her in any way. "You'll find the road we need around that large oak."

"Thanks." He walked into the woods where he'd left his horse, then brought him to the wagon. Tying the animal securely to the back, he glanced up at Lacey.

She was looking closely at his mount. "That's an excellent horse." She hadn't seen such a fine animal since before the war, nor such good equipment. The saddle, bedroll, canteen, and saddlebags all looked new as well as expensive. Suddenly, she became suspicious. Her eyes narrowed. "That looks like Union gear."

"You're right." He casually patted his horse on the nose, then pulled a rifle out of its leather sheath attached to the saddle. "Ever seen one of these?"

She ran a finger down the sleek wood frame. "No. What is it?"

"It's called a Spencer repeating carbine. Only some of the Yankees had them toward the end of the war." He slid it back. "It's fast and accurate. I was damn lucky to get it and this whole outfit."

"You sure were." She relaxed. Of course, he had

15

Yankee equipment. By the close of the war, Confederate soldiers were using as much Union clothing and weapons as they could get off battlefields. Otherwise, they went barefoot and wore homespun, butternut-dyed clothes, if they could get them.

"But I've still got my CSA belt."

She looked at him more closely. He wore Union blue trousers and a tattered Confederate gray shirt. Around his waist was a black leather belt with a CSA buckle. Attached to the belt was a black leather holster carrying what was probably a fine Union pistol, as well as a sheathed knife. His black leather boots were scuffed and worn.

Glancing at the men in the back of the wagon, two of them barefoot, she immediately saw the contrast. The other former soldiers wore ragged butternuts and carried no weapons. And then she remembered that upon surrender, Confederate soldiers had had to give up their weapons. She didn't know how they would now hunt for food or defend themselves.

"You know the price you'll pay if Yankees catch you carrying weapons like that, since you're a former soldier." She was worried. "It could affect us all." And she was even more concerned about how a weaponless Rebel had overpowered a Yankee so well armed.

"I know. But I think it's worth the chance if we get these men to safety." He nodded curtly, then walked to the front of the wagon, sat down, and started the mules forward.

Silently agreeing with him, she turned back to the wounded. They'd be safer with the weapons, no matter how he got them. She wished the men weren't wet, for that condition could weaken them. But as long as it rained, there was nothing she could do about it. At least the weather was warm, but flies and other insects were attracted to wounds. Talking soothingly, hardly aware of her words, she began to work, doing the best she could with the limited supplies she had.

Clint followed a narrow, rutted road, the rain making the ground soft. The wagon kept sinking into holes, and he wondered what he would do if it got stuck or they broke an axle. The only good thing about the weather was that if the Raiders decided to look for any survivors, their trail would be almost impossible to find. How Lacey was able to work with the movement of the wagon and the rain was beyond him.

Much later she joined him, handing him a hunk of bread. "This'll keep you going till we stop. It'll be night soon."

"Thanks." He took a bite, savoring the flavor and freshness. "It may not be safe to stop."

"I know, but we're all tired. And in the dark with this rain, the road will be dangerous." She leaned back against the seat and shut her eyes, obviously exhausted.

Clint rubbed the scar on his face, thinking about sleeping, thinking about the rain covering their tracks. "Okay, but we'll be up at first light." Glancing at her, he felt a sudden need to comfort her. But he pushed the feeling aside. He was all out of practice. "How're the men?"

"I've done what I can. One has me worried, but I think they'll all make it if we get to the cottage soon."

"Good."

"They'll sleep for a while now."

"So should you."

She noticed again how tired he looked and shook her head. "I'd better stay awake to help keep you going."

"I look that bad?"

"You mustn't have slept much in days. You can't keep on like that."

"Just get me to Whitmore cottage."

She shivered. "You don't know how many men muttered that in their sleep, delirium, or on the cutting table. Over and over they'd say 'Whitmore cottage,' as

17

if the words themselves could somehow keep them safe."

"It's had that effect on me and these men."

Pushing strands of wet hair back from her face, she gave him a questioning look.

"When you're out there, no place is safe. You're either hunted or hunting. When you're strong and rested, it's not so bad. But that doesn't last long. It's hard to keep going when there's not much food or sleep or hope." He slanted a glance at her. "So somebody tells you about Whitmore cottage and how the women will feed and heal you. With a vision like that in your head, you can keep going a lot longer."

She nodded, understanding.

"It was your father who told us how we'd get to Whitmore cottage safe."

"And we will."

"I'd like nothing better than some hot food."

"There'll be plenty of hot food and soft beds for you and the other men when we get there." She smiled wistfully. "And it'll be safe, too."

It was the first smile he'd seen from her and it made her suddenly beautiful. He wanted to touch her more than ever. Instead, he clicked to the mules. "Go on to sleep. You can take over later."

Hesitating, she decided she'd be of more use to everybody if she were rested. "Don't let me sleep too long." And shutting her eyes, she was quickly asleep.

He watched as her chin bobbed forward to her chest. She was obviously used to catching a few minutes sleep wherever she could get it. So was he. He glanced in back. The men were asleep. The forest was silent except for the rain, and it seemed as if they were suddenly adrift in a land untouched by war or strife or pain. Hidden in the trees, protected by the curtain of rain, he felt a tension ease in him and he relaxed in a way he hadn't in years.

Chapter Two

Early dawn light filtered through the trees, the songs of birds filled the air. Lacey jerked awake as someone called her name. For a moment she didn't recognize the man looming over her, then she remembered the day before and felt despair at the loss of her father and so many men.

"We've got to get going." Clint watched her, knowing she'd have been shocked if she'd realized how he'd thought of her during the night. If she hadn't been a lady, he'd have paid her price, any price, to ease the itch in him. It'd been long, too damn long to go without a woman.

Sitting up, Lacey pushed her hair back from her face and glanced around in concern at the wounded men. She stood up, then quickly checked each one until she was satisfied all would probably live, except for a man who'd developed a fever during the night. For him, she felt deeply worried. She turned to Clint, frowning. "We've got to get these men to the cottage soon."

"Let's get packed and on our way."

It didn't take long to reload. Clint drove while Lacey checked her patients, rebandaging wounds, trying to reduce the fever of the worst man, and in general doing her best to encourage them. When her patients drifted to sleep, she moved to the seat beside Clint.

"We should arrive by this afternoon." She smoothed

back her hair, suddenly realizing how dirty and un-kempt she must look. But what did it matter how Clint McCullough saw her?

"Will they all make it?" Clint's hands tightened on the reins.

"I don't know, but the sooner we get them out of this moving wagon the better."

"If you'll drive, I'll go back and check our trail."

"Raiders?" She watched his hands holding the reins, liking the long, straight fingers, thinking how strong they would feel if he touched her. Surprised at her own thoughts, she shook her head to dismiss them.

"I want to make sure we aren't followed."

"Go ahead. I'll take care of the men."

He glanced at her. "If I don't come back, keep go-ing."

"What do you mean?" She tried to hide the sudden concern in her voice but didn't succeed very well.

"I don't want you to wait in case I meet up with the Raiders and—"

"Don't say it." They shared a look. "Come back."

He nodded and handed her the reins, intentionally touching her fingers.

She stopped the wagon. "Take care."

Jumping down, he walked to the back, untied his horse, then rode off the way they'd come.

Worried about him, she pulled on her driving gloves and started the mules down the road anyway. She had five wounded men to think about, not one healthy one. But still she couldn't help wondering about Clint, having little else to occupy her mind except worry, loss, and pain, and not wanting to think about any of those things.

She tried to distract herself with thoughts of the cot-tage, of the warm welcome that would be waiting for them. She could enjoy a hot bath, eat good food, and relax, for Kate, Martha, and Jeb would take over as soon as they arrived. She thought of her home and how the windows would be open to allow cool forest breezes inside.

Of course, her mother wouldn't be there, nor her father. That would hurt, but they would be buried together in the small cemetery in back. She'd known she would lose them someday, but she had hoped it would be much later. The war had taken so many and her parents were definitely the casualties of war, even though it was officially over.

She would go on as she had during the war, helping the former soldiers as they made their way home. Later there would be fewer wounded to help and her life would return to normal. The cottage was mostly self-sufficient and she could continue to doctor people in the area. It seemed like a good life and one she had been raised to live. Yet she felt a loneliness contemplating it, and that was something she'd never felt before.

Her mother had often mentioned marriage and children, but Lacey had seen too many husbands and children die in the war. She was afraid of any more heartbreak. Perhaps it was better to have a safe, emotionless life helping others than to hazard the chance of more loss and pain.

Yet the loneliness remained, and nothing her rational mind conjured up could ease it. Finally, she decided it was because of the loss of her parents. Naturally, she would be lonely without them. Naturally, she would miss them. Still, something nagged at her, something undefined, a feeling of something growing within her yet unnamed. And she didn't like it.

Finally, she pushed all thoughts from her head and glanced around the forest, enjoying the fragrance, the sounds, the beauty. She had grown up in the thick northern Georgia stand of trees, ranging from pines to cedars to hardwoods, and she loved the area. It was home and she couldn't imagine being happy anywhere

21

else.

But there were still Randolph's Raiders. They had to be caught and brought to justice. Yet, with the end of the war and the collapse of the Confederacy, law was uncertain. The Union was only beginning to step in and take control, and people were mostly left to fend for themselves. Still, somehow, the Raiders had to be stopped.

She hoped the Raiders hadn't found Clint. She hated to think what they would do to a lone man. And the worry came back. He had been gone quite a while. Looking over her shoulder, she checked the men in back, then watched the road behind her. Still no sign of Clint.

As she was trying to decide if she should search for him after she got the wounded to the cottage, she glanced back again and saw him. Relief washed over her as she stopped the mules. He rode up to the back, tied his horse, then walked up and sat down beside her.

She started the wagon forward.

"I didn't find any sign of the Raiders."

"Good."

"I don't know. It doesn't make sense." He ran a hand through his hair in agitation. He didn't tell her he had worried about her the whole time he was gone, imagining the Raiders sneaking up and kidnapping her. At that point, he had shut his mind to what they might do to her.

"The rain probably washed away our tracks and they decided we were all dead like we planned."

"But where the hell are they?" He wanted to take the reins from her to be back in control, but he didn't think she'd take kindly to his interference.

"I don't care so long as they stay away." She flicked the reins over the mules' backs, obviously an experienced, competent driver. "We'll be home soon. There's nothing to worry about now."

"I damn well hope so." He glanced at the wounded.

"How are they?"

"Sleeping."

"Want me to drive?"

"No thanks. You can rest."

Relieved he was back safely and they were so close to home, she let herself relax. It would all be well now. She hadn't realized how worried she'd been. Shrugging the tension out of her shoulders, she watched as they passed familiar landmarks.

Suddenly, her vision tunneled and she was no longer seeing the road but Whitmore cottage. It was burning. A group of men, maybe ten or twelve, were yelling as they rode around her home. All had bulging saddlebags. Her three friends lay on the steps, their bodies bloody and still. A man rode close, his savage face surrounded by wild black hair, a full beard, and mustache. His piercing black eyes gazed right at her. Then he rode away, calling the men after him.

Just as suddenly as the vision came, it went and she could see the road again. But her hands were shaking, the reins loose.

"Lacey!" Clint grabbed the reins, stopped the mules, then took her hands, rubbing them hard. "What is it?"

Confused, not knowing quite what had happened, she immediately sought to protect herself. "Tired, I guess. Could you drive?" She pulled her hands out of his grasp, fighting the urge to let him comfort her. She had to be self-reliant, especially now.

He made her face him and looked into her dark blue eyes. "Are you sure you're okay?"

"Yes. Please, let's go on. Hurry." She was now filled with an overwhelming urgency to reach the cottage.

He snapped the reins over the mules' backs, and they moved ahead. But the dread he'd felt since not finding the Raiders' trail was stronger than ever. And Whitmore cottage no longer seemed a haven.

As he drove, she tried to collect her thoughts, repeatedly reliving what she had seen . . . or thought she saw. Lacey could come to only one conclusion: She had finally experienced what her mother had told her would happen when she met her soul mate, for she would always know when he was in danger.

She glanced at Clint. Surely the man responsible for failing to save her father couldn't be the man destined for her. She looked in back, realizing any of the wounded might be the one. Or someone at the cottage.

And then she rebelled at the idea of having no choice in the man she was destined to love. She would be no pawn of fate or her supposed legacy. She was probably simply overly tired and worried, especially after losing both her parents.

Still, a part of her was cautious, raised to believe in the Whitmore legacy. She turned toward Clint. "I think we should leave the wagon in a glade I know near here, while I go in on foot and make sure everything is all right."

"You sensed something earlier, didn't you?"

"I just think we should be careful."

"After four years of war, a man learns to depend on his instincts. Mine saved me more times than I want to remember. We'll hide the wounded and sneak up to the house."

"You don't have to go. Someone should stay to protect the men in case—"

"If the Raiders find them, it won't much matter. And there's no way in hell I'm letting you go in there alone."

She took a deep breath, reluctant to admit she wanted his help.

"The men can take care of each other. Dave's only got a leg wound."

"Then around the next bend in the road, turn off in front of a large pine. The road's overgrown but it'll take us back into the glade."

They rode on in silence. Lacey felt more uneasy all the time. She wanted to run the rest of the way to the cottage just to make sure it was the way she had left it, but she couldn't leave her patients and she had to be cautious. Tense and hot, she tugged off her gloves and dropped them to the floor of the wagon.

When Clint turned off, the wheels bucked over ruts and undergrowth, but he kept the mules moving and she clung to the side of the wagon. Soon they came to a small glade and he drove down toward it, limbs scraping the sides of the wagon. He stopped the mules near a pool of water, and she jumped down. He followed her to the back of the wagon.

"Dave, I'm going to leave you in charge." Clint handed the wounded man his pistol. "Do what you can if it comes to that, but we should be back soon."

"Trouble?" Dave glanced from Clint to Lacey.

"Just cautious." Clint slipped his rifle out of its sheath and took Lacey's arm.

She hated to leave the men, for they were her responsibility. "There's food and medicine in the wagon."

"Don't worry about us." Dave looked determined. "Make sure nobody hurts Whitmore cottage."

Lacey nodded, then started down a narrow trail that led from the glade to the house. Clint followed, and they both moved quietly through the woods, pushing aside clinging tree limbs, vines, and bushes. But soon they smelled smoke. Horrified, Lacey started to run, for she could see a reddish glow ahead.

Clint caught her arm and pulled her back. "Careful!" He hated knowing what they were going to find, but he didn't believe there was any chance of the cottage surviving now.

Swallowing hard, she realized they must be careful if they were to be of help to anyone. She cautiously began moving toward the house. When she knew they could be seen from the cottage, she knelt and crawled. Stopping behind an ancient live oak tree, she glanced back at Clint. He joined her and they slowly rose to their feet, concealing themselves behind the trunk of

25

the tree, then looked into the clearing.

Whitmore cottage was burning. At least a dozen men rode around it, their saddlebags bulging, their voices calling in triumph. And on the front steps lay three people, almost certainly dead.

Horrified, Lacey started forward, but Clint caught and held her.

"You can't help." He held her back as she struggled to get free. "The Raiders'd kill you, but not till they'd made you want to die."

She turned toward him, her eyes filled with pain. "Shoot them. You've got a rifle."

"No." He gritted his teeth. "One shot and they'd know we're here. I'd get some, but I can't get them all. If they find us, they find the others."

"Surely there's something we can do."

"We wait. I know it's hard, but we'll get them later."

Frustrated, Lacey stood still, unwilling to endanger the men in the wagon but also barely able to stand the sight of the Raiders circling her home. What she saw was her vision come true, although she could hardly endure its reality. Now she could no longer imagine away the truth of Whitmore legacy.

Watching the Raiders, Clint growled to himself. He suddenly realized there must have been a traitor on the train. It would have taken only one man to set the dynamite and that same man to pace them through the forest, sending messages to the main band of outlaws. Scouting ahead, they could have found the cottage.

"Do you know which is Randolph?" Lacey searched the face of each Raider as he rode by.

Clint pointed out a man, recognizing Shelton Randolph from a group photograph of Union officers he'd seen.

Lacey committed the Raider's face to memory, although she had already seen it in her vision, for this was the man with cold black eyes and wild black hair and beard. This was the man she would bring to jus-

26

tice, one way or another.

Clint felt her body stiffen, and he knew how much she wanted to get Randolph, make him pay for his crimes, somehow make everything all right. But it didn't work that way. Nothing would be like it was ever again. The injustice made him furious, but he controlled his temper. He had to, or he'd never complete his mission.

For, despite what Lacey Whitmore thought, he was not a former Confederate soldier. He was a Union officer. Born and bred in the North, he'd fought the war on the side of the United States, and he believed the right side had won. But that didn't mean he wanted Southerners hurt. He wanted the wounds healed as quickly as possible. And that was why he was here.

When news of Randolph's Raiders had reached Washington, he'd been offered the assignment because he knew the South well. His mother, who had died when he was still a child, had been from southern Alabama, so his father had let him spend many summers visiting his kin there. With that background, he'd been the right man to come South and hunt down the Raiders, either bringing them to justice or killing them if there was no other way. Right now he wanted to kill them, although he'd thought he'd seen enough death during the war to last a lifetime.

Watching the Raiders, he thought back to the beginning of his journey south. He had joined a group of wounded former Confederate soldiers making their way home from prisons in the North. It was a slow, agonizing journey, and he had decided to help them as well as build a cover while he gathered news of the Raiders who were last reported to be in northern Georgia.

He and the Rebels had been offered the use of a train if they could make it work. With horses and wagons scarce, they were desperate to get it moving. It hadn't been easy, but with his own skill and some parts he'd managed to get without anybody knowing where they came from, they'd headed out, often stopping to repair the track and pick up other former Confederates.

However, they had all known the track ended in northern Georgia. From there they didn't know how the worst of them would survive, for many couldn't walk. That was when a man, who Clint now realized was Lacey's father, had told them about Whitmore cottage and how he could get them there. The other men had heard tales of wounded soldiers going into the woods to the ladies of the cottage and coming out well and strong. With that waiting for them, they'd had renewed hope and determination to continue.

Clint gritted his teeth. But there had been a traitor among them, somebody who had stayed a step ahead of them all the way. And now Whitmore cottage was burning.

He focused on the Raiders again, determined to remember every face. When the outlaws finally began riding away, leading stolen horses, Clint looked down at Lacey. He was with the last Whitmore woman, watching as her haven burned to the ground.

Caressing her shoulder, he realized he now had another problem. Lacey Whitmore. He wanted her. But she was a Southern lady and he was a Union spy. If she ever found out the truth, she'd probably try to kill him.

Exactly why he felt so strongly about her, he didn't know. Maybe it was guilt. Maybe it was being too long away from women. Or maybe it was just pure lust. But whatever the reason, he intended to have her.

Chapter Three

"I've got to check my friends." Lacey stepped away from the tree, hoping against hope that even one of the people she loved might still be alive.

Clint let her go, but he stayed close on the chance Randolph had left somebody behind to watch the place or might decide to return. He figured the outlaws were long gone, but he wasn't taking any chances, not after losing the train and the cottage.

The heat from the burning house was intense, but Lacey ignored it as she hurried to where her friends lay. Kneeling, she checked Martha, then Jeb and Kate. All dead. Now there was no hope. Her parents gone. Her friends. The cottage. Tears burned her eyes. She wanted desperately to cry, but what point was there in that? It hadn't saved her father and it wouldn't bring back her friends.

Furious, hurting, she wanted to lash out and vent her anger, her frustration. But the Raiders were gone and out of reach. Suddenly, she felt so weak she couldn't stand and abruptly sat down near Jeb. His face was familiar, so dear. He'd been like a second father. She brushed smudge off his cheek, humming a Rebel war song he'd favored.

Clint knelt beside her. "It doesn't help how many times you see it, does it?"

She shook her head, continuing to hum.

29

"But it hurts worse when you know them."

Nodding, she smoothed Jeb's shirt. How many more would die before the war was truly over? How many times could she keep patching up the wounded and burying the dead before she was so hurt herself she couldn't give any more? Now she felt burned-out, just like her home. And yet there were more waiting to be helped.

She didn't feel as if she could continue, yet she knew she couldn't stop. There were wounded waiting for her in the wagon. Her father had to be laid beside her mother. Her friends must be put in their final resting places. And they had to move on to safety. Still, she didn't see how she could do any of it. Not now, not ever.

Clint squeezed her hand. "You're not alone, Lacey. You can trust and depend on me. Whatever you have to do, I'll help."

Even though she didn't answer him, she heard his words. It was good not to be alone, but who was he? A stranger who'd first appeared to her as the specter of death. Did death follow him? She looked around. Did it follow them all? No matter. She needed his help now. When she was stronger, when the pain of loss had lessened, she could go on alone.

"Come on." Clint lifted her to her feet, knowing he had to get her moving or she might simply give up. "You can mourn later. Right now we need to bury your friends and get away from here."

Standing, she forced her mind to work. "There's a cemetery near the old oak tree in back. It used to be a small family plot, but since the war it's gotten bigger."

"I'll carry your friends over there."

"Wait. There're shovels in the barn. I'll get them if you'll go for my father and tell the men what happened." She hesitated, trying to think of all that must be done. "And would you see if Dave can water the mules?"

"Okay, but be careful while I'm gone."

As she watched him walk away, she felt terribly alone. Everything she'd known and loved was gone. How could she carry on? Tears burned her eyes, but she fought to control them. Then she remembered her mother's words: *Daughter, you get through life one step at a time.* Yes, that was it. One step. She turned and headed for the barn.

Inside, little had been disturbed except that the horses were taken. Most of the chickens had also been stolen, but the ones that were left could take care of themselves since they roosted high in the barn. She set the cow free, knowing it would wander to the nearest neighbor.

Finding two shovels, she carried them outside, then went back and filled a bucket with rainwater. She carried it to her friends. Kneeling, she pulled a handkerchief from her pocket, then realized the stains on it were from her father. Blood. So much blood.

She felt weakness run through her body again as she looked at the handkerchief, then she remembered the strength of her family and friends. Nothing must stop her. She dipped the white cloth into water and carefully began washing their faces and hands. When she had cleaned them as much as she could, she straightened their clothes and hair.

Lacey swallowed hard and stood up. Rinsing out the handkerchief, she twisted it to get most of the water out, then put it back in her pocket. She dumped the bucket of water and set it near a tree. Glancing around, she saw Clint leading his horse into the yard, with her father wrapped in a blanket and strapped across the saddle.

He stopped beside her. "Let's take your father to the graveyard, then I'll come back for your friends."

"Were they all right at the wagon?"

"Yes, for now."

"Then let's hurry." She picked up the shovels and led

him toward the cemetery.

Stopping under the shade of the old oak tree, she glanced around the area, suddenly realizing how many dead had been buried over four years. Too many. And still more to go. She shook her head, feeling the pain of loss twist inside her.

She watched as Clint laid her father's body on the ground, then led his horse back toward the burning house to pick up the others.

Walking to her mother's grave, she bowed her head for a moment, feeling the smooth wood of the shovel's handle under her hand. How many times had she stood like this, smelling the rich soil, feeling the wind against her face, knowing she had to deaden her emotions a little more to keep going. . . .

And now it was time to put her father beside her mother, put her friends in the ground where they had helped to bury so many. For a moment she wished she were lying there, too. So still, so calm, so free of pain. Then it would all be over and she could rest. But she thought of Randolph and his Raiders, and she hardened inside. No, it was not yet her time to be laid here. It was not yet her time for peace. There was still unfinished business.

Taking another deep breath, she placed the shovel's tip against the earth, put her foot on the curved metal lip, and pressed. The shovel easily pushed into the rain-softened ground, then she pulled it out, feeling the strain across her back. But she was used to the aches and pains that came from digging graves, used to the rhythm of digging one spadeful after another. Now she was even glad of the physical release, glad to be the one to perform the last duty for her father and friends.

And she knew exactly how deep to dig to keep predators away, because she'd had so much experience. That was a sad realization, but reality nonetheless. She kept shoveling, determined to let nothing break her rhythm until she had the topsoil broken to perfectly fit her father's body.

Clint saw what she was doing as he led his horse back to the graveyard. Concerned, he dropped the reins and hurried toward her. "Lacey, I can dig that." He tried to take the shovel from her. "You're tired. Why don't you rest?"

"No." She pulled the shovel back, hardly breaking her rhythm. "I can't stop now. It has to be done right."

He hesitated, seeing her determination, knowing what it must be costing her emotionally. "Damn it, Lacey! You don't have to dig your own father's grave."

She glanced up, her blue eyes hard. "And who better to dig it?"

If he hadn't been through four years of war and untold deaths, he might have fought her, might have insisted she let him do it because he wanted to save her the pain. But he understood her need, and maybe digging the grave would help. "I'll go get the others, then start their graves. Where do you want them?"

"Near Papa's. They were all like family."

He nodded. "I'll be right back."

Lacey hardly noticed him leave, for her thoughts were on the job ahead, on memories of her father, of her mother, of the life they'd lived before the war. Happy times. That was what she wanted to remember.

Later, when Clint began digging near the head of her parents' graves, she glanced up and nodded in encouragement. It was going to be a long, hard job for both of them, and the wounded in the wagon waited, hopefully safe, hopefully still alive.

Clint settled into the digging and noticed the redness of the soil. Suddenly, he was reminded of all the blood he'd seen spilled on the earth and how it had soaked into the ground. But here it would have blended in, hardly noticeable. He felt his gut twist and knew he couldn't think of blood, or death, or Raiders.

Instead, he thought of Lacey, of her beautiful smile, of how much the war must have changed her. He won-

33

dered how she had looked as a young girl, and envisioned an open, smiling face and bright, questioning eyes. But then the war had come and she had become closed, protective of herself. What would it take to free her of the past? What would it take to free them all?

He dug silently, watching her, thinking about her. As the sun began its descent in the west the wind picked up, bringing the scent of wildflowers and grass to mix with the pungent aroma of freshly turned earth. And smoke continued to drift toward them as the cottage burned.

Lacey was aware of little as she dug her father's grave, and by the time she finished, she realized her hands were red and blistered. She should have worn her gloves as she always did, but she had left them in the wagon.

Noticing she'd finished, Clint stopped and helped her lower her father into the grave. Suddenly, he saw her reddened hands, but before he could do anything, she started shoveling dirt onto her father's blanket-covered body.

"Lacey, stop." He put a hand over hers, keeping her from shoveling. "You're hurting yourself."

"Please. I must do this. And do it alone."

"But you're tearing up your hands." He lifted one for their inspection.

"They'll heal."

"You need gloves."

"Mine're in the wagon and there's not time to go back."

"There must be some in the barn."

"I don't know." She hesitated, trying to think. "Maybe."

"I'll go look. Rest while I'm gone." He realized she wasn't thinking clearly, or else she wanted the pain in her hands to cover up her emotions. Either way, it'd do them no good for her to ruin her hands. She had wounded to heal and they needed her whole.

34

She watched him walk off toward the barn. He was right about the gloves, but it didn't much matter. She was going to finish her father's grave and that was that. Shoveling harder and faster, she felt her clothes stick to her body. She was hot, tired, and dirty, but nothing mattered now except making sure her father was safely buried.

When Clint returned, he was surprised to see how much she'd done. He took the shovel from her, then turned her hands over and looked at them. They were bloody.

"Damn! We don't need you wounded, too."

She looked at her hands in surprise. Now she could feel them burning, but before she'd felt nothing.

"I found a pair of work gloves. They're a man's but they'll do." He grimaced. "You can't put your hands in them like this. The wounds'll fester and—"

"I've got a handkerchief in my pocket." She pulled it out. It was damp and stained.

"I can't use that."

"It'll only be for a while. I'll take it off as soon as we've finished the graves."

He took the cloth and ripped it in half. "You're going to rest while I wrap your hands."

Leading her to the oak tree, they sat down. He braced her right hand on his knee, then tore narrow strips into one half of the handkerchief so he could tie it around her palm.

Halfway into bandaging her hand, he suddenly wondered if he was either a coldhearted Yankee with no feelings for her recent loss or if he'd been so long without a woman that this kind of nearness to female flesh was enough to drive him crazy. He was getting so hot he wanted to either throw her back into the grass and bury himself deep inside her or get as far away as he could. Keeping any kind of neutral ground seemed impossible.

Gritting his teeth, he finished wrapping her right

hand, then reached for the left. Touching her was getting so bad he felt sweat break out on his forehead. He didn't know how much longer he could control himself. But he held on long enough to complete what he'd started, then threw the gloves in her lap and stood up, making sure his back was to her.

He took deep breaths, willing his body to control, knowing if he moved now he'd never be able to walk in a normal manner. Finally, when he felt a little steadier, he glanced down at her.

She looked into his eyes and smiled.

He was almost undone, for she appeared so vulnerable, so trusting, so like *his* woman that he took a step back to widen the distance between them. It was either that or take her in his arms, and if he did that, he'd never be able to let her go until he had, in fact, made her his woman.

"Thanks, Clint." She stood up, pulling on the gloves. "You did a good job."

"Let's get back to work." He knew he spoke gruffly but didn't care. He had to get away from her. Hurrying back to the grave he'd been digging, he started shoveling hard and fast. He was amazed at the energy he suddenly had, and he realized that with Lacey around he'd probably be able to keep going forever.

Puzzled, she watched him a moment, then shook her head at the mystery of men. He'd been warm one minute, then cold the next. But she had no time to ponder his actions. She had to finish her father's grave. Walking back, she picked up her shovel and began working. When the earth was finally piled high, she stopped and leaned against her shovel. Done. Her father laid to rest.

She glanced from her mother's grave to her father's, then back again. She'd managed to join their gold heart and bury them side by side. It was what they had wanted and the last she could do for them.

After a quiet moment, she turned to Clint. He was

36

watching her with a hard glint in his eyes. Again she wondered what he was thinking, feeling, but knew she had no time to pursue it. Instead, she began digging the next grave.

As the sun set, they laid the last body in its grave, covered it with red earth, and glanced at each other in exhausted triumph.

Lacey looked out over the graveyard for a long time, thinking of each mound, each person who had passed through her life, some only briefly. Too many had died too soon and too violently. Now she must do something to stop the destruction. Instead of being the one who healed and buried, she must become the predator, the one to stop the senseless violence before it started.

Making a personal commitment to each and every grave, she turned to Clint. "I'm going after Randolph and his Raiders just as soon as we've taken the wounded to safety."

"You don't have to do that, Lacey. I'm going after them."

"This is personal, and I'm going to see those men don't destroy anyone else."

"I don't want to see you hurt."

"I'm already hurt. Can't you see that?"

He wished he didn't understand, but he did. They all hurt from the war. "We'll talk about it later." He had enough problems without dealing with her while he stalked Randolph. Besides, he wanted her someplace safe.

"Fine, but my decision's made." She put her shovel on her shoulder and started for the barn.

Clint followed, wondering how he was going to talk her out of going after Randolph's Raiders and how the hell he was going to keep his hands off her, if he even could. She was obviously not an easily swayed woman, and once she got the bit between her teeth, he wondered if anybody could stop her.

In the barn she set aside her shovel, then pulled off

the work gloves and dropped them. The handkerchief bandages around her hands were soaked with blood and stuck firmly to her skin. She would have to soak them loose or risk starting the bleeding again. But she would take care of that later. Now there was something more important to do.

She walked to a far corner of the building, knelt, and pressed one of the floorboards. It popped up. Inside was a darkened oil cloth, which she carefully turned back to reveal a large knife. She lifted it from its hiding place, set it beside her, then withdrew a pistol and several boxes of ammunition. Last, she took out a leather sheath for the knife and a leather holster for the pistol. Satisfied, she replaced the board, recovered it with straw, then picked up the weapons and turned to Clint.

"I'm ready to go now." There was a glint in her eyes that challenged him or anybody else to try and stop what she was going to do.

"Let me carry those for you." First things first. They'd get back to the men, make sure they were safe, then make plans. Right now, he was just damn glad to see more weapons.

She handed him the gun, holster, and bullets. "I need the knife. Come outside and I'll show you why."

He walked beside her to a hickory tree in front of the collapsing cottage. Carrying his shovel, he decided to keep it with them. It was hot near the burning house and he watched flames continue to consume what little was left. Then his attention was drawn to Lacey.

She was cutting symbols in the trunk of the tree. When she finished, she turned to him, placing the knife in its sheath.

"Whitmore isn't the only safe house for the wounded. There's a network, and anyone coming here who is part of our group will be able to read this and know what happened. They will also know where to go next."

Surprised, he raised a brow.

"But we've got to make sure the Raiders don't trail us, if they're still in the area."

"I'll make sure." He was glad she trusted him enough to take him to another safe house, glad to know there was one. And he'd make damn sure nobody tailed them this time.

"There are also some supplies hidden nearby in a cave. We never knew when we might be found, so we always kept fresh food, medicine, and quilts in case somebody had to escape. It seemed like a lot of trouble at the time, but now I'm grateful for it."

He slipped the pistol into its holster. "And I'm glad we've got the extra gun and knife."

"Right. I can use them, too. Papa made sure I could defend myself." At the thought of her father and all he had meant to her, she once more felt tears sting her eyes. She turned abruptly away. "The cave's over here."

Chapter Four

After loading Clint's horse with supplies, they started back down the narrow trail leading to the glade. Silent, they listened for sounds of predators, Raiders, or other danger. But all was still except for the noise of their passing.

As shadows lengthened around them, Lacey wanted to be at the glade before it was completely dark, for in the forest there would be little light from the moon except in open areas. She glanced down at her hands. They hurt. She gripped the knife with her right hand and felt fresh blood dampen the handkerchief. But pain was a small price to pay for knowing her loved ones were safely buried.

She glanced behind her, noticing how tough Clint looked. A stranger. A dangerous man. She must remember that. If she had met him under other circumstances, she wouldn't have trusted him. As it was, she had no choice because she needed his help. But that didn't mean she shouldn't be cautious.

An owl hooted in a tree close by, and she hoped the eerie sound wasn't a bad omen. So much had already gone wrong. So many were dead. Now all she could hope for was getting the men still alive to safety. If the Raiders had found the glade, killed the men, and gone on, she didn't know how she could bear it. But she wouldn't think about that. All would be well. Still, she walked faster, more apprehensive than ever.

"Who goes there?" a voice called.

Startled, Lacey stopped.

Clint put a hand on her shoulder and squeezed, recognizing the voice. "Dave, it's us."

Lacey relaxed. Not the Raiders. One of their own. She glanced around for signs of the wounded man but saw no one.

A moment later, Dave limped into sight. "Sure glad to see you two."

"Are the men all right?" Lacey realized she was holding her breath.

"Yes, ma'am. That is, all except Billy." He paused, clearing his throat. "He didn't make it."

"I'm sorry." She felt a sinking sensation in her heart. If not for the Raiders, Billy would be alive. She struggled to control her renewed fury.

"We're all sorry," Dave said. "And you don't know how we hated hearing about Whitmore cottage. They've about got us all."

"No." Lacey's voice held determination. "There's another safe house. We're going there. You men will be all right."

"Bless you." Dave rubbed his wounded leg.

Lacey looked at him in concern. "Let's get you back to the wagon. We brought more food and medicine."

"I'm okay. But the others sure could use your touch."

"I'll bury Billy while Lacey takes care of the wounded," Clint said as they started down the trail.

When they stepped into the glade, Lacey looked at Clint. "Do you think we'll be safe here for the night?"

"If the Raiders had found this place, I think they'd have attacked."

"It's well hidden."

"They must have been satisfied with looting the cottage." Clint glanced around the area. "I think we're as well off here as anyplace."

41

Lacey felt a sense of relief but knew she wouldn't completely relax until they reached the next safe house. She followed Dave to the wagon. Clint helped her up, then handed her the kerosene lantern they had brought from the cave. She wouldn't use it long for fear of its light attracting predators or the Raiders. But she needed to see the wounds if she was going to treat the men.

While Clint and Dave went to take care of Billy, she lit the lantern, opened her medicine bag, put the knife inside, then began checking her patients. They were stable. What they needed now more than anything was peace and quiet and lots of rest. They could get that where she was taking them. She rebandaged the wounds, murmured words of encouragement, then closed her bag. It was all she could do for now.

Stepping down from the wagon, she went to Clint's horse and pulled off the bundle containing fresh food. It smelled delicious, for Kate had left fried chicken, biscuits, cheese, beef jerky, and bread. Once more she was grateful for the foresight. Her stomach rumbled with hunger, but she would eat last. First her patients needed food. She turned toward the wagon.

"Can I help you?" Dave limped toward her.

She shook her head in concern. He was going to hurt himself permanently if he didn't get off his leg. "Yes. I've got food for you and the men. If you'll get in the wagon, I'll have a look at your leg while you hand the food around."

"You don't have to ask twice." He hobbled to the wagon, then managed to lever himself upward.

Lacey quickly joined him. When he was seated, she handed him the bundle of food.

"Men, look at this!" Dave said as he passed around fried chicken. "I ain't seen nothing this good since before the war. And biscuits. I must've died and gone to heaven."

The others murmured agreement, then all were silent except for the moans and groans of satisfaction as they ate.

Lacey started to laugh at their happiness, then choked off the sound as she opened the bloody bandage on Dave's leg. He must have been on his feet most of the afternoon, taking care of the men and watching out for the Raiders. The wound looked bad. She'd have to be very careful now or he could get gangrene. And she wasn't equipped to cut off his leg, not physically or emotionally.

"How's it look?" Dave asked around a mouthful of biscuit.

"I'm ordering you off your leg for the next several days," Lacey said sternly.

"I don't want to go against your word, but if those murdering Raiders show up, I'll be up like a shot." Dave's eyes narrowed and he swallowed hard.

"In that case, yes," Lacey agreed, "but otherwise you're confined to the wagon." She finished rebandaging his leg.

"How're the men?" Clint asked, stopping beside the wagon and sliding his shovel along the inside.

"All right." Lacey pushed back a strand of hair.

"Best vittles I've had since my mama's cooking," Dave said as he bit into a chicken leg.

"You going to save some for me?" Clint grinned.

"Only if you hurry." Dave reached for another biscuit.

"Billy's taken care of, so I'm going down to the pond to wash off," Clint said, "but I expect some food when I get back."

"We'll save you some." Lacey glanced at her hands. "In fact, I need to wash off, too. Why don't I bring some food down to the pond."

"Good idea." Clint gave her a considering stare. "I'll take a quilt with me." He walked away.

"If you don't mind my saying so, you look plumb tuckered out." Dave stopped eating long enough to speak.

"Yes, but I'm hungry, too."

"Here." Dave bundled up the food and handed it to her. "We've had enough. We'll want some tomorrow." Then he lay down. "I'm all for sleep."

"You rest well. Clint and I will keep watch." She pulled a quilt over Dave, blew out the lantern, and picked up her medicine bag.

She left the wagon and glanced around, noting there was enough moonlight to see by now. She wanted nothing more than to relax, eat, and sleep forever, but first she had to take care of her hands. They were burning, aching, and by tomorrow would be stiff. She should have been more careful, but Lacey realized she hadn't been thinking clearly since she'd found her father dead. It was still hard to believe both her parents were gone, as well as her friends and the cottage.

As she walked toward the pond, she noticed Clint had spread the quilt near the water, then stretched out on top of it. As she watched him, he ran a hand through his damp hair, pushing it back from his face. Moonlight turned everything silver, casting long shadows. Again she thought of the specter of death. But no, he was Clint McCullough, and he'd been through the war just the same as she had. They were both simply trying to survive. No more, no less.

She set the bundle of food and her medicine bag by the quilt, then walked on down to the pond. Kneeling, she sat back on her heels, splashed water on her face, then held her hands in the cool, soothing liquid.

"How're your hands?" Clint watched her.

His voice was a low rumble that caused a tingling sensation up her spine. Surprised, she looked back at him. Moonlight glinted off the long scar on his face and she suddenly wanted to touch it, to comfort him, to take away the old hurt. She wished she'd been the one who had stitched up his face. Perhaps she could have done it better, perhaps not. And then she wondered at her thoughts.

"Lacey?"

She shook her head, bringing herself back to the present. "My hands?" She tested the bandage on her left hand. It had loosened, and she slowly began unwinding it. "They'll be all right, Clint."

"If you can't take care of yourself, I'll have to do it for you."

Again a shiver ran up her spine. She looked over her shoulder at him once more. "Who are you to talk?" And before she could mention his face, she bit her tongue, suddenly realizing he was probably sensitive about the scar. Turning back, she jerked the bandage off her right hand, felt the pain, and didn't care.

"I guess you mean my face."

She straightened her back, rinsed out the bloody strips of handkerchief, then walked back to him and sat down. "I'm sorry. I shouldn't have—"

"It's all right. It's not the only scar I've got, and it's probably not the last one I'll get, either. This one just shows a whole hell of a lot more."

She rung out the pieces of cloth, then neatly folded them in squares. Anything to keep from looking at him. "How did it happen, if you don't mind?"

"Saber cut. During the war."

"Damnyankees." She clenched her fists, felt the pain, and stopped. "They were determined to destroy the South, not just win. And anything they couldn't kill, they tried to maim." She turned to him. "Even now, they're still at it. Those Raiders!"

He'd never seen her so passionate before. Angry, hurt, determined, but not filled with passion. Suddenly, he wanted that passion for himself. He looked away, to keep from pulling her into his arms. "All Yankees aren't bad."

"How can you say that?" Her eyes gleamed. "Have you ever known a good one?"

He cleared his throat, wishing they were talking

45

about anything else. Keeping his heritage a secret was going to be much worse than he'd thought. "As a matter of fact, one saved my life during the war." And that was sure the damn truth.

She was silent for a moment. "I suppose they have family and loved ones the same as we do, but we didn't go up there and burn their homes, murder their women, children, and elders, or ravage their land. And then afterwards turn loose the Raiders."

He wished he could defend the North, but if she knew who he really was, she'd probably want to kill him. And he understood her pain. "Both sides lost a lot during the war. Fact is, estimates are a hundred thousand more Northerners died than Southerners."

"That many more Yankees died?" She was surprised to learn that, because the North had won the war. But perhaps it was simply wishful Rebel thinking.

"Looks like it. But now we need to go on and put the war behind us."

"With men like the Raiders running free? With carpetbaggers stealing what little is left?" She searched his face, suddenly realizing he'd always carry the pain and tragedy of the war for all to see. If he could put it behind him, perhaps she could, too. "Yes, we need to go on, but how?"

He took her right hand. "Give me some ointment and bandages, and we'll start here and now."

Tears suddenly filled her eyes. "You're right. One step at a time, as my mother always used to say."

She found what he needed in her medicine bag and handed it to him. She also found relief in having him take over for a while. He was gentle as he spread the ointment over the blisters, then expertly began wrapping gauze around her palm. When he'd finished, he started on her left hand.

"You're good at that." She liked his touch.

"Experience. Couldn't depend on a doctor being around, so we learned to take care of each other."

46

"And with so little food and medicine."

Again he knew she was talking about the Confederates, but Yankees had had to do without sometimes, too. It'd been hard on both sides. "We made it, Lacey. That's what counts." He finally let her hand go. "You'll have to wear gloves when you drive."

"I will." She hesitated. "I'd say I'd be more careful in the future, but I hope to never have to dig that many graves again. Ever."

"So do I." He pulled the bundle of food toward them. "Now, let's get some food down us."

Lacey was glad to change the subject, glad to eat, and she helped him unwrap Kate's cache. When she sank her teeth into a flaky biscuit, she murmured in contentment. And smiled.

Clint caught her expression, and as he bit into a tender piece of chicken, he winked.

Surprised to see this side of him, she realized just how hard life had been for so long. When she had been in the thick of survival, it had become a way of life, but now she could see how it might be different. What if there were time to simply enjoy being with someone else, sitting by a pond of water, eating, smiling, being close? Very close.

And then she felt a strange yearning to be closer to Clint, to be held by him, perhaps kissed. Surprised, she looked away. This was not the time for emotions or for getting involved with a man, especially a stranger. Wounded men still depended on them, and Randolph's Raiders had to be brought to justice. Still, there was something about him that called to her at a deep level.

"Lacey?" Clint had stopped eating and was watching her.

She quickly picked up a piece of chicken and began eating ravenously. Anything to stop him from looking at her, from perhaps realizing that for a moment she had wanted him as a lover. It was just the tension, the worry, the pain. The feeling would be gone tomorrow.

"I'm sorry about your family and friends." He rubbed the scar on his face.

"Thanks." She felt her chest tighten, unable to forget he hadn't helped save her father.

"There's not much I can say to help, but I can go after Randolph."

"I'm going to do that." She looked into the distance, her chin raised.

"You can trust me to do it, Lacey." He watched her profile.

"It's not that I don't trust you. I have to do this for myself." She glanced back at him, picked up a biscuit, then put it down.

"I understand, but it won't be easy." He wanted to keep her safe, but he knew how she felt. He just wished like hell he could tell her the truth . . . could be the former Confederate soldier she thought him to be. But, no, he had made his choice at the beginning of the war and it was the right one for him.

Moving closer to her, he took her hand. She didn't withdraw it, and he rubbed his thumb across the back of her knuckles.

"I've been wondering." She knew she should remove her hand from his, but she felt mesmerized by his touch. "Do you think the Raiders attacked the cottage because they thought we had hidden Confederate gold and valuables?"

"It makes sense."

"But there would have been no need to kill defenseless men and women. They could have stolen what they wanted. Besides, there wasn't much of value in the house. A few pieces of Whitmore heirloom jewelry would have been worth the most."

"Maybe they wanted revenge, too."

"But they won the war. That doesn't make sense to me." She felt renewed bitterness at the horror of the war.

"A lot of Union soldiers died, too, Lacey." Her skin was soft and he clasped her hand.

"Yes, of course, but—"

"I think your idea is the best answer we're going to come up with." He hesitated, wondering how much she would trust him. "And I think we should leave at dawn for the next safe house. Where is it?"

"Alabama."

"Exactly where?"

"I can't tell you that."

"You don't trust me enough?" He tightened his grip, then realized he might be hurting her hand and eased his touch.

"That's not information I would give anyone. I'll show you the way, but you don't have to feel you must stay with us. I can get the wounded there alone."

"With the Raiders on the hunt?"

"I'll be careful."

"You need a scout, Lacey, and help. Besides, I've been with these men a long time and I'm not going to abandon them now." He knew he shouldn't let the Raiders' trail get cold, but he couldn't leave Lacey and the wounded, either.

"Thanks. I admit you'll make the trip easier."

"Good. Then we'll go together."

Clint raised her hand to his lips and kissed the tip of each finger. She felt the sensation throughout her body. Without realizing it, she leaned closer, unresisting. He kissed the fingers of her other hand, then stopped and looked at her face to judge her reaction. Touched by his gentleness, she raised a hand to his face and lightly ran a finger down the scar.

"Are you repulsed by it?" He hated himself for asking.

"Oh, no. How could you think that?"

"Some women are."

"They're wrong." Her eyes narrowed. "It's a symbol of all you fought for."

49

"But you've seen much worse. Maybe that's the difference."

"Maybe. But it suits you."

He shook his head. "Thanks. Even if you're being polite."

Hurting for him, she leaned forward and lightly kissed the scar. Surprised at herself, she started to move away, but he caught her chin with his hand and held her face close to his.

"Careful, Lacey Whitmore." His nostrils flared, as if catching her scent. "I may be more than you bargained for."

Their eyes locked, communicating silently, then he lowered his head and captured her lips with his mouth. Heat leaped between them, and she moaned softly. He quickly put his hands on her shoulders, holding her, drawing her closer, feeling the heat of her body, feeling his own response.

Passion blazed between them. He deepened the kiss, pressing his lips harder, opening his mouth, seeking entrance while pulling her so close her breasts were crushed against his chest. He felt her respond, her lips parting for him, soft and pliant. Plunging inside, he tasted her sweetness, reveled in the feel of her, the power, the heat she created in him.

But suddenly she pulled away, breathing fast. Lacey looked surprised, confused, embarrassed, and she studied his face as if to find some answer to her sudden passion.

Clint controlled himself as best he could, but he hurt in his need for her. "It's been a long time." He searched her face for acceptance or condemnation. He found the ice queen again.

"And it's been a long day." She looked away, as if dismissing what they had shared. "We have the wounded to think about and the trip ahead of us. We should get some sleep."

"I'll make us a place under the wagon."

"I don't think that's a good idea." She didn't want to be with him when she was relaxed, for he was becoming more dangerous to her all the time. How could she have suddenly wanted him with such a fierce longing? Yet it had felt so good to be in his arms, to be wanted, to belong.

He took her hand, knowing he had to regain her trust. "Look, we've got a hard drive ahead of us. The Raiders may be out there looking for us. We've got to stick together and keep each other safe. And we're going to sleep side by side under that wagon. If anything happens, I want you close."

Again she searched his eyes for truth. But how could she trust a stranger, a man who made her senses spin? Still, there was practical sense. He was right. And for some strange reason, she did almost trust him. She squeezed his hand, feeling his warmth, his strength, and smiled.

Part Two

Trail of Tears

Chapter Five

Lacey snapped the reins over the backs of the mules, not surprised they moved so slowly. It felt as if the heat and humidity were drawing the energy right out of them all. She glanced around. The day was too quiet. Clouds hung heavy and low in the sky. Rain threatened at any moment. Instead of a refuge, the trees towering over them felt like a prison, with danger lurking behind every broad trunk.

Maybe she was being fanciful, but after what she had witnessed at the train and Whitmore cottage, she didn't feel she could trust anything or anyone again. Yet if she didn't have faith in herself or Clint or the safe house where they were heading, how could she go on?

Maybe she simply had to believe in herself, in what her parents had taught her, in her own skills, her own experience. But she wasn't used to being without friends and family, and it made her feel vulnerable.

At least Clint was with her. He had fought in the war. He was experienced in the outside world. And he wasn't wounded. She only hoped her trust in him was justified.

She glanced behind her. Still no sign of Clint. She hoped he was safe. He'd been gone since dawn, scouting for sign of Randolph's Raiders.

Clint McCullough. She thought of him more than

she had any man, worried about him when he was away, and worst of all, her body craved his touch. She didn't know how she could even think of physical pleasure when they were in so much danger, when others depended on her for their very lives, and yet she did.

Her sudden passion for Clint confused, frustrated, and frightened her, but still excited her beyond anything she could possibly have imagined. Finally, she understood why women went through so much for the men they loved and wanted.

But she didn't want to dwell on Clint or the Whitmore legacy or events beyond her power to control. She wanted to take charge of her life. And she wanted her parents. She hesitated, clenching the reins in her fists. But they were gone forever.

What she must remember of her parents was their love, their caring, and their happiness together no matter how difficult life became. She must also remember that they had wanted the same for her and had worried when she had found no one to love. They would have wanted her to carry on, to save lives, to stop the destruction.

Suddenly, the wagon hit a deep rut, bounced out, then continued on down the narrow, overgrown road. She glanced back at her patients. They lay still, sleeping or resting. Dave had wanted to help her drive while Clint scouted, but she had insisted he rest. Nevertheless, he kept her pistol by his side and she guessed he slept little, ready to defend them if necessary.

They had been traveling for days, following a winding road through the woods. There was a more direct route, but because of the Raiders she was afraid of taking a well-known road. Instead, she had directed them the long way, up through Georgia, then into North Carolina through the foothills of the Great Smoky Mountains. They had skirted the town of Chattanooga and were finally nearing the Tennessee River in Alabama.

During this time, Clint had found no sign of the Raiders, but there was destruction everywhere from the war. It pained Lacey to see it, knowing how many lives had been lost. But she could do nothing about the war now. She had to think of the men in her care.

Glancing around, she watched for Clint. It was time he returned. The sun would be setting soon, and she wanted to make camp. Her hands ached from driving the mules all day, and she knew her palms weren't healing well since they stayed hot and damp within the leather gloves. She was tired, but before she could rest she would need to tend the wounded again. Yet it would be worth every moment of the tiredness and pain if they could reach Marsden cottage safely.

She urged the mules onward, knowing there was a cabin up ahead where they could spend the night. At least the place had been there the last time she and her father had taken this road to the safe house. The cabin was part of the network, and it was kept stocked with wood and usually some food for travelers.

Thinking of hot food and a dry place to sleep, she was startled at the sudden jingle of a horse's bridle. She looked behind and sighed in relief at the sight of Clint. She was relying on him too much and knew it, not only for the safety of the wounded but for her emotions as well. But none of her rational reasoning seemed to make a bit of difference.

As he rode up to her, she noticed the weariness seemed to leave him. He straightened in the saddle, ran a hand through his thick dark hair, and smiled. Watching him, her heart suddenly beat faster. Even with the scar on his face, even though he was dusty from travel, and even if she couldn't quite trust him, she still felt a response she had never felt with anyone else.

"How're you doing?" He searched her face.

"Fine. But we're ready to rest."

"You look tired."

She nodded, feeling the intensity of his gray eyes on

her, enjoying his concern. "No sign of the Raiders?"

"Far as I can tell, we're safe tonight."

"Want me to stop so you can ride in the wagon?"

"No thanks." He looked down the road. "I'll go on to the cabin and make sure everything's safe."

"Do you remember the area I described?"

"Yes." He gave her a hard stare. "Be careful." Then he rode on ahead.

She watched until he disappeared into the trees, not knowing whether to fight her feelings or give in to the pleasure that beckoned. Of course, he might not be interested in her. But then she remembered the look she'd frequently seen in his eyes. Hunger. And he had not been thinking of food.

She started the mules forward, and they continued their slow pace down the rutted road. A light rain began to fall, and she glanced in back. Dave smiled at her, then carefully began pulling quilts over the other men. She nodded, glad she'd had him to help her. Clicking to the mules to hurry, she was more anxious than ever to reach the cabin.

By the time she arrived at the haven, smoke curled from its chimney. She knew Clint was taking a chance, but with no sign of the Raiders and with the trees to conceal the smoke, they should be safe. And she knew her patients needed hot food. She stopped the mules and set aside the reins.

Clint stepped out of the weathered log cabin, and as the rain became heavier he hurried to help her down. She didn't protest as his arms went around her, for she had been sitting still so long her legs were stiff. Besides, she enjoyed the brief moment of closeness before he set her on the ground.

While he helped the wounded from the wagon, she carried her medicine bag into the cabin, along with several quilts. She was touched to see Clint had picked wildflowers and put them in a chipped pitcher in the center of the rough pine table. In the summer they had

58

always kept wildflowers in Whitmore cottage, and she felt the loss of her parents all over again.

The aroma of brewing coffee filled the room, and she was grateful for Clint's thoughtfulness. But she suddenly wondered how a man, surely hardened by four long years of war, could be so concerned. Maybe like many Southerners, he thought they must preserve and protect what little was left after the war.

Glancing around the one room cabin, she noticed a pile of wood in one corner and straw in another. She set her bags down on the table, then spread a quilt over the straw. At least there would be a fairly comfortable bed for the two sickest men. There were four straight-back chairs in the room, along with a low cabinet. Inside she found a few tin plates, spoons, coffee, sugar, and biscuit-makings.

She wished there was more food, but at least she could make biscuits and with the last of the jerky they could have something filling and hot.

Clint came in, carrying one of the wounded. Dave followed, supporting another man. She motioned toward the pallet and Clint eased the wounded man down. Dave and the man he supported sat down at the table, while Clint went back for the last patient.

Picking up a wooden bucket by the door, Lacey stepped outside. The rain was only a drizzle now, and she was glad since she wanted to get water from the stream in back so she could make biscuits and clean the men's wounds.

As Clint carried the last man toward her, he stopped, noticing the bucket. "Wait for me."

She opened the cabin door for him. "I'll just be a moment."

"I don't want you going anywhere alone."

"But the wounded—"

"Dave'll take care of them."

She waited while he went inside, not knowing if she liked this much concern or not. She could take care of herself. After all, she'd been doing it a long time and Clint should realize that. Still, Randolph's Raiders were now a constant threat.

He returned soon, and they followed a narrow, over-grown trail behind the cabin to a small creek in back. Water bubbled over smooth stones, and crickets chirped loudly. Night was falling rapidly, and the forest cast dark shadows.

Taking the bucket from her, he dipped it in the stream.

"I think I could stay here forever." She enjoyed the beautiful setting, the peace and quiet, the seeming safety of the area.

Turning toward her, he set the full bucket down and stepped close. He pushed a strand of hair back from her face. "I can take care of the men tonight. Why don't you rest?"

"Thanks." She glanced away, watching the shadows play over the water, knowing she should step away from Clint, go back to the house, anything, yet she didn't want to break the spell. "But you're tired, too. We've all got to pull our own weight. Besides, it's just one more day and night till the Marsdens take over."

"If they can."

"Don't say that." She felt a sudden chill invade her. "I won't believe they aren't all right."

"I just didn't want you to—"

"Hope. I'm living on that now. Please don't shake it."

"We lived on a lot of hope during the war. Some-times it worked, sometimes it didn't." Now it was his turn to watch the water, his thoughts running back in time.

"I know. Maybe it's luck for some people, maybe it's destiny. I never understood why some made it and others didn't."

"I've seen men go down right beside me, the bullet so close it was a matter of inches. Why they're dead and I'm alive I'll never know."

She touched his arm, felt his warmth and strength, and squeezed, comforting him as she had so many men during the war. "You must simply believe you were destined to live."

"And make the most of it."

"Yes."

"I guess that's what keeps me going. A lot of men died around me, a lot of good men, better men than me. I owe them and I'm going to repay."

Smiling, she thought how much he sounded like her father, like so many of the men who had lived and died fighting the war. And yet there were men like the Raiders who had turned the other way, turned to preying on the weaker ones who were left.

Still, she must remember that she didn't know Clint McCullough. He hadn't help save her father. Why he was helping her now she didn't know. And it worried her, especially because she wanted him and was afraid she would come to care too much.

Crossing her arms under her breasts, she felt chilled, although it was hot. So much had happened so fast. How was she to know what or whom to believe?

"Lacey?" Clint put a strong, warm hand on her shoulder and turned her to face him.

She didn't want to, didn't want to acknowledge the hot, aching current that was flowing between them. How far could she go and still be able to return? Or want to return?

"I want you to know I'm your friend and you can trust me." His gray eyes were steady.

"How can I?" She exhaled sharply, twisting her shoulder out of his grip. "I'll see that train blowing up in my mind for the rest of my life."

"Your warning didn't come in time." He clenched his fists.

"You didn't believe me. You held me back. You—"

"Damn it, Lacey!" He took a deep breath, trying to

control his temper. "There wasn't time. I'd never seen you before. We were running from the Raiders. How could I trust you instantly?"

"And do you now?"

"Yes. And we'll get these men to safety." He exhaled sharply. "I'm sorry about your father. You don't know how sorry. But there wasn't a damn thing either of us could have done at that point."

Pewter-gray eyes clashed with midnight-blue, then he pulled her against his chest, feeling her breasts press against him, soft and round. He wanted her badly, could hardly control himself, but he didn't know how to break through the wall she had built between them.

Wanting to tell her the truth, to have it all out between them, to let her know he was a Yankee and even now worked for the United States Army, he instead pushed strong fingers into her hair and pulled it free from the tight chignon, sending pins flying. Long, thick dark blond hair cascaded down her back and he grabbed a fistful of it, then tugged back her head so he could control her more completely.

She gazed up at him, her eyes wary, confused, and yet deep in their depths flickered a flame. Desire. And that was the flame he wanted to fan. He wanted her inflamed only for him. To hell with who he was or her past either. The only thing that mattered was their passion.

Bending his head downward, he captured her lips with his, feeling their warmth, their softness. And then he could stand it no more and crushed her to him, clutching her head in his hand, her back with his arm, and demanded entrance to her mouth.

She moaned and opened to him. He pushed inside, his tongue hot and greedy to taste her, to test her, to begin their union. From everything he knew of her, she was innocent, and the kiss began like that before it heated as she started to awaken to the passion sizzling between them. Suddenly, her arms were around his neck, her fingers in his hair, and her tongue invading his mouth.

Excited at her response, his body tightened, hardened, and he moved his hands over her, unable to get close enough. He left her mouth to bite down the smooth column of her throat, where he stopped and pressed hot kisses. But fabric bared his way. Frustrated, he started to unbutton her gown and she moaned, unresisting.

Suddenly, he stopped. She had been with soldiers, lots of soldiers throughout the war. And they would have been putty in her hands—alone, wounded, doctored by a beautiful young woman. Jealousy flooded him. He could see her taking long walks among the wildflowers, lying down under ancient oaks, and then the soldiers would undress her, caressing her naked body until finally they would move over her and thrust deep inside.

He saw red. She couldn't be innocent, no matter her response to him. He jerked away, pushing her from him.

Startled, she could only stare at him in shock as she tried to recover her balance.

"I guess you've known a lot of soldiers, haven't you?"

Further shocked, she stepped back, feeling as if he'd slapped her. She had never been with a man so intimately before, never felt the sting of passion before, and now he was accusing her of . . . of what? "I beg your pardon?"

"Soldiers! How many men have you led down the garden path, little miss prim and proper?" He was surprised at himself, saw the hurt in her eyes, and tried to stop. But the jealously was too powerful, the pain at thinking of her with other men too overwhelming.

"You, sir, are insulting." She turned to go.

He grabbed her arm. "Not so fast." He swung her back against him. "If they've had it, why shouldn't I?"

He crushed her against him, seeking her mouth.

"Stop!" She kicked out, hit his shin, and felt satisfaction when he grunted in pain.

But he didn't let her go. Instead, he lowered her to the ground and anchored her with his body. Jerking her hands up over her head, he grinned down at her in triumph. Finally, he had her where he wanted her.

Suddenly she was afraid, for the man she had come to almost trust and certainly want had become a horrifying stranger. He could have been one of Randolph's Raiders. Maybe he was. Perhaps she was leading him straight to a safe house where he would destroy everybody in it. He hadn't saved her father, had he?

Desperately, she began trying to get away, but she was no match for his strength and size. She kicked out, bucked, twisted, tossed her head back and forth. All to no avail. Finally, exhausted, she lay still beneath him, her eyes dark and mutinous. But she could feel the hardness of his body, hear his ragged breathing, and suddenly she wanted him again, despite everything. Then she was as furious with herself as with him.

"You feel good." He moved his hips, pushing against her, taking her stillness for acceptance. "There's no need to wait, is there?"

"Not if you're one of Randolph's Raiders."

He froze. "What do you mean?"

"You said I could trust you. You said you were my friend. I think instead you're a Raider. That's what you're acting like."

"Hell and damnation!" He released her and sat up.

Thankful he'd listened to her, she quickly moved away from him and stood. Brushing at her clothes, she realized she was wet, dirty, and in no condition to return to the cabin. She tried to put up her hair, but the pins were lost. What would the other men think?

"I'm no Raider." He stood, too. "I'm jealous. Tell me you haven't been with another man."

"It's none of your business." She hesitated, seeing

the suddenly dangerous glint in his eyes. But she couldn't let him frighten her. "Perhaps we both got a little carried away. It's been a trying time. We can put this behind us. In fact, I'd like you to leave. I can take the men on in from here."

"I want you." And his eyes said how much.

"And I want you to leave."

He stepped closer to her. "I can take you."

"And I can scream. Dave will come." She moved back, not trusting either of them.

"No. You're alone with me. All alone."

She shivered, knowing he was right. Dave wouldn't hear her in time, or Clint could simply overpower her again. Could she have been so wrong about this man? "Then you're a Raider?"

"No." He touched her face gently, controlling himself with effort. "And I won't force you. I've never done that to a woman and I never will. But, Lacey, I want you so bad it hurts. And I can't stand the idea of you being with another man. Tell me you haven't."

She was tempted to tell him the truth. Instead, she looked away. She must remain rational, calm. She mustn't let ridiculous emotions overwhelm her. And she mustn't let this man she couldn't trust control her. "You can stay the night in the cabin, but I'm going on alone in the morning."

"We're close enough that I can find Marsden cottage now. You can't keep me away from it or from following you."

"But I can't trust you." She could still feel the imprint of his body on hers, feel the weakness that had overcome her in his arms.

"Yes you can." He looked at her for a long moment. "But I'm going to have to prove it."

"Please go your own way. I've got to get those men to safety." She looked in the direction of the cabin in frustration.

"That's what we'll do. Tomorrow."

"But—"

"It's going to be my way, Lacey, at least for now." He took her hand and wouldn't let her pull away. "I'm the strongest. You need me. The men need me. We're both taking them in."

"I don't trust you."

"I know. My fault." He quickly placed a light kiss on her lips. "But before it's all said and done, you will."

Then he led her toward the cabin.

Chapter Six

Clint rode up to the wagon and paced it. "Tennessee River's around the next bend."

Relief ran through Lacey, but she merely nodded. She wouldn't soon forget his threats of the night before or the way she had succumbed to him.

"So where to, Lacey, or do you want me to find it on my own?" Clint slapped the ends of the reins against his leg.

She gave him a cold look. "I want to see the Tennessee, then I'll get my directions."

"Get them quick. This close in, we'd have a hell of a time losing the Raiders." Clint knew she was stalling, not trusting him. But he could play a waiting game. He'd had plenty of experience during the war.

They moved on in silence, the smell of water making the mules walk faster. The sky had cleared, becoming a beautiful blue, and the sun was hot, warming the land. The scent of evergreen and wildflowers was on the wind. And birds sang from the tops of trees.

Lacey ran a hand through her wild, matted hair, held back loosely with a pale yellow ribbon from her chemise. After Clint had scattered the pins from her hair, she'd had to make do. She knew she was going to present a dirty, unkempt, ragged appearance to the Marsdens, but she also realized they'd seen plenty of that during the war. It wouldn't shock them.

"There's the Tennessee," Dave called from the back of the wagon.

Lacey pulled the mules to a stop on a bluff overlooking the river. Every time she saw the Tennessee she was surprised anew, for it was a great wide ribbon of water. Huge. Boats plied it. Sunlight sparkled over its dark depths. But it showed no scars of the war, although Lacey knew terrible battles had been fought to control it.

She sat still a moment, watching the river, wanting to simply let it take her away, to anyplace without pain, memories, and responsibility.

"Where to, Lacey?" Clint saw the longing on her face and knew what she was thinking. But the war wasn't over yet, not for them.

Shaking her head as if to bring herself back to the present, she indicated a narrow road running along the top of the bluff.

Clint started down it and Lacey followed, urging the tired mules to finish the last of their journey.

In back, Dave kept his finger near the trigger of Lacey's pistol, scanning constantly for any sign of the Raiders.

After they'd ridden less than a mile, Lacey pointed to the left, back away from the bluff. "That way, Clint. I know it doesn't look like much, but it'll take us in."

Clint turned his horse, pushing passed tree limbs and overgrown shrubs that partially blocked the entrance to another road, little more than two ruts for wagon wheels through dense forest. Lacey followed, struggling with the mules, trying to keep the wagon on track.

It was cooler in the shade of the forest, pleasant out of the heat of the sun, but Lacey grew more and more tense as they neared Marsden cottage. What would they find?

But she didn't have to ponder that question long, for suddenly they came upon a small cottage set in a glade.

68

Gardenia bushes had been planted around the house while several huge magnolias shaded the yard. The cottage was made of wood turned gray by the weather, and three faded rockers set on its wide front porch. Smoke curled from the house's brick chimney, chickens scratched in the front yard, and a goat ran past chasing a small dog.

It was such a homey scene that Lacey stopped the mules and stared, feeling tears of happiness sting her eyes. Marsden cottage was safe.

Just then a boy of about nine ran out of the house, slamming the door behind him. "Goober, you leave Rattail alone." He headed after the goat and dog as fast as his legs could carry him.

Clint chuckled and glanced at Lacey. Their eyes met, held, and heat radiated between them. Unspoken, but in their eyes and minds, was the idea of a son of their own and how that child would be conceived.

Lacey looked away, shaking her head, still angry about his accusations. Other soldiers, indeed!

Suddenly, the front door opened and an older woman stepped onto the porch. She wore a flowered print dress with a large white apron over it. Her iron-gray hair was pulled back into a tight chignon.

"Joel!" she called. "Get back in here. You're not through with your lessons." She looked in both directions. "Joel!" And then she noticed the wagon and the rider in the shade of the trees. She stepped back into the house and slammed the door.

Lacey urged the mules forward. She hadn't meant to frighten her friend.

The front door opened again and the woman stepped onto the porch, carrying a shotgun. She aimed it at the group slowing moving toward her. "Hold it right there," she ordered.

"Sarah, it's me. Lacey Whitmore." She stopped the mules, and Clint guided his mount near her.

"Lacey?" Sarah looked at Clint, then back at Lacey.

69

"Where's your pa? Are you all right?" She didn't lower the gun.

"Yes." Lacey stepped down, motioned for Clint to stay where he was, and hurried up to the porch.

Still, Sarah didn't lower the shotgun. "Are those men forcing you, Lacey, or did you come on your own? Tell me quick while there's time."

"I brought them. Randolph's Raiders got Whitmore cottage. Mama's gone. Papa, too. Everybody." Tears blurred her vision.

Sarah set the gun against her house and took Lacey in her arms, enveloping her in a scent of bread and lilacs. "You can cry, honey," Sarah crooned, patting Lacey's back, holding her close.

"No." Lacey stepped away, straightening her back. "Not yet. I've got wounded in the wagon. They need your help. We all do."

"You brought them all this way alone?"

"Yes." Lacey raised her chin.

"Who's the man on the horse?"

"He's a former Confederate soldier, and—"

"Well, of course he was a soldier. Every able-bodied man was. But who is he?"

"Clint McCullough."

"You know what I mean, Lacey." Sarah frowned. "Who's his kin?"

"I don't know. But he helped me save these men."

Sarah gave Clint a hard stare. "Hale will take care of that when he gets back." She wiped her hands on her apron. "We'll get the men inside first and see what needs to be done." She looked toward the woods and called, "Joel, come here. We need you."

Lacey walked back to Clint. "You can carry the men in now."

"Trouble?" His eyes narrowed.

"No. Sarah's rightfully cautious."

Dave tucked the pistol under his belt, eased down from the wagon, and began gathering quilts. Clint tied

70

his horse in back and picked up the first man. Lacey got her medicine bag, then led the way. She held open the door to the cottage, then followed the men inside.

Simple handmade pine furniture filled the room, from rocking chairs in front of a central fireplace to a sturdy dining table with six straight back chairs around it. All the furniture was decorated and made comfortable with brightly colored cotton print pillows. Print curtains were tied back from open windows, allowing forest breezes to cool the house. A rough wooden ladder led to a sleeping loft above.

A door was open to the single room in back. Lacey entered, thinking how much the cottage reminded her of her former home. A double bed and dresser were shoved up against one wall to make room for a row of six cots. All were made up and ready for use.

"You can put your wounded in any of the beds," Sarah said, waiting for them. "Our last patient left a few days ago. We aren't getting near as many now as we were right after the war."

"We weren't, either," Lacey agreed, suddenly remembering a similar sickroom filled with wounded men, some dying, many moaning in horrible pain, and the constant smell of medicine and sickness. She shook her head to dispel the thoughts.

Clint carefully put down the man he held, then left for the other wounded. Dave set aside the quilts and followed.

Sarah began checking the first patient. "You've done a good job."

"Thank you."

Sarah sniffed. "First thing we'll do is get these men cleaned up. I don't allow dirt in my sickroom."

"There wasn't much we could do about that."

"I understand." She stopped and looked at Lacey. "So what happened?"

"You know about the Whitmore legacy?" Lacey pulled the gloves off her hands, glad to feel dry air against her damp skin.

Sarah nodded, then returned to her patient. He moaned as she peeled back the bandage.

"Mother caught a fever from one of the wounded and she wasn't strong enough to fight it. As she died, she saw Papa in a vision. He was on a train coming home. You know, those tracks ending near our cottage."

"Yes, I know the area." Sarah continued working.

"Mama saw Papa's train explode, then she died. I tried to get there in time to save him, but I didn't. That's where I met Clint. We put the men still alive in my wagon and drove to our cottage. But again I was too late."

"The Raiders?"

"Yes." Lacey twisted her gloves, then thrust them in the pocket of her skirt.

"I'd heard they were bad, but I thought they were after money, not poor cottages." Sarah stood, looking confused.

"All I know is they destroyed everything we had." Lacey's voice quivered. "I'm going after them, Sarah. They've got to be stopped."

Sarah grasped Lacey's shoulders. "Honey, you're only one woman. Sure, you can heal the sick. But you don't know a thing about killing." She shook Lacey. "And you don't want to know."

Lacey turned away, then looked back. "They killed my family. They've killed others. Somebody's got to stop them."

"The law—"

"What law?" Lacey ran a hand through her wild hair.

"Let the men do it."

"What men? I'm the only one left in my family." She looked at her wounded palms, reminded of the graves she'd had to dig. "I'm going after the Raiders, Sarah, and nobody's going to stop me."

Sarah smiled gently and lifted Lacey's chin. "You always were a determined little thing. Maybe if I was young enough, I'd go with you."

"Really? But I thought —"

"I told you what I knew your parents would have wanted me to say." She hesitated. "I agree the Raiders have to be stopped, and no one seems to be doing it. But, Lacey, you'll need help."

"Clint wants to go after them, too."

"Are you involved with him?" Sarah was shrewd.

"No." Lacey's blue eyes darkened. "And I'm not sure I want to be."

"Just remember, whatever you do will change you. But if you don't do what you think is right, you'll never rest easy in your old age."

"I hadn't thought of it that way."

Sarah raised a brow. "I don't much like to give advice, but I've lived a lot longer than you. I do know when it's all said and done, each of us has our own personal code we live by. If we violate that code, it wounds us deep inside and it festers. That's a wound won't hardly heal."

"Thanks for the advice." Lacey kissed Sarah's cheek. "And for encouraging me."

Sarah put an arm around Lacey and held her close. "Don't thank me yet. Remember, you might not come out alive."

Lacey shivered. "I know, but I have to try."

Nodding, Sarah was misty-eyed.

Suddenly, Clint walked into the room. He carried another wounded man, with Dave right behind him supporting the last. The wounded were eased onto cots and Sarah took control.

"I want all you men to rest now. You're safe. And, like it or not, I'm in charge while you're in my care." She gave them all a hard stare. "You'll do what I say when I say it. I'm your commanding officer till you leave here. My husband Hale and my grandson Joel

73

will be working with you, too. But you got any questions, any complaints, come to me."

"I'm not that sick, ma'am." Dave touched his bandaged leg.

"You're to lie down, young man, until I've had a chance to look at your injury. You don't want to lose that leg, do you?"

"No, ma'am." Dave looked pale, and he sat down on a cot.

"You sick?" Sarah fixed her eyes on Clint.

"No."

"But you're tired. Lay down, too."

"It's not dark yet." He didn't like the older woman's attitude. "I think I'll—"

"Grandma, there's a wagon in the yard." The boy came to a quick stop just inside the room. "Soldiers!" He was a slim youth with blond hair lightened by the sun, bright blue eyes, and freckles dotting his nose. Barefoot, he wore faded trousers and an equally faded plaid shirt, both too big for him.

Sarah put a hand on his shoulder. "This is my grandson, Joel. Last of my line."

"Hello, Joel." Clint hunkered down to be at eye level with the boy. "How would you like to help me scout around the area? My horse can carry us both."

Joel looked at his grandmother.

She smiled and nodded.

Joel grinned at Clint, then saluted.

Clint stood up. "I want to make sure the Raiders didn't follow us."

"Is there a chance of that?" Sarah's eyes narrowed.

"Yes, but slim."

"Go then. Joel knows the area. But both of you be careful." Sarah squeezed Joel's shoulder.

"I'm taking Rattail." He ran after Clint.

Sarah grinned. "A lot of good that mongrel'll do on a hunt. Let's just hope the pup doesn't get eaten by something twice its size."

74

"There's not a chance of that, is there?"

"On, no. If there's any danger, Rattail will put that long tail between his legs and be back home and under the shed before anybody knows what's happened."

"Smart dog." Lacey wished she could still run home to safety.

"But no hunter. Joel will never accept it, of course. But as long as they have fun, it doesn't matter. That's what childhood's all about."

Lacey nodded, thinking of all the people who had lost childhoods due to the war. She glanced down at the wounded. "You were pretty tough on the men, weren't you?"

Sarah chuckled. "Have to be. It's the only way to keep them in bed long enough to heal. Otherwise, they're up and around, under my feet, pulling out stitches, whatever. But you know all about that."

Smiling, Lacey nodded.

Sarah knelt and checked the other patients. "You've done a fine job, Lacey, and I know it wasn't easy. They'll heal now and be on their feet in no time."

Dave sat up, smiling.

"Not you, young man. I want you off that leg."

"My name's Dave and I've been helping."

"You've done a good job, Dave, but now you rest." Sarah stood up and put an arm around Lacey as she led her from the room. "Come on, my dear, and show me your hands."

"It's nothing."

"You can't go after the Raiders wounded."

They sat down at the dining table, and Sarah looked at Lacey's hands.

"Keep the gloves off, let the air get to them, and they'll be fine." Sarah leaned back in the chair. "You look worn out."

"I am. We all are." She smiled. "And filthy. I can't tell you how much I want a bath."

"Hale's over at a friend's house trading vegetables

and news. When he comes back, he'll help me clean up the men."

"I can do that."

"No. You've done enough. Leave it to me now."

Lacey nodded in relief. "All the way here I kept thinking, if I get to Sarah, she'll take over."

"That's right. Now, I want you to have something to eat, then take a towel down to the river. There's a narrow branch of the Tennessee just in back. You can bathe there, relax. It's private and safe."

"But—"

"No buts!" Sarah put her hands on her hips. "You don't know how bad you look. And you're going no place till you're in better shape."

Lacey bowed her head in agreement, wanting nothing more than to do as her friend requested. "Thanks."

"Lacey, you're like my own daughter. I'd known your parents most of my life. I can hardly believe they're both gone. So fast."

"I know." Lacey wiped at the sudden moisture in her eyes. "But I carried Mama's half of the heart to Papa. He knew before he died."

"And now they're together."

"Yes. I buried them side by side. That's how I got the blisters on my hands."

Sarah's fist came down hard on the table. "Didn't enough die in the war? Aren't the Yankees satisfied?"

"I don't know. But the Raiders are out there and I'm going to stop them."

"Did you get anything from the house?"

"No." Lacey turned her palms up, indicating empty. "Just some food and quilts from the cave."

"Then I'll give you what money we can, and I've got some clothes stashed away for the wounded. There should be a dress or two we can alter to fit you."

"One dress will do, Sarah."

"That may be all I have."

"I won't take much money."

"You'll take what we can give you." Sarah stood up. "And that's that. Now, let's get you down to the river, and I'll see to the wounded."

Lacey hugged her friend close. "We'll get the Raiders, Sarah. And they'll never hurt anybody again."

Chapter Seven

Lacey relaxed on an outcropping of rock jutting over a narrow inlet of the Tennessee River. Sunlight warmed her. Trees and bushes protected her. She could hear birds chirping as they flitted from tree to tree. And her stomach was satisfyingly full from the cold biscuits and rabbit she had eaten earlier.

She felt refreshed after her long bath in the clean water of the stream and a good scrubbing with sand afterward. Brushing her damp hair, she let it fan out to catch the breeze and heat of the sun to dry more quickly. Sunlight had highlighted her hair, leaving golden streaks amid the darker strands, and as she brushed, it waved and curled and thickened until it formed a golden mane extending to her waist.

Wearing a white cotton chemise with a pink ribbon threaded through the eyelet trim, drawers, and one petticoat, she was pleased the clothes fit as well as they did, for Sarah had done quite well from her cache of clothing. They had also found a cotton summer dress of dark blue flowers on an ecru background, and although it was more of a party dress with its low, ruffled bodice than the serviceable gown she had hoped to find, it fit relatively well, even without a corset. But then it had been some time since she had bothered with that confining piece of clothing.

She smiled, fingering the soft fabric of the dress beside her and thinking how long it had been since she'd worn anything as playful as the gown, obviously left over from the days before the war.

What would Clint think when he saw her wearing it? He'd never seen her cleaned up before or dressed in anything except the gray high-necked dress she'd worn since she met him. Would he find her more attractive, striking even? Would he desire her? Her fingers tightened on the fabric and she frowned. How could she even think such frivolous thoughts, especially about a man who believed she gave herself to every soldier she met?

Then she threw back her head, letting sunlight warm her face, and gloried in the feeling of peace as the heat relaxed her. A slight smile hovered about her lips as she thought of how bad she was being by letting sunlight shine directly on her pale complexion. But after being good for so long, controlled for so long, at the call of so many others for so long, she was delighting in the feeling of being lazy and alone.

And then she laughed at herself. Yes, she was really being bad by sitting in the sunlight. But she had been raised to protect her complexion, and the instinct was strong. However, that life, that young woman, seemed a long time ago, much longer than four years. Now a pale, perfect complexion was so far from important that it was laughable. And *bad* was defined in terms of Randolph's Raiders.

She shrugged, determined to push away thoughts and feelings of pain and sorrow. When she had bathed she had let the water cleanse her, washing away the old to make way for the new. It was what her parents had planned to do. They were going to leave the past behind and make the most of what was left of their lives in the aftermath of losing the war.

And that's what she had to do. She had done what she could for her dead parents and friends. She had done what she could for so many wounded soldiers.

Now she had to go on. She was free from old responsibilities, but she was taking on new ones. Randolph's Raiders.

Her breath caught in her throat as she felt raw, savage anger burn through her at the thought of the Raiders' destruction. But she controlled her emotions, as she had contained them for so long. She had to be levelheaded and smart to catch Randolph and his outlaws.

A frown marred her face as she watched the stream below run toward the great river. Where were the Raiders now? How could she pick up their trail? And once found, how could she catch and take them to the law?

She'd been taught by her father basic self-defense and to use guns, but she was unprepared for going after the Raiders and knew it. How then did she complete her quest?

Clint McCullough.

Could she trust him to help her? Would he? Could she trust him not to attack her again? And did she dare spend any more time alone with him, for he had a strange and strong impact on her senses, even when he was insulting her. Yet where else could she turn for help?

If Clint were going after the Raiders, perhaps they could combine forces. He hadn't helped save her father. But could he have been right that there had been no chance to rescue the train anyway? Perhaps it was true, now that she was thinking more clearly, for since that time he had been a strong, reliable partner. But could he be playing some secret game of his own?

Shaking her head, she ran fingers through her tangle-free hair, delighting in its cleanliness, its softness. And thought of Clint's hands in her hair. She shivered, feeling an inner heat begin to glow. Could she trust herself around Clint McCullough?

And that thought brought her to the Whitmore legacy. Could Clint be her soul mate? He certainly affected her strongly. And he'd been there when she'd had the vision, but the other wounded had been with her, too. She didn't want to believe she was destined to love a man she couldn't trust, didn't understand, and knew little about. She was too practical for that.

Setting aside the brush, she looked at her palms. They were beginning to heal, although they were still sore and she would have to be careful not to hurt them, especially in the next few days. But with Sarah taking care of things, she felt she could give her hands a chance to heal.

Picking up her brush, she began on her hair again, feeling the sun warm, relax, and cleanse her.

Suddenly, her vision tunneled and she could see deep woods. A massive boar was charging, its eyes wild, its tusks huge. Then she saw Clint in its path.

Just as suddenly, she could see the stream again, but now she was trembling, her body was covered in a fine moisture, and she was terrified. Jumping up, she hurriedly pulled on her gown, fumbling with the buttons up the front.

She had to get help for Clint. She froze. The vision. Clint. Whitmore legacy. She bit her lower lip, looked wildly around, then grabbed her towel and started running toward the cottage.

As she hurried into the clearing, Clint and Joel walked out of the woods, leading Clint's horse. She heard barking, and Lacey turned to see Rattail poke his head out from under the shed to bark furiously at Clint and Joel before hiding again. When she got close enough, she saw there was a dead boar tied to the back of Clint's mount. The horse edged sideways as it walked, snorting and tossing its head at the smell of the strange animal.

"Clint!" Lacey called, relief washing through her.

He grinned. "There's plenty to eat tonight."

"Grandma!" Joel shouted. "Grandma, come see what we got!" He took several running steps toward

81

the cottage, then ran back, unable to leave the boar.

Sarah stepped onto the porch, looked around in concern, then smiled as she walked briskly toward the group.

"Grandma, look!" Joel pointed toward Clint's horse.

"Well, look at the size of that." Sarah put her hands on her hips as she took a good look at the boar. "Fresh boar meat. It's been a long time." She smacked her lips in appreciation. "Good shot, too."

"Great hunters, me and Clint," Joel agreed, then shyly smiled at Clint.

"That's right." Clint nodded at Sarah. "Took us both to bring down the boar."

Sarah hugged Joel, then smiled at Lacey. "How're you doing, my dear?" She looked at Lacey more closely. "Are you all right?"

"Yes, of course." Lacey felt a little disoriented. Her vision had been so real. And she'd been so afraid for Clint.

Clint pulled the ropes loose and lowered the boar to the ground. Then he led his horse to the wagon and tied him there. As he walked back, he caught Lacey's eye, then stopped, suddenly realizing how she looked. Gone was the ice queen. In her place was a seductive siren, with golden hair like a halo around her.

He looked her over from head to toe, then wanted to follow that look with his hands and lips. Now he was even more proud of the boar he'd killed and brought home, for it made him more worthy of her.

Sarah saw the look in Clint's eyes, then glanced at Lacey. And she nodded in understanding.

"Do we get a reward?" Joel looked around at the group.

"Sure." Clint walked back, momentarily breaking Lacey's spell. "What do you want?"

"My own bow and arrow, so I can track and hunt."

"Not a rifle?"

"No." Joel shook his head violently. "Got to be quiet."

Clint glanced at Sarah, realizing how hiding from enemies during four long years of war had affected the young boy. "Then a bow and arrow it is."

"Don't promise him things he can't have." Sarah's eyes were fierce. "We've never lied to him, not about his parents or about the war."

Clint squeezed Joel's shoulder. "We'll make our own, Joel. Tomorrow we'll go out in the woods and pick the right branches. Then I'll show you how."

"Grandma?" Joel's eyes gleamed.

"You're a man of many talents." Sarah considered Clint a moment, then nodded at Joel.

Joel began shouting and twisted around in the air. "I get a reward," he singsonged. "I get a reward." Suddenly, he turned solemn. "I'm going to get all bad boars."

"What do you mean?" Lacey asked, touched by Clint's concern for Joel.

"It was close," Clint admitted, raising a brow.

Lacey felt a chill invade her. So Clint *had* been in grave danger, just as she had seen in the vision. And that meant he was supposed to be her soul mate. But Lacey was skeptical and wished desperately to talk with her mother, to know how she had reacted to her father in the beginning.

"You've got to be quick with a boar and you only get one chance." Sarah pointed at the dead animal. "If you'll drag that boar back to the shed, I'll ask Hale to butcher it when he gets back."

"Okay." Clint glanced at the mules and his horse. "But I've got to take care of the animals, too."

Sarah nodded in approval. "Everything you'll need is in the shed."

As Clint leaned down to pick up the boar, the jingle of harness reached them. Alarmed, he stepped to his horse, jerked out the rifle, and leveled it across the

83

back of the saddle.

An older man, almost bald but with a full gray beard and bushy gray eyebrows, rode a swaybacked horse into the clearing. When he saw Clint, he calmly raised his own rifle and aimed it at the stranger.

"Now, ladies, will you please tell me if this man is friend or foe." Hale Marsden's eyes narrowed.

"Grandpa!" Joel called. "We killed a boar!"

"Very good." His rifle remained trained on Clint's heart. "I hope that's the last of the killing today."

"Hale, get off your horse and come here and greet Lacey." Sarah was impatient.

"Not till you explain this stranger with the rifle."

"That's Lacey's friend." Sarah put her hands on her hips in exasperation. "Both you men lower your guns."

Eyeing each other, they slowly lowered their rifles at the exact same pace. Finally, still watching one another, they sheathed their weapons.

Hale got off his horse, and Lacey hurried to embrace him. He held her long and hard, then set her back. "Where's your family, Lacey?"

Tears filled her eyes.

"Damn Yankees!" His voice was filled with pain.

"We got a boar." Joel put his small hand in Hale's large one and squeezed, trying to comfort his grandfather.

"Good boy." Hale returned the squeeze. "Why don't you introduce me to your friend, Joel?"

Clint walked closer, judging the older man with each step.

"This here's Clint." Joel grinned proudly.

"Clint McCullough," Lacey added. "Randolph's Raiders got the cottage . . . everybody. Clint helped me get the wounded here."

Hale nodded, taking stock of the younger man. "And the boar?"

"Went scouting around to see if the Raiders had tailed us. Didn't find them, but got the boar." Clint finally spoke for himself.

"Alabama boy by your accent," Hale remarked, looking Clint over. "You looked strong, healthy. Not scrawny like most of our starved boys."

"I was in a Northern prison. But I've got kin down in southern Alabama—or at least I did. My mother was an Everett. There's no telling what I'll find there now."

"That where you heading?" Hale's voice was stern.

"Yes. But first I'm going after Randolph's Raiders."

Hale raised a bushy eyebrow. "Nobody's been able to catch them."

"I'm going after them, too." Lacey was a little put out that Clint had gotten to tell first.

Turning, Hale fixed a hard stare on Lacey. "Now, missy," his chin jutted forward, "I'd be right off my rocker if I let a little thing like you take on Randolph. Besides, your father would turn over in his grave if I let his daughter do anything that foolish."

"She's got a right to revenge, Hale," Sarah said quietly.

"Revenge, hell!" Hale's bushy brows rose. "We spent four years trying to get justice and revenge. What we got was death. And more death. No, ma'am, Miss Lacey Whitmore best stay right here."

"But, Hale—"

"No, Lacey. That subject's closed." Hale took a deep breath, glanced around the clearing, and focused on the boar. "Right now we're going to get that boar cleaned. Then we'll sit down to a good meal." He smiled at Lacey. "Go on with Sarah like a good girl." Turning away, he motioned for Clint to follow him.

They picked up the boar and began lugging it toward the shed. Joel kept pace, regaling his grandfather with tales of stalking the wild boar. When they had disappeared inside the shed, Lacey turned to Sarah.

"He's not going to stop me from going after the Raiders."

"Don't worry, honey." Sarah took Lacey's arm and

85

led her toward the house. "It'll just take him a while to get used to the idea. We lost all our babies to that war and Hale doesn't want to chance losing you, too."

"But I've got to do it."

"I know." She squeezed Lacey's arm. "We'll talk more about it later. Right now, let's enjoy some peace and quiet and family time. Let's put aside our grief and worries."

"You're right." Lacey didn't want to upset Sarah, so she decided to worry about Hale and the Raiders later. "How are the wounded?"

"Just fine. I gave them all a sleeping draught and they'll be out for a while." She opened the door to the cottage and they stepped inside. "How was your bath?"

"Wonderful!"

"The dress looks good on you."

"You don't think the bodice is too low?"

Sarah chuckled. "Not on someone with your figure."

"It makes me feel like a woman." Lacey stroked the smooth skin above her breasts. "I guess I haven't felt like that in a long time."

"The war changed us all." Sarah smiled. "But now's the time to be a woman again."

"I don't know. There're still the Raiders."

"But not right now." Sarah stepped into the sick room, made sure all the men were still sleeping well, then opened the bottom drawer of the dresser. She pulled out a shawl and walked back to Lacey. "Take this. It belonged to my mother. Now I want you to have it." She chuckled. "If you get to feeling too immodest, wrap it around your shoulders."

Lacey shook out the shawl. It was crocheted of dark blue silk in a pattern of twining roses and leaves. "Oh, Sarah, it's beautiful. But it was your mother's. I can't."

"Of course you can. I'll never need anything so fine again, and you're the closest I've got to a daughter left."

"Thank you." Lacey hugged her friend close, tears misting her eyes.

"Besides, you lost everything in the cottage and you need some heritage."

Lacey smiled.

"Now, young lady, let's get to fixing supper. We're going to make this a feast. Roast boar, corn on the cob, bread, butter, whatever vegetables Hale brought. And fresh peach pie."

"Is that what smells so good?" Lacey sniffed the air.

"Yes. I thought we should have something special. Besides, those sick men need good food to stick to their ribs."

"Where did you get the sugar?"

"It's the last I've got."

"Oh, Sarah."

"But it's well worth it." Sarah looked determined. "I want to celebrate your visit."

"I'm not complaining. But what can I do to help?"

"First, get on out to Hale's horse and bring in the food. Then I'll get you to help me in the kitchen. Like I said, it's going to be a feast."

Lacey kissed Sarah's cheek. "Thanks."

"Go on now."

Wrapping the lovely shawl around her shoulders, Lacey stepped onto the porch. The sun was setting, the day was cooling, and soon they would all be inside, together, almost like a family. Her heart ached for a moment as she thought of all she had lost.

But she had to go on now. At least she had friends like Sarah, Hale, Joel, and . . . Clint. Her soul mate. That still seemed hard to believe. But if tales of the Whitmore legacy ran true, then she had met the man she would love and live with the rest of her days. Clint McCullough.

She shook her head, driving away her thoughts. Sarah was right. It was time to take pleasure in what she had. There would be plenty of time later to worry. About the Raiders. About a soul mate. For now, she was going to enjoy a delicious supper and wonderful company.

Smiling, she drew the shawl closer and stepped off the porch.

Chapter Eight

"Lacey, I want you and Clint to take a walk." Sarah pushed her chair back from the dining table and stood up.

"But I was going to help you clean up," Lacey protested, feeling a little groggy from having eaten so much. She stood, too, and looked at Clint for moral support.

"Hale and Joel will help," Sarah insisted.

"But—" Lacey began.

"It's no good, Lacey," Hale interrupted. "Sarah got me to promise I'd send you two outside after dinner."

"I want you to relax." Sarah looked determined. "You got the wounded here, now let us take over."

"I haven't eaten anything that good in years." Clint smiled. "But I agree with Lacey."

"You killed the boar. That was the hardest job." Sarah's eyes turned fierce. "Now you two go on before I get my shotgun." Then she chuckled.

"Oh, all right." Lacey joined the laughter. "If you're so set on working, then I'll let you." She pulled her new shawl more tightly around her shoulders, nodded at Clint, then stepped away from the table. "But, Sarah, I don't want to hear you complaining tomorrow."

Clint opened the front door for Lacey and they moved outside. Although the air had cooled since the heat of the day, it was still warm and humid near the Tennessee River. The sounds of crickets and frogs came from the stream, and little bursts of light broke the darkness as fireflies flitted around the yard seeking mates.

Lacey took a deep breath, inhaling the sweet scent of magnolias and gardenias. She felt relaxed and wonderfully full. Still, there was an inner tension inside her caused by Clint's closeness. The man had an incredibly strong effect on her that she couldn't seem to control, no matter how many times she reminded herself he hadn't helped her save her father and that he was a dangerous stranger.

As for the Whitmore legacy, she admitted she had seen a vision that involved Clint and danger twice. But she'd given the situation some thought and decided the visions still didn't mean she would instantly fall head over heels for Clint McCullough. There was an attraction between them, yes, but it didn't necessarily mean love.

Besides, right now she didn't have time for soul mates, or visions, or love. She had to catch the Raiders. And she didn't want to chance any heartbreak after seeing so much during the war.

As they walked around the side of the house, Clint stopped and plucked a small white gardenia from a bush. He turned to Lacey, a rueful smile on his lips, then leaned forward, pushed her loose hair aside, and tucked the fragrant blossom behind her left ear. He placed a soft kiss on her cheek, then pulled her hand into the crook of his arm and led her away from the house.

"If you think that'll make me forget your behavior last night, it won't." Lacey's words were harsh and she knew it, but she didn't want him thinking he could get around her that easily.

"No." He paused, suddenly cautious. "It's simply a pretty flower for a pretty lady."

"Really! Do you think I'll succumb to sweet words?" Lacey felt insulted, then stopped and gave him a hard stare, her blue eyes narrowed.

In the moonlight his face was all hard planes and angles, with the scar a savage slash across his left cheek. His gray eyes suddenly glinted silver.

He plucked the flower out of her hair, dropped it to the ground, and crushed it with the toe of his boot. "Of course, you aren't a woman who likes pretty words or flowers. What would you know about that?" He turned on his heel and strode away toward the stream.

Shocked, Lacey stood watching him, suddenly wondering if he were just as lost as her at this type of thing. Did they now know nothing of love, of soft words, of soft touches, but of only war and blood and death? Was she being too hard on him, on herself? Suddenly feeling guilty, she hurried after him, pulling her shawl tightly around her.

When she caught up, she cleared her throat. "I'm sorry. I — I don't know — "

"Don't be sorry. You have a right to be offended. What the hell do you know about me?" He whirled abruptly to face her, his eyes glowing hot and savage.

"Or about myself?" she murmured, suddenly realizing that while she knew a great deal about healing a man's body, she knew nothing about healing his soul. And after the war there must be a great many souls in need of healing.

He looked down at her, his silver-gray eyes intent. "I'm not used to women anymore, Lacey. Before the war I could have treated you like a lady and you would have responded like one. Now I don't know what you are, or me either. I give you a flower and you hate me. If I slapped you, would you love me?"

She lifted a hand toward him, then dropped it. He

seemed capable of doing either, and she didn't know how to reach him, didn't even know if she wanted to. She had enough pain of her own. She didn't need to try to deal with his, too. Besides, she'd done enough healing. She had other things to do now.

And yet she *did* want to ease him, heal him, bridge the gap between them. Suddenly, the Whitmore legacy no longer mattered. Neither did love. What mattered was putting behind the sorrow, the pain, and the loneliness.

She reached out again and caught his hand. Her eyes never leaving his, she raised his hand to her lips and kissed each fingertip gently, as he had done for her after they had buried the last of her family.

He trembled, and she felt it. Looking into his face, she saw pain and longing.

"I don't know how to be gentle anymore, Lacey." His voice was full of sorrow. "I'm a beast. And you're so beautiful. So good. So sweet." He turned his back on her. "I'm no longer fit for a woman like you."

"Clint—" She clutched the sleeve of his jacket.

"No!" He jerked away. "Listen to me. You don't know what I've done, what I've seen, what I've thought." He inhaled sharply. "You spent the war healing broken men. I spent the same time breaking them."

He turned back, looking at her from head to toe. "In that dress you appeared so much like women before the war that it took me back in time. I wanted to take care of you, protect you, keep you safe, innocent. I still do. But you've seen too much, haven't you?"

She nodded, speechless in the face of his pain.

"We can't ever go back to those days. I realize that now." He clenched his jaw, then released it. "We thought we were so brave, so strong. We thought the war would be over in months. Fools!"

"Not fools. Brave soldiers. But it's over, Clint."

"Do you think so? Will it ever be over so long as it lives in our minds, our memories? How do you forget the screams of pain, those men and women who gave their lives for us?" He grabbed her shoulders and shook her. "How do I forget what I've done? What other men have done? Tell me!"

She shook her head, having no answer for him, no words, no comfort, nothing. She was hollow inside from the pain, sorrow, and giving she had done for four years. All she had left was her body. And the tiny flame of her spirit.

Perhaps they would be enough. Slowly, ever so gently, she raised to her toes and spread her fingers over his chest. Feeling his heat, the rapid beat of his heart as it shook his chest, she moved her hands upward.

And she looked at him, really looked, as if to carry the sight of him in her memory forever. She noticed the results of his bath, for his face was clean shaven, smooth, and sleek under her fingers as she stroked it, carefully tracing the pale scar. He'd left his dark hair long to his shoulders and she touched it, feeling its thickness in comparison to her own silky fine hair. He was wearing clean clothes, with no trace of a soldier left except for the CSA buckle of his leather belt.

"What do you see?" His voice was tense.

"A man I want." She was surprised at her wanton reply, but he seemed desperate to know he could still be desired, no matter the horror he had been through. And she wanted to comfort him. Besides, it was the truth, no matter her misgivings.

Then he pulled her close, slowly easing her toward him until her full breasts brushed his chest. "I don't know if I can be gentle."

Smiling, she traced his lips with the tip of her finger, then clasped the back of his neck with her in-

93

jured palms and pulled his head toward her. She kissed him, lightly as a butterfly touch, then slower, harder, more possessively. And she felt his hands tighten on her, one slipping down to her waist, pulling her closer.

She could feel his heat, his strength, all barely restrained as his passion rose. Did she dare bait the beast? But did she have a choice, as her own desire soared higher and higher?

Moaning, she opened her mouth and felt his tongue slip inside, push deep into her, tasting, testing, determined to conquer. And she responded, feeling her body grow hot, languid, and the heat centered in her, twining, twisting, making her burn with need.

"Lacey," he groaned, running his hands down her back to clasp her hips and pull her against his hardness.

Now she had no doubt as to his need of her, nor her own sharp desire. She gloried in his strong hands kneading her, pulling her into him so she could feel his arousal. Excited, she moved against him, wanting desperately to slake the burning that was growing hotter and hotter.

He groaned and pulled away from her mouth to trace the contours of her jaw, then pressed soft, hot kisses over her face. He tenderly kissed each eyelid. She shivered under his touch and felt her knees grow weak. Then he moved back to her lips, tracing their shape with the tip of his tongue. She opened her mouth and he thrust inside, harder this time, as if he could not drink his fill.

Finally, he left her mouth and nibbled down her throat to her shoulder. There he bit her sensitive flesh, felt her shudder in reaction, then touched his tongue to the area, soothing her, exciting her, making her want more. He pushed the shawl back from her shoulder, baring the smooth skin from her neck to the slope of her breasts.

His hand shook slightly as he touched her, letting his fingers caress her skin. Then quickly, as if he could no longer restrain himself, he cupped her breast and felt it exactly fit his hand. He squeezed gently, then with more force, feeling her nipple harden under the thin cotton fabric.

He wanted her desperately, but he abruptly pulled her against him, hugged her hard, then set her away.

Swaying, she tossed her head as if to clear it and reached for him.

"No." He was breathing hard. "I can't take any more, Lacey. You don't know how long I've been without a woman and how much I want you."

"I want you, too."

"This isn't the time or place." He paused, running a hand through his hair. "And I'm not the right man for you."

"And who *is* the right man?" Her voice was husky, daring him to find another one more worthy. She didn't think she'd ever spoken in that tone of voice before in her life, and yet it felt right. She wanted to tempt him, taunt him into losing all control and giving her that incredible inner glory she knew she was so close to feeling.

"Almost any Southerner," he said bitterly, clenching his fists.

"You're the Southerner I want." She moved close again, her voice still husky, luring, daring.

Again he stepped away. "Leave me some respect, Lacey. If I take you now, last of the Whitmore women, I don't think I can ever forgive myself."

"I'm just a woman."

"No, you're a mystique." He grabbed her left hand and held it up to the moonlight. "There!" He traced the spidery-shaped birthmark in her palm, careful not to hurt the wounds. "Men would have destroyed heaven and hell to have protected Whitmore cottage

95

and its women. I couldn't save the cottage, but I can damn well save you, at least from myself."

Lacey took a deep breath, her body cooling. "I won't force myself on you."

"It's not that. You know I want you."

"You wanted to hurt me. That's all." Her voice was suddenly hard, cold.

"I hurt, too."

She walked to the stream and watched the moonlight glint on the water. He followed her.

"Lacey, I'm going to leave soon and go after Randolph's Raiders. I'll leave you safe with the Marsdens." He put a hand on her shoulder. "When the Raiders are behind bars, I'll come back to you . . . if you still want me."

Jerking away, she looked at him, her eyes narrowed. "This was all just some clever game to remind me that I was a woman, soft, vulnerable, easily swayed by her emotions. You thought I'd docilely stay here if you plied me with kisses and promised to return."

"No, I—"

"Well, you're wrong!" Her eyes glinted savagely. "I'm no soft Southern Belle. I'm an Iron Magnolia. And you'd better get that through your head right now. I'm going after the Raiders. And nothing will ever change my mind."

"Lacey, be sensible. The country's crawling with half-starved former Confederate soldiers. And Northerners can't get down here fast enough." He glared at her. "Do you have any idea how vulnerable a beautiful, young woman like you would be?"

"I don't care. The Raiders killed all I loved. They have to be stopped."

Clint took a deep breath, looked around in frustration, then stuck his hands deep in his pockets. "Hale won't let you go." The last thing he needed was Lacey along while he was trying to do his job.

And if she found out he was a Union officer, she'd probably waste no time turning him over to a Confederate lynch mob.

"He can't stop me. Sarah will help. She's already agreed."

"Damn stupid women!"

"We are not. We know what has to be done and we're going to do it."

Clint paced away, then turned back. "What if I let you come with me?"

"Let me come with you? Well, thank you for small favors. If I went with you, it'd be as partners. Nothing less." She tossed her head, her hair flying out in a wild mane of silvery gold.

"Damn it, Lacey." He rubbed the scar on his face in frustration. "All right. We go together. It'll be the only way to keep an eye on you and keep you safe."

"Thank you very much, but Papa taught me to use a gun and take care of myself. I may not have been a soldier, but I can shoot straight if I have to."

"I'm glad to hear it. But can you track?"

"What do you mean?" Her voice was suddenly defensive.

"I mean, how do you plan on finding the Raiders?"

"Oh, I'll ask around."

"You'll ask around! Just like the Raiders announce their plans to everybody."

"Stop making me sound like a child. I don't know how I'd find them, but I would." She crossed her arms under her breasts. "And I'm not going anywhere with you if you treat me like this."

He exhaled sharply. "All right. We probably each have skills the other needs."

"Exactly."

"I just don't know what yours are yet."

"I'm sure you'll find out."

"Too soon, I'm afraid."

"Look, Clint. I mean it. If you're going to treat me like I'm a weight around your neck, I'll go on my own."

"Lacey, I'm going to explain something to you and explain it once." He pointed a finger at her. "There's no way in hell I'd let you loose alone in the South."

She put her hands on her hips. "This is a free country. Or at least it was. I'm a grown woman. I'll do what I want and where I want."

He reached and snagged her wrist. "You're baiting the beast." He squeezed hard. "Don't."

Jerking her arm, she tried to get free. But he was too strong. She frowned.

"We'll go together after the Raiders, but I'm in charge."

"No one has to be in charge. We can be partners."

"No, we can't. I'm the leader and you have to acknowledge that now."

"No." She tried to pull away.

"Lacey, don't make me prove it."

"Let me go. You're hurting my wrist. I don't think I need you after all."

He twisted, and she slowly went down on her knees in front of him. "Now, who's in charge?"

"This isn't fair. You're stronger and that doesn't count."

"It counts." He held her down.

"No."

He didn't want to hurt her. Otherwise, it would have been easy to break her, body and soul. But that was far from what he wanted. He wanted her cooperation, and he wanted her spirited. "Lacey, agree and we'll each do what we do best on our hunt. If there's a medical problem, you'll be in charge. I'll handle what I know best. Is it a deal?"

Hesitating, she chewed her lower lip.

"You agree?" He didn't trust her.

"Yes."

He loosened his hold, then helped her up. Rubbing her wrist, he watched her, wondering what he was letting himself in for. But if he left her with the Marsdens, she'd simply strike out on her own.

"You didn't have to hurt me."

"I wanted you to understand there's a big, bad world out there. You aren't used to it. You've been protected."

"But I've seen the results of that war." She tried to pull away again, but he continued massaging her wrist.

"Yes, but you've been safe. And I'll try to keep you safe, but you've got to trust my judgment. Okay?"

"I agree you've had more experience."

"Good. Now let's go back. I could use some more peach pie."

He tucked her hand in the crook of his arm and headed toward the house, thinking that if he could tell her the truth about himself, he wouldn't have any more problems with Lacey Whitmore wanting to travel with him. But he was under orders to keep the mission secret, revealing nothing that was not absolutely necessary to complete the task.

Randolph's Raiders. If not for his memories, it would be easy to forget the Raiders and stay with Lacey and the Marsdens in the peaceful, happy life of the glade. He looked forward to teaching Joel to make a bow and arrow, and they would no doubt have to take Rattail along to teach him how to hunt. Thoughts of Joel made him think of children he might have with Lacey if they lived in the safe world of the Marsdens.

But safety was an illusion. And the Raiders were out there burning homes, killing families. Somebody had to stop them and it was his job. A job for the beast.

Covering Lacey's hand with his own, he saw soft

lights in the cottage and heard muted voices on the front porch. He would give a lot to stay there forever, but it wasn't for him . . . not anymore.

Part Three

Beauty and the Beast

Chapter Nine

Bridgeport, Alabama had seen better days, much better days, and Lacey shuddered at the thought of the number of lives that had been lost there during the war.

For this was where the Memphis-Charleston railroad, considered the backbone of the Confederacy, spanned the Tennessee River. The bridge had been burned several times during the war before finally being captured by Union soldiers in July 1863. After that, Bridgeport became the key base of operations in the United States victory of Chickamauga and the lifting of the siege of Chattanooga.

Those events were burned into Lacey's mind, for they had happened so near her home and because they had been so important in the victory of the North.

Glancing at Clint as they rode down the main street of Bridgeport, she knew he must feel the horror of the war all around them. As a light rain began to fall, she almost felt as if it were blood, come to once more soak the land red. Reaching out to Clint, she squeezed his hand, not wanting him to feel his fight for the Confederacy had been in vain.

Surprised, he glanced at her and smiled, returning the pressure of her hand.

As she looked around, she wasn't shocked to see

a lot of Yankees, easy to spot by their attitude, their clothing, their money, or their weapons. But she felt renewed anger burn through her at their presence. She might have been protected during the war, spared the battles, the occupations, the burnings, but she had still seen Yankee handiwork in the wounded soldiers she'd tried to keep alive. And finally Randolph's Raiders in her own backyard.

But before the Raiders, she'd only confronted a few Northerners in her entire life. And she certainly hadn't missed them. As she glanced around at the people in the street, she was surprised to notice the Yankees looked human enough, despite their notorious inhumanity in the South. But no matter how they looked, she would never count one as a friend.

She hoped they could find a cheap, safe place to spend the night, although from the looks of things it might be better to sleep in the woods. Back in civilization, or what counted as that now, she had a better idea of what Clint had meant when he had insisted she would be vulnerable in the new South.

They had a little money. She hadn't wanted to take it, but Sarah and Hale had insisted. In exchange, she'd left her mother's quilts. They also had a change of clothes. And food. They had traded the mules and wagon with Hale's neighbor for a good horse and a little cash. But money was scarce among Southerners, and Lacey wondered how they were going to afford to follow the Raiders.

But she wasn't going to let herself worry about it now, not when their quest had just begun. Somehow, they had to keep going till Randolph was caught, and that was that.

She wished Dave had come with them. He was a good buffer between her and Clint, as well as a good friend. But his leg simply wasn't strong enough, and Sarah had insisted he stay at the cottage. She had hated to leave her friends, and only something as important as Randolph's Raiders could have made her.

Patting the neck of her horse when he shied at a loud noise, she noticed Bridgeport had become a raw, rough town, with buildings going up fast and white tents wedged in here and there. Freed black men lounged in front of stores or tended jobs. Drunken men stumbled along the road, some collapsed in the mud, some still on their feet. A fancy surrey pulled by a sleek, handsome horse spun past, and Lacey was surprised to see several painted, gaudily dressed women in back.

Yes, Bridgeport had changed, and she was anxious to be out of it and on her way.

Suddenly, a large man in filthy clothes stumbled onto the street, grabbed the reins of Lacey's horse, and jerked her to a stop. He was followed by two cronies, both holding near empty bottles of whiskey. They crowded up around Lacey, the stench of their breath almost overpowering.

"Unhand my horse," she demanded, trying to turn her mount away.

But the man held onto the reins, tightly controlling her horse. Then he spoke fast. And leered.

Lacey simply stared at him in amazement, trying to understand what he had said. It had been English, but so fast and with such a strange accent she couldn't make out his words. Then she realized he must be a Yankee.

He repeated himself, moving closer.

"Release my horse!" But she was beginning to understand his accent, and his words weren't something she wanted to hear.

Grabbing her thigh, the man squeezed, then grinned up at her.

She kicked out at him, but one of the others caught her leg and held it. She looked over her shoulder at Clint. He had moved his horse in close, and his face was full of fury and menace.

"Let the lady go." Clint spoke in a voice used to command.

"There ain't no more ladies in the South." The man laughed. "They're all whores now. Scarlet women for the brave soldiers of the North."

"Step back." Clint's eyes were steely gray. "Do it now."

"Now look here, mister. There's plenty for all."

Clint drew his pistol and aimed it at the stranger's heart. "Let go of her or you're a dead man."

Surprised, the man frowned and dropped his hand. "You're the dead man, mister. Don't you know better than to talk back to your betters?" He laughed loudly and pounded his two friends on their backs. "Looks like we got ourselves some Rebel stew."

Clint kept his pistol trained on the leader. "Get out of here."

"You got the gun now, mister, but the law's on our side. You're the dead man and your lady's gonna whore for us tonight." He took a good look at Clint and Lacey, gave them a curt nod, then turned and stalked away, his two friends swaggering after him.

Clint grabbed Lacey's reins and pulled her horse after his as he hurried them down the street. At the first alley, he turned off and made his way back between some tents and wagons. Stopping, he looked around, then slipped his pistol back in its holster.

"Hell and damnation! It's what I was afraid of when I agreed to bring you with me."

"But, Clint, we were minding our own business."

"That doesn't matter. You're a fine woman, a Southern lady. Drunk carpetbaggers are going to want you first and a shot at a Rebel second." He clenched his fist and hit his thigh. "Damn!"

"Well, excuse me, but they were in the wrong."

"Yes, but they won the war."

Lacey suddenly realized she knew nothing about the world her South had become. "I'm sorry. I didn't understand."

"No reason for you to. It's as much my fault. I should have chopped off your hair and dressed you like a boy. But that'd have made you vulnerable, too."

"I'm not going back to the Marsdens."

They looked at each other.

"All right. But we've got to get out of here. They can tail us. That guy's bound to have friends and they'll hunt us down like rabbits. It'll be sport to them."

"We've got guns."

"So will they. Besides, I don't want us drawing attention or getting thrown in jail. We've got to get out of here without a trail."

"What about the river?"

Clint looked out toward the wide Tennessee. "It'd have to be something downriver, undercover, and quick."

Lacey nodded in agreement.

Taking care to avoid being noticed, they rode down to the Tennessee, but stayed away from the main activity of flatboats, keelboats, and steamboats loading and unloading. Clint kept checking their trail, afraid he'd see the carpetbagger and his friends riding up on them. But nobody seemed to be following as they made their way down to the bank.

A light rain was falling as they looked around for transportation. There were a few boats, but most looked like they would never leave land again.

Then they noticed a keelboat riding low in the water. It was smaller than a flatboat and tapered to sharp points at bow and stern. Long poles indicated it could be poled upriver or down, and its deck was made of heavy oak keel-timbers and partially roofed. Several tough-looking bully boys were loading the boat with a variety of barrels, sacks, and bales of cotton.

Clint had seen better-looking crafts, and he glanced upriver at the jumble of boats, wishing they could board one of them. But they couldn't afford to be seen. And the keelboat looked in better shape than the others around them.

"Stay here," he ordered, glancing at Lacey.

"But—"

"Keelboatmen are a tough and reckless lot. They've got a reputation for loving nothing better than roaring brawls, hard drinking, and gambling. Getting a woman like you anywhere near them is asking for trouble."

"It seems my existence is asking for trouble."

Clint looked her up and down. "That's about right. But it'll be safest if you stay here while I try to buy our way onto that keelboat."

Lacey watched him ride away, angry at the injustice of their life and society. She wished more than ever to be back at Whitmore cottage, where she had never been considered anything but a help. Yet that life was gone and she knew it, so there was no point in wishing for things that couldn't be.

Sighing, she watched as Clint haggled with a tall, heavily built man with flaming red hair and beard. She didn't want to ride that boat. She didn't like its look or its men. She glanced back at Bridgeport, at the better boats, and frowned in frustration. There didn't seem to be much choice.

Clint motioned her forward and she clicked to her horse, wondering what kind of reception she was going to receive this time. As she rode down the slight embankment, the crew of the keelboat stopped their work and stared. Raising her chin a little higher, she was determined not to let them make her angry or intimidate her. She had a lot more important problems than some woman-hungry bully boys.

She stopped her horse by Clint's, and he helped her down. Pulling her hand into the crook of his arm, he lead her over to the red-haired man.

"This is the lady," Clint said, then glanced around, obviously staking his claim before all the other men.

"Captain Redbeard at your service, ma'am." Doffing his cap, the tall man grinned, showing blackened teeth. The stench of his unwashed body was strong, and his clothes were grimy with dirt and ragged with use.

Lacey inclined her head regally, not sure what she was supposed to do at this point. But she knew she didn't want to be far from Clint.

Clint covered her hand with his and pressed it in encouragement. "This crew's headed to Guntersville at the bend in the Tennessee. They'll take us and our horses."

Captain Redbeard nodded, then glanced at his bully boys. "Get back to work, you lazy lot!"

As the men returned to their labors, Lacey squeezed Clint's arm, relieved that they had a ride out of Bridgeport. But she couldn't help wondering how safe they would be on the keelboat.

"Go ahead and board your horses." Redbeard looked at Clint. "We're gonna cast off soon."

Clint hated to leave Lacey but knew he didn't have a choice. "I'll be right back." He walked over to the horses and picked up their reins, then led them toward the boat.

As Lacey watched Clint, the captain stepped close to her. "Randolph's Raiders are raiding and burning up and down the Tennessee."

"What?" She turned intense blue eyes on him.

Pleased he'd caught her interest, he stuck his hands in his belt and inhaled with pride. "That's right. But with me at the helm, you don't worry 'bout nothing." He leaned closer, his breath fetid. "I take good care of my women."

"How nice, but my companion—"

"Told me he was your husband."

Lacey flushed. "Yes. Of course. But recently. I still haven't adjusted to my new status."

Captain Redbeard smirked. "Husbands change." He pointed a finger at her. "Just remember, I take care of my women real good." Then he turned and boarded his boat.

Lacey's eyes narrowed. Could the captain have been suggesting that he planned to take Clint's place as her *man?* She'd better warn Clint, if he didn't already suspect trouble. At the moment she didn't know which was more dangerous, the town or the boat. Still, the captain and his bully boys were obviously Southern, so surely they could be counted on to restrain themselves with a lady.

She watched as Clint settled the horses, then turned back toward her, leaving the noise and activity on the keelboat. When he reached her side, he took her hands.

"The keelboat's not much, but it'll get us away from Bridgeport."

"Thanks." She hesitated. "The captain said Randolph and his men were raiding up and down the Tennessee."

Clint's eyes narrowed as he gazed out at the river. "This boat'll be stopping at small towns along the river. They used to stop at the plantations, but I doubt if there's much of that going on now."

Lacey felt a tightness in her chest. How much more destruction would they see along the riverbank? And how much of it would have been caused by the Raiders?

"We'll ask at every place we stop, and as soon as we get word of a recent raid, we'll be after the Raiders." Clint looked determined.

She squeezed his hand. "Do you think it could all be over soon?"

He shook his head. "No way to know."

They both fell silent, watching the bully boys load cargo, calling out to each other as the captain bellowed commands.

"It'll be time to board soon." Clint's gray eyes showed concern. "Stay still and quiet. Don't draw any attention to yourself."

"I don't think there's much way to avoid that."

"Maybe not, but be careful."

"I will. And, Clint. That captain. He said—"

"What?" Clint gripped her hands.

"You know, about your being my husband."

"Do you mind? I thought that'd be safest."

"It's all right." In fact, the idea made her feel strangely warm. "It's that he said husbands could change and he took good care of his women."

"Damn!" Clint gritted his teeth. "Don't worry, he won't get his hands on you."

"Thanks."

"Come on. Redbeard's motioning us to board."

Reluctantly, Lacey let Clint help her onboard. There wasn't much room in the keelboat and it stank of fish, something rotten, and unwashed bodies. She knew she would be grateful for a breeze once they got started. Since there weren't any real places to sit, Clint spread his blanket roll in front of a bale of cotton.

Lacey sat down, glad to be partially concealed by the barrels, boxes, and bales around her. At least now the Yankees from the town wouldn't be able to see her. When Clint sat down beside her, she put a hand on his arm, once more glad of his presence.

"Are we safe?" She knew it was a stupid question

but still couldn't resist asking.

"We should be." He glanced around, watching the crew finish their loading and preparation to shove off into the wide river. "But don't relax around these men."

Lacey hugged her knees to her chin, careful to make sure even her toes were covered by her skirt, then pushed damp hair back from her face. Would it never stop raining? She wanted a clear sky and bright sunlight to lift her spirits, but she felt as if she would never see the sun again.

Suddenly, the keelboat shuddered as the bully boys used their long poles to push them away from the bank.

Clint squeezed Lacey's hand and watched as they slid past other keelboats and flatboats making their way into the wide Tennessee. He didn't see the Northerners who had accosted them earlier. Good. That danger was over. As they headed downriver, he finally began to relax.

Stroking Lacey's hand, he thought of all they had yet to do and wondered if it would change her. He wanted her safe, innocent, sweet. But she was bent on revenge. In the end, would it be a shallow victory, the cost too high? There was no way to know. But they were set on their course. The Raiders had to be stopped. If all went well, they should get word of Randolph soon. Then their hunt would really begin.

He glanced at her. She was so beautiful, so pure, her hair all golden, her skin pale and pink. In contrast, he touched the scar on his face, thinking of all the wounds he carried. The contrast between them was greater than she could ever imagine.

And soon he'd have to let the beast in himself free to hunt down and capture or kill the Raiders. He didn't want her to see that part of him, and yet there was no way to avoid it and still catch the

Raiders.

Gazing out over the Tennessee, turned gray by the heavy clouds, he suddenly wished he was anywhere else.

Chapter Ten

For Lacey, the ride down the Tennessee was smooth, the skies clear, the wind a cooling breeze. She enjoyed the sun, even though it was hot and humid, with buzzing insects and the occasional sting of a mosquito. They had stopped at a few towns, most dying a slow death in the wake of the war. It seemed the Raiders had been everywhere, but not recently enough to pick up a trail.

Discouraged but not daunted, she tried to relax, and it could have been a peaceful time if not for the smoldering, possessive looks she received from Captain Redbeard. If Clint were aware of the situation, he showed no indication, so she followed his actions, pretending unconcern with any of the men onboard the keelboat. Still, she wished the captain would restrain his interest.

There wasn't much to do, except watch the passing coastline and other boats on the river. If she hadn't been so anxious to catch the Raiders, she might have enjoyed the restful time more. Besides, Lacey realized she wasn't used to being motionless, and she grew cramped from being unable to move around much. Clint sometimes paced the deck, but he wanted her to sit still, arousing as little attention as possible. And she reluctantly agreed.

Signs of the war were all around them, from ragged boats to burned houses and towns along the riverbank. In places, dark green trees and bright green grass and wildflowers stood out in sharp contrast to blackened land, where Yankees had burned crops and forest. She wondered sadly how long it would take the South to recover, if they ever could.

Feeling a breeze cool her face, she saw Clint stride aft, carefully making his way around coils of rope, barrels, boxes, and bales. He was graceful like a wild animal, and she felt a shiver run through her. They'd had no opportunity to be alone since boarding the keelboat and perhaps it was best, since passion wasn't something either of them needed to deal with right now. Randolph's Raiders were all that mattered and she must keep that foremost in her mind.

Still, she watched Clint and remembered the feel of his lips on hers, the heat of his body, the strength of his hands as they stroked her back. Desire ran through her like molten silver and she shuddered, feeling her body grow languid, her inner core hot and damp with need.

"You gettin' too hot?" Redbeard stood over Lacey, his gaze roaming her body, his hands behind his back.

Embarrassed, she felt heat warm her face and looked away, willing herself to coolness. "It's hot, but I'm fine."

"I take care of my women." He grinned, showing his blackened teeth, and suddenly produced a fan from behind his back. He held it out to her. "This'll help you."

Horrified, she glanced toward Clint, but his back was to them as he gazed out over the river. She didn't want to accept anything from the captain,

115

but how could she refuse without insulting him? The last thing she needed was for the huge man to be angry with her. "Really, I'm fine."

"Go ahead. Take it."

Still, she didn't move to accept the fan.

He frowned. "It's not stolen." Then his face cleared and he smiled. "You think it's another woman's, don't you? Don't worry your pretty head 'bout that. There's lots of damnyankees selling stuff." His eyes narrowed, as if he were remembering. "Sure, Yankee's stole it, but it'd please me if I knew it was back in a Southern lady's hands where it belongs."

Lacey felt her resolve melt. His words were touching, even if he were manipulating her. And the breeze from the fan would feel good. She held out her hand. "Thanks. I'll just borrow it for the trip. Some other woman might need it another time."

He let her take the fan without touching her, then walked away.

Unfolding it, Lacey smiled. The fan was beautiful, with ivory sticks and a colorful scene of flowers painted on a vellum mount. It was obviously quite old but still in almost perfect condition. She had no doubt it had been stolen from one of the rich plantation mansions where it had been in the family for generations.

She fanned her face, enjoying the cool breeze. What had happened to the fan's family? Were they still alive? Was their home burned, their possessions scattered? She shivered, thinking of her own family's few possessions. She was sure the Raiders had taken all that was of value. Had Randolph already sold the heavy gold ring with the single large emerald that had been handed down in her mother's family? Did some Yankee woman now show it to her friends as the spoils of war?

116

Tears stung her eyes. She mustn't think this way. She mustn't allow herself to get soft. So what if she had lost the physical possessions of her family? The Yankees could never take away the memories, the dreams, the love.

She snapped the fan closed. Wherever the fan's family was, whatever had happened to them, they had not lost, either. They, too, would always have the memories. Opening the fan, she began cooling her face again.

Clint walked back to her and sat down. He noticed the fan and frowned. "Where'd you get that?"

"Redbeard."

"Damn!"

"It's all right, Clint." She smiled softly. "I just realized we can't start thinking everyone's bad because of the war. We've got to remember the good things before so much was lost."

"That's hard to do."

"I know. But look at this fan. Think of the women who held it, fanning themselves at parties, talking to beaus, husbands, children. Think of the happiness that goes with it."

Clint looked at her skeptically.

"Just because we've lost our possessions and our loved ones doesn't mean we've lost our dreams or hopes. We're alive and we mustn't ever forget the good things from the past. It can be our legacy to the children of the South. Even a fan speaks its own language, carries its own story, and we mustn't turn away just because our past now carries such painful thoughts."

Clint shook his head. "I don't want the memories. All I want is to catch Randolph."

She touched his arm, felt the warmth of him, and smiled. "I understand. I can't go on with my life either till that man is stopped, but I won't forget

117

the good things, Clint. There was horror, yes. There are bad people, yes. But I *must* believe good will eventually prevail."

Covering her hand with his, he looked at her as if he could readily drown in the clearness of her blue eyes. "With women like you around, Lacey, there's hope for us all." He took the fan from her hand, touching it gently as if remembering much of what he had pushed from his life. "I'd almost forgotten about art and love and gentleness. Where I've been, there was no place for anything except survival."

"I know. I've been there, too. Clint, we must go on now. We must rebuild. But we must also remember. We can't let people like Randolph destroy our belief in good, in beauty, in kindness, or our past."

Clint handed the fan back to her. "You take my breath away, Lacey." He hesitated. "When I'm with you I can almost forget all the ugliness, the horror, the blood, the screams." He touched the scar on his face. "But I can't let myself forget it. Not now. Once I've caught Randolph and his Raiders, then—"

She put a fingertip to his lips. "Yes. Until then, there's nothing for us except the past."

He kissed her fingertip, then pulled her hand down so he could trace the faint spidery birthmark. "Whitmore cottage. We'll get him, Lacey, then we'll talk about the future."

Smiling, she fanned herself, wondering what her future would bring but for the moment content to simply enjoy being close to Clint, in the sunlight and at peace. "Did your mother have a fan like this?"

Surprised, he glanced at her. "Maybe. I don't remember. She died when I was young."

"I'm sorry you didn't get to know her."

"I remember her as a beautiful Southern lady.

118

But I was close to my dad before he was killed in the war. He was a hardworking man from Scotland. He had some land of his own, and he was determined I'd be properly educated. You know, a real gentleman. Just like my mother wanted. He never did stop loving her and didn't remarry."

"Perhaps they're together now, like my parents."

"I'd like to think that."

They grew quiet, their thoughts drifting farther into the past, until suddenly a wild wind sprang up and dark clouds began moving in from the north.

"Looks like a squall." Clint turned to keep an eye on the quickly developing front.

"Is this boat safe?"

"Better be." He watched as the bully boys ran around the deck, tying down as much as they could. "I'm going to check the horses."

As he walked away, Lacey stood up and put a hand on the bale of cotton to balance herself against the rocking boat. She put the fan in the pocket of her dress as she watched Clint calm their animals. She also noticed that, despite appearances, Captain Redbeard and his crew seemed to know exactly what to do. Somewhat relieved, she watched the storm gather strength.

Soon the sun was obscured by heavy clouds. High waves rocked the boat and splashed over the sides, soaking whatever they reached. Lightning streaked through the thick clouds, bright and dangerous, then thunder followed, rumbling loudly. Suddenly, rain fell, big, heavy wet drops that drenched everything in their wake, and the boat was quickly enveloped in fog when the cool rain hit the heat of the afternoon.

"Clint?" Lacey called, unable to see more than shadowy shapes onboard. Suddenly, her vision tunneled and she saw Clint desperately bailing water

119

from a sinking boat. Water was around his ankles and was rising fast. Then her vision cleared and she was caught in the fog surrounding her. This time she understood the vision, knew they were all in grave danger. Yet what could she do about it?

"Clint!"

"Over here."

Then he was beside her. Placing a warm arm around her shoulders, he led her to the center of the keelboat under the roof. He lifted her to a bale of cotton, letting his hands linger on her waist before sitting down beside her.

She shivered, unused to being on a river, especially in a storm, and terrified of what would happen since the vision. Yet she must be strong and believe they would come through the danger unscathed.

"Magnificent, isn't it?"

"Dangerous, you mean."

"Both. But if this boat's seaworthy, we should be all right."

"That's a big *if*."

Clint laughed. The weather excited him. He looked down at Lacey. Right now he wanted to make love to her, bury himself deep inside her, with the rain and wind and lightning all around. Then she would turn wild and wanton in his arms, just as the storm around them. Laughing again, he hugged her tight, then held her hand as the weather raged.

Lacey clung to him, not in the least enjoying the stinging spray that hit her, nor the roaring of the water, nor the thunder and lightning. Besides, the rocking of the boat was making her feel sick in her stomach.

She shook her head. So she was soaked to her skin. So she was frightened of drowning. She had known it wouldn't be easy to trail and capture Randolph and his Raiders. Later, she might look back on this as easy in comparison to what was to come. But she hoped not. And she hoped most of all that Clint would be safe.

Suddenly, there was a loud crunching of wood as they were rammed by another boat. Bully boys cursed and called commands across the water. As the crew ran toward the problem, Clint stood up, ready for action, but still held tightly to Lacey's hand.

In the fog and rain, it was hard to tell exactly what had happened or how bad the damage was, but Captain Redbeard shouted commands until there was another loud crunching sound, the deck heaved, and the boats separated. Then Redbeard gave a loud, ragged cry of pain, followed by silence.

"He's hurt," Lacey said, tugging at Clint's hand. "Get my medicine bag off the horse."

"Wait, Lacey. We don't know what's happened."

She stepped out from under the protective roof and glanced around. It was still impossible to see much. "Bring your captain here! I'm a doctor."

"I'll get him." Clint stepped away, determined to keep her from doing anything more dangerous.

But she caught his arm. "No. Please stay where it's safe."

"This boat may be sinking for all we know."

"But you could be washed overboard." Rain hit her face and water foamed up over her feet.

"Wait here." Then he was gone into the fog.

She clenched the cotton bale, her mind racing ahead to what she'd need. She would have to have a light, as well as her medicine bag. Waiting, she imagined the worst case possible, until finally several of the crew dragged the captain, still barely on his feet, to her. Clint was right behind them with her medical bag.

"Captain, I will need a light." Lacey used her most professional tone to elicit confidence in the men around her.

Redbeard nodded at one of the men. As the man rushed away, the captain put a hand on the cotton bale to steady himself. "Get back to work, boys. Save her."

The crew quickly left, and the captain slumped against the bale.

"What happened?" Lacey dreaded to see a wound she couldn't heal.

"Leg." He took several deep breaths to control the pain. "Got caught 'tween . . . boats when we shoved them apart."

"Can you sit on the cotton bale? You'll be out of the water that way and I can see your leg better."

Redbeard started to hoist himself up, then shuddered and leaned weakly against the cotton.

Clint thrust the medicine bag into Lacey's hands, then helped the captain up on the bale, realizing the man had to be losing a lot of blood to be so weak.

"Here's the lantern," one of the crew said as he returned, thrusting a battered shape toward them.

Clint took it, shielded the lamp from the wind with his back, struck a match, and lit the lantern. The flame wavered, then held. He raised the lamp up to the captain's legs and Lacey groaned, for there was a long, jagged gash clear to the bone along the fleshy part of Redbeard's left calf. And he was bleeding freely.

Clint unbuckled his belt and pulled it off.

Nodding in approval, Lacey took his belt, wrapped it just above Redbeard's knee, and pulled it taut. With the tourniquet holding back the blood flow, she could clean the wound, then stitch it up. But it wouldn't be an easy or quick task, not with the storm raging and the boat tossing. Still, she had

122

to do the best she could.

She glanced up at Clint. "Have you got some whiskey for him? This is going to be painful."

"I'll get it."

"Be careful."

"If you've got the blood stopped . . . I'll get back to my command." Redbeard took quick, shallow breaths.

"You won't do this boat any good dead, Captain. And I can't leave that tourniquet on long or you'll lose the leg."

"I *can't* lose this boat." He stifled a groan. "It's all I've got."

"You're more important than the boat. And that's that."

Clint handed her a small bottle of whiskey, then held the lantern in front of the wound, balancing himself as the boat tossed.

"Here. Drink some of this, Captain, because I'm not letting you resume command till I've got that leg stitched."

"You sound like my mother." He shook his head, then raised the bottle to his lips. "Once she set her mind, that was it." He took a long drink. "Go ahead, but it may be the death of us all."

Lacey clamped her lower lip between her teeth, took back the bottle, and poured it down the length of the gash.

Redbeard groaned, clenched his fists, but only jerked his leg slightly. "I've seen worse. On the battlefields."

"So've I," Clint agreed, "but the doctors didn't have to work in conditions like this."

"What doctors?" Redbeard took the bottle back and drank more.

"You're lucky." Clint held the lamp, watching Lacey use tweezers to pull out bits of wood and

123

hemp from the wound. "You've got the best this time. Ever hear of Whitmore cottage?"

"Sure. What soldier in these parts hasn't?" There was a touch of awe in the Captain's voice.

"This is Lacey Whitmore."

Redbeard stopped breathing for a moment, then the harsh, shallow breaths continued. "I won't worry 'bout nothing now. This boat'll sail through just fine."

"I'll do my best." Lacey shivered, wondering how former Confederate soldiers could put so much faith in tales of Whitmore cottage.

"Whitmore," Redbeard repeated, then choked and coughed at the sudden pain as she pulled a chunk of wood from his leg.

"You don't have to be quiet." Lacey didn't want him to hurt himself by being so brave he didn't cry out.

"If I'd known you was a Whitmore woman from the first—"

"It doesn't matter now. Please save your strength. You're going to need it."

The captain clamped his teeth together and held onto the cotton bale as Lacey dug deeper, poured more whiskey on the wound, then began carefully stitching. The wind howled around them and water slowly rose up to Clint's ankles. Kneeling, Lacey felt it around her knees and hoped there weren't snakes or other dangers crawling nearer and nearer her. But she put those thoughts aside as she concentrated on her job, the lantern's light flickering in the wind even with Clint to shield it.

Suddenly, Redbeard growled in pain and collapsed into unconsciousness. Clint quickly gave the lantern to Lacey, then lifted the captain so he was lying across the bale of cotton, his legs dangling over one side. She handed back the lamp and Clint raised the injured leg so she could finish her work.

Some time later she stopped, poured whiskey down the stitches, then cleaned her equipment and closed her medicine bag. "That's all I can do."

Clint blew out the lantern, set it aside, and took her in his arms. "You did a good job. Saved his leg and probably his life."

She felt exhausted. "We'll have to watch him. He might develop a fever. In fact, he probably will due to this weather."

"He'll make it. He knows he's got you on his side."

Lacey shook her head. "I don't work miracles, but I do my best."

"You've got the Whitmore touch. That counts for a lot, doesn't it?"

"Oh, Clint." She rested her head against his chest. Even wet, his body was warm. Too warm? No, she mustn't think in terms of patients. Clint was fine. They'd all be fine if they could just ride out the storm.

Suddenly, there was a commotion at one end of the keelboat as the crew rushed to that area. Then one of them shouted, "Taking on water fast."

Lacey felt despair, remembering her vision.

"You stay here." Clint placed a quick kiss on her forehead. "Watch Redbeard. I'll help bail." He took her medical bag. "First, I'll tie this to your horse."

"But, Clint—"

"Put some of that Whitmore luck to work, Lacey. Start praying for clear weather."

And because there was nothing else she could do except watch over the captain, she began to think of clear blue skies, calm waters, and a safe port nearby. Maybe she could *be* Whitmore cottage and take the power with her wherever she went. Maybe it didn't have to be confined to one place.

125

Whitmore cottage, she thought, just as she had heard so many soldiers whisper in the depths of pain. Whitmore cottage. And then more fiercely. Whitmore cottage.

Chapter Eleven

A bright streak of lightning, a tremendous crash of thunder, and the keelboat tilted dangerously. Water rushed over the deck in a fierce wave, carrying much in its wake. The avalanche hit Lacey, knocking her to her knees. She grasped the cotton bale to keep from being swept overboard, but the wall of water washed up and over the bale, catching Captain Redbeard and carrying him with it.

Horrified, Lacey grabbed his ankle and clung to the cotton to keep them both from being flung into the river. Then she felt the bale slip just as her own strength began to ebb. She knew if the water carried the bale of cotton overboard, they would go with it. In the fury of the rain, she could see nothing else to stop their slide.

But suddenly the avalanche flowed on, the boat righted, and she and the captain were lying on the bottom of the keelboat, covered in water. Redbeard sputtered, then coughed as he weakly raised his head above the high water. She crawled to his side, grabbed his shoulders, and lifted him so he rested against her body.

For the moment safe, she wondered if anyone else on the boat had survived. And most of all if Clint were safe.

"Lacey?"

She felt the sudden sting of tears in her eyes. Clint. He *was* alive. So close to death, she realized how much he had come to mean to her. Whitmore legacy. She'd had another vision of Clint in danger. And the way she felt right now, he could *be* her soul mate. "Clint, over here!"

As he hurried to her, the storm rapidly began to recede. The sky lightened, the wind died, and the thunder faded away as he reached her side. He knelt, took her hand in his, and suddenly the sun appeared, bathing him in a rosy halo.

She reached out to him, no specter of death now but the harbinger of life. He pulled her into his arms and hugged her close. "I thought I'd lost you."

"Not so easily." She smiled as they loosened their grip and looked deep into each other's eyes.

"What about me?" Captain Redbeard complained, slowly maneuvering himself to lean against the bale of cotton.

Lacey laughed. "You'll be lucky if we don't blame you for the storm."

"Nature." He shook his head and glanced at Clint. "How's the boat?"

"We're bailing and losing ground."

"Rot! Any other boats around?" Redbeard frowned and gingerly touched his injured leg.

"Don't know yet." Clint was so relieved Lacey was safe he could think of little else. She looked half-drowned, but solid, real, alive. He didn't think he'd worried as much during the war as he had in those few minutes when he thought he'd lost her.

"Land!" a bully boy shouted, followed by triumphant cries from the rest of the crew.

Clint stood up and looked around. "Big town up ahead." He could see a narrow outcropping of land at the bend in the Tennessee, and a town nestled among trees, low hills, and laid out close to the water's edge. Boats were lined up along its shore.

"I'll be damned." Redbeard grinned. "Must be Guntersville. We made it." Then he gave Lacey a considering stare. "It pays to have a Whitmore woman with you, all right. I bet there's plenty boats don't make it in."

Lacey shivered, remembering her fervent thoughts of Whitmore cottage. Was there some special power of the Whitmores she brought with her, or had their survival simply been coincidence and expertise?

Redbeard started struggling to his feet. "I'm going in standing or not at all."

Clint helped him up, wondering how the man could stand after so much loss of blood. But he'd seen men do miraculous things during the war, so he wasn't totally surprised.

Standing, Lacey looked at the port coming closer on their left. "As soon as we get to land, Captain, you're going to be on your back for a while. I don't want you losing that leg after all my work."

Redbeard growled and looked disgusted.

Lacey felt the fan in her pocket. "Oh, Captain." She handed the delicate fan toward him, now wet but still in one piece. "I'm sorry, it seems to be damaged. But I won't be needing it now."

"Keep it. You got us through the storm."

"But I don't—"

"Ask any man on this keelboat and they'll tell you a Whitmore woman brought us in. It's little enough to thank you." Then he turned away.

Lacey was touched. "Thank you. I'll keep the fan as a memento. It's very lovely. But I still think your skills had a lot to do with our survival."

Redbeard looked at Clint. "Women! They don't

never want to let a man win." He limped away, with Clint helping him through the water on deck.

Lacey followed, pushing strands of wet hair out of her face, hoping she hadn't been too hard on the captain. But she knew if she didn't insist, he'd never stay off his leg.

The keelboat had been hit hard, but she was relieved to see their horses had made it through all right. She stopped to stroke their noses and speak softly to them until they calmed. Much of the cargo had been lost or damaged, and she knew Redbeard and his crew would be hard pressed to recover the loss. Still, they had all survived and that was what counted.

Approaching Clint and Redbeard, she noticed some of the bully boys were bailing water while others poled toward shore. Several other boats were limping in around them. Sighing in relief, she thought of the future, of a hot bath, a good meal, and Clint. She glanced at him, noticing how tired he looked, how bedraggled, then realized his appearance had absolutely nothing to do with the way she felt about him.

Captain Redbeard didn't head them toward Guntersville but to the nearest shore, for the boat was taking on water fast and they didn't have long to make land. Holding steady, the boat finally scraped bottom.

A loud cry of triumph erupted from the crew, and inwardly Lacey hoped she never saw a large body of water again.

The bully boys quickly pulled the keelboat as far onto shore as possible, then began unloading. Clint helped Redbeard walk ashore, then went back for Lacey. But she had already started leading the horses aft, so he helped her get them to steady ground. They watched as the boat was emptied and slowly rose in the water. The men pulled the keelboat farther onto shore, then firmly secured it to land.

Redbeard turned toward his crew. "Men, we ain't got much left. But if we get what we've got into Guntersville and sell it, we'll get maybe enough to fix the boat and get a few drinks under our belt. Are you with me?"

There were some muttered curses, a quick discussion, then the bully boys nodded in agreement.

"Okay. First, we got to get a wagon from town. No drinking till the work's done. And no leaving the boat unguarded."

Lacey watched the captain's face get paler the longer he talked, and she wondered how he could keep going. Then she realized his entire life, as well as his crew's, was riding on the boat and cargo. He had no choice.

"Captain," Clint said, "we'll take you and one of your mates into Guntersville on our horses."

"Thanks." Redbeard's eyes said much more than his words. He was weak, but he didn't want his crew to know how bad. The horses would take him where he couldn't walk. "I got a friend owns a stable. You can fix up your horses there and I'll get a wagon."

"Sounds good." Clint was anxious to get into town and find a safe, clean place for Lacey, and he wouldn't be averse to resting either.

Loading up double on both horses, they started toward Guntersville. As they rode, Lacey wondered how they'd be received at establishments in town while in their present condition. Then she realized they wouldn't be the only ones coming in looking half-drowned from the storm.

131

As they neared town, it was evident the storm had pounded Guntersville, too, for grass and wildflowers were flattened, roofs damaged, and debris strewn about the streets. There was evidence of Yankee infiltration here, too, for again Lacey saw people who by their dress could only be Northerners. They passed a few white tents, mostly collapsed from the storm, new buildings in progress, and then older wooden and brick structures as they rode farther into the town.

Turning down a side street, Redbeard directed them toward the rivermen's part of town. They guided their horses around tree branches blown down in the storm and arrived at a stable. Although not fancy, it was a clean and well-kept establishment, as were the buildings around it.

Hearing their approach, the stable owner came out. He was a short, wiry man with grizzled hair and smooth, dark skin. Seeing their bedraggled condition, he stopped short in surprise.

"Got caught in the storm, Manny," Redbeard said as he carefully dismounted.

Clint got off his horse, then looked around for Lacey. She guided her mount close to his and stopped. The man behind her got off, and Clint helped her down.

Manny looked around the group. "Angels of Mercy, looks like you all drank more water than you floated."

Redbeard ran a hand through his wild hair. "Hell of a storm. My friends want to stable their horses and I need to rent a wagon."

"How's the boat?"

"Been better. Had to put in downstream."

"No charge for the wagon if you got that case of whiskey through."

Redbeard chuckled. "Your whiskey made it, but not much else."

"Your friends need a place to stay?"

"Right. I was thinking about Kate's place."

"Good choice." Manny gave Clint a hard stare. "Kate's got an inn. Clean, reasonable, good food. She stands for no trouble, no law."

"Sounds fine." Clint wanted nothing better than a quiet inn.

"Down the street, fifth house on your right," Redbeard said, then limped over to lean against the front of the stable.

Lacey watched him take a deep breath and knew he was in pain. She hoped he hadn't pulled loose his stitches.

"You'll groom the horses, feed them, and—" Clint started.

"You got the money, I do the work." Manny held out his hand.

Clint gave him what he thought the service was worth and a little extra to insure the horses would be there when they returned. Fine mounts were so scarce in the South they were bringing a high price. "Could you hire somebody extra to watch the horses all the time?"

"Sure thing. Fine animals. You'll be lucky somebody don't kill you for them." Manny took the money and nodded in satisfaction.

"By the way," Clint looked as casual as he could, "you heard anything about Randolph's Raiders?"

Manny hawked and spit on the ground. "Them devil spawn! Got a family in here yesterday. If they hadn't been out in the woods hunting, they'd have had been home and dead. As it was, Raiders took all they had, then torched the house."

"How do they know it was Raiders?"

"Who the hell else is going round these parts doing that?"

"But it could have been—"

"Raiders!" Manny looked grim. "That's their mark. They take it all, then torch the place."

"Where was the home?"

"South of here. Just off the main road." He spit again.

"Those damnyankees aren't gonna leave us with nothin'." Redbeard's eyes were fierce.

"Is somebody trying to catch them?" Lacey asked, wondering if they could join forces with a bigger group.

"Sure." Manny looked completely skeptical. "What local law's left. A few Yankees. And Southerners. You know how much good that'll do. We're half starved, not much for horses, too few guns, and those Raiders don't wait around to be caught."

"Surely the Union will—" Clint started.

"We'll get old waiting for that," Redbeard said, then turned toward the entrance to the stable. "But we don't got time for Raiders now. I've got to get my stuff in town before dark."

"Captain, there'll be a room for you at Kate's inn," Lacey said, not knowing how they could afford it. But somehow she was going to make sure Redbeard had at least three nights in clean, dry surroundings.

He looked surprised. "I'll sleep near the boat."

Lacey's eyes narrowed. "We're going to pay for a room for you whether you use it or not." Then she stepped forward, placed a light kiss on his dirty cheek, and smiled. "Good luck. And thanks." She glanced at Manny. "Thank you for taking care of the horses."

Clint pulled the saddlebags off the horses, anxious to scout around town for more information about the Raiders. They were getting close. He could smell it. He would have given a lot to tell these people the United States government looked after its own. But that wasn't possible. And they'd have found it hard to believe anyway.

Shifting the saddlebags to his left shoulder, he held out his arm to Lacey. She put a hand on his arm and they left the stable.

As they walked down the boardwalk, she noticed the people they passed gave them strange looks, then stepped around them. Some even walked onto the street to avoid being close to them.

After a while, Lacey began to chuckle under her breath, then her amusement grew until she was laughing out loud.

"What's so funny?" Clint looked down at her, puzzlement in his gray eyes.

She laughed even harder, leaning against him.

"Are you sick?" He frowned.

"No." Slowly, her laughter turned to giggles, and she stopped to look at Clint. "Do you have any idea how funny we must look?"

"No."

"But everybody we pass moves out of our way with sneering glances."

"And you think that's funny?"

"At one time I would have been horrified. But after what we've been through, a few upturned noses is absolutely funny."

Chuckling, Clint shook his head. "You're right. But I'll feel a hell of a lot more like laughing when I've got my feet planted firmly on a solid floor with a locked door between me and danger."

Suddenly sobering, she nodded. "You're right. It's just that—"

"I know. It's a damn relief to be safe." He hesitated, thinking of the Raiders as he glanced around the street. "For now." He took her arm. "Come on. Let's get to Kate's."

A short while later they stopped outside a two-story dark green wooden building with pale green shutters, open glass windows, and a shake shingle roof with two red brick chimneys. A wide porch sported several rocking chairs and spittoons. And a hanging wooden sign, painted in shades of green, announced: KATE'S PLACE, A Fine Inn For Fine Folks.

"Think we can get a room?" Lacey grinned, for some reason continuing to be amused at their situation.

Clint shook his head at her. "You still want to get one for Redbeard?"

"Yes. If we don't, he won't eat right or get a chance to heal."

"Okay. But it'll mean one for us."

She raised a brow.

"We can tell them we're married. The money's limited, Lacey, and we need some supplies to go after the Raiders."

Making up her mind, she nodded. "I can't think what difference a room makes in comparison to a wagon or horse or boat, so it'll do. I want the captain to keep that leg."

As they stepped up to the porch, Clint thought that a room with a feather bed made a hell of a lot of difference and he was almost glad the captain'd had an accident if it gave him the opportunity to be alone with Lacey. Really alone.

Clint opened the front door, and they stepped inside a small common room. Two straight-leg wing chairs in worn green plaid and a matching camelback sofa in dark green faced each other in front of a fireplace. Across from that was a heavy walnut table used as a desk, with a ladder back chair behind it. The table was littered with paper and books, and a kerosene lamp with a clear glass base and a green glass shade was set on one corner.

A bell tinkled as Clint shut the door behind them, and a tall, gaunt woman stepped into the room. Her graying auburn hair was pulled back severely in a chignon, and she wore a simple dark green dress with ecru lace at collar and cuff. She looked her guests up and down, then sniffed.

"More poor souls out of the storm." She stepped behind the desk. "One room or two?"

"Two." Clint stepped forward. "One for me and my wife, and another for Captain Redbeard. If you're Kate, the captain recommended your place."

A slight smile touched her lips, then she was back to business. "Yes, I'm Kate. So Redbeard made it in safely. I'm surprised. That scrap heap he calls a boat shouldn't be allowed on the Tennessee." She pushed the ledger forward, then dipped a pen in ink and handed it to Clint. "But that's none of my affair."

As Clint signed, Kate looked Lacey over, shook her head, then turned the ledger around and read the names. "Mr. and Mrs. McCullough, I suppose you'll want hot baths. Meals are taken in the dining room." She pointed at two glass doors to her right.

"Thanks." Clint handed her money and watched as she made change. "Go ahead and send up hot water. And some bread and cheese. Something to drink, too." He handed her back some of the money.

She took it. "Lemonade all right?"

Clint nodded.

137

"Up the stairs, second door on your left."

"Thanks." Clint took the key and turned to Lacey.

They climbed the stairs together, Lacey stifling laughter as she wondered if they were leaving a wet, muddy trail all the way across the spotless wooden floor up the carpeted stairs. For some reason, it seemed hilarious and terrible all at the same time. And suddenly she felt like crying as well as laughing.

They walked down the hall, then Clint unlocked and pushed open the door to their room. Lacey stepped inside and stopped. The double bed with the colorful quilt, the washstand with white porcelain pitcher, bowl, and hand towels beside it, and an oak scroll rocker with mauve cushions in one corner were suddenly so homey, so comfortable, so *normal*, that she simply froze.

Unable to move, laugh, or cry, she just stood there, wondering how she could have come so far from her former life in so short a time. She heard Clint lock the door behind them, then watched him lay their saddlebags on an oak dresser with a crochet-edged white cloth across its top. She stifled a sudden sob. Who was this man? He'd been a total stranger not long ago, coming into her carefully controlled life as it was suddenly turned upside down. Why did she trust him? And could she really?

Suddenly, she felt wetness on her cheeks and realized she was crying. She hiccupped, surprising herself at the sound. She began to laugh, a low keening sound that was more a cry of pain than of humor. Then she abruptly sobbed.

Clint whirled around and took several long strides to her side. Taking her in his arms, he led her to the bed. They sat down and he held her, patting her back as he pressed soft kisses to her face.

"It's all right, Lacey. You're having a delayed shock to what you've been through. It's normal. I saw it time and again after a battle. Go ahead and cry, laugh, whatever it takes, then you'll be all right."

"But," she hiccuped, "what about you?"

"Me?" He shrugged. "I'm used to it."

She lifted her face and looked at him. His gray eyes were warm, a dark molten silver, and she felt a deep peace invade her. Pushing back a strand of hair, she smiled tentatively. "I don't understand."

He pressed her face to his shoulder, feeling the stirrings of desire begin to build. The last thing either of them needed right now was passion. He'd have to get away from her, or he didn't know what he'd do. He needed a release, too, but he wasn't going to get it by using Lacey. As soon as he could, he'd go out, find a bar, have a few drinks, then get a bath in one of the places that sold them cheap. While he was out, he'd ask around about the Raiders.

Then, when he was calm and in control, he'd come back to her. And beyond that he didn't dare think.

He raised her head from his shoulder. She looked better. "What you need is a bath, some food, and sleep."

She nodded, suddenly feeling exhausted.

"I'm going out."

"What?" Her body was instantly tense.

"You'll be safe here. Kate'll bring up the food and bath. Meanwhile, I want to hunt down more news on the Raiders. We can't wait. If their trail's hot, we've got to move soon."

139

"You're right. It's just that—"

"You don't want to be alone. I understand." He stood up, hating to leave her but knowing he had to or he wouldn't be responsible for his actions. "I'll be back soon."

He got up and walked across the room. Opening the door, he looked back. "Get some rest." Then he resolutely shut the door behind him.

Chapter Twelve

By the time Lacey pulled open the drapes in her room, the sun was setting. She yawned, feeling wonderfully refreshed after a bath, food, and sleep. Glancing in the oak framed oval mirror over the washstand, she pushed fingers into her damp hair as she combed it back from her face. Her hair had been lightened by the sun and a spattering of freckles marred the skin across her nose, blending with the slight tan she had acquired on her journey.

A little concerned because Clint had yet to return, she glanced around the room. Suddenly, she wondered if he had simply left her and gone on after the Raiders himself. A shiver ran up her spine. What if he had sold one of the horses, then taken the other on the trail? She would have nothing left except two saddlebags. What could she do? Alone. Far from friends.

She shook her head at her irrational fear. Before Clint had come into her life, she had existed quite well alone. She could get back to the Marsdens if she decided to do that. Or she would find some way to go alone after the Raiders. Anyway, Clint had proved himself dependable and trustworthy up to now. Why was she suddenly worried? She had no answer, except that Clint had been gone a long time. What if he had found the Raiders in town

141

and they'd killed him?

A pain seared her heart. The thought of losing him, after all she had lost, was almost impossible to imagine. She glanced back in the mirror. Life was changing her. She looked more mature. Maybe Clint was changing her. She no longer felt so in control. Her emotions were continually threatening to overcome her. What was this man making her feel for him, for life?

She was afraid to answer that question. She couldn't accept him as her soul mate, not now, maybe never, because she couldn't make any plans for her future until the Raiders were brought to justice. And she might not live through that ordeal. No, right now she had no future, no right to private emotions until Randolph was stopped.

But her heart, her senses, didn't want to accept that fact. Suddenly, Lacey saw visions of Clint partially clothed, at work, laughing, kissing her, holding her close, his face changed with passion. No! She mustn't let herself become weak over this man. She mustn't let herself be hurt or prevented from reaching her goal. She must remember the horror of the Raiders. She must.

Pacing the small room, she put her mind to practical matters. Kate had taken her soiled, wet gray dress and underthings, promising to return them all cleaned and pressed first thing in the morning. Sarah had already turned that gown into a split skirt so she could ride astride more safely and comfortably. It wasn't proper riding attire for a lady, but maybe there was no longer a place for ladies in the South after the war.

She checked the fan Redbeard had given her. Before she had gone to sleep, she had dried it off, then set it out to finish drying. Now it was only

142

damp. The color had held and the vellum was only slightly warped. She would keep it forever, just like Sarah's shawl, as she rebuilt what she had lost to the war.

Picking up the shawl, she wrapped it around her shoulders, luxuriating in the soft, silky feel of it. Earlier, she had donned the cotton summer dress of dark blue flowers on an ecru background that Sarah had given her. It was her only other gown, and it made her feel almost young and carefree. But underneath that illusion was a growing concern for Clint and the need to go after the Raiders.

She sat down in the rocker, feeling tense. If Clint didn't return by dark, she'd have to go after him. Or should she wait until morning? No. There was no need to be concerned yet. But, unable to sit still, she jumped up and checked her boots. They were still wet but hopefully would be dry by morning. She was wearing a pair of soft natural kid slippers that had been protected in the saddlebags. But tomorrow she would need the boots.

Lacey returned to the chair and sat down. She shouldn't be so tense and she knew it. Clint would be back soon and all would be well. It wasn't like her to worry so much. She had trained herself to be cool, to get the job done under pressure. Maybe it was that so much was suddenly out of her control. She didn't know how to cope well in her new situation, but she was determined to learn.

Suddenly, she heard a key turn in the lock of the door. She jumped to her feet.

Opening the door, Clint stepped inside, quietly shutting the door behind him.

"Where have you been?" She was suddenly consumed by fury.

Surprised, Clint glanced around as if he had

missed something. "Like I told you before I left, I've been—"

"It couldn't have taken this long." She frowned, her voice hard, cold.

"If you'll notice, I had a bath, a few drinks."

"How could you leave me alone this long?" She clenched her fists. "I've been worried sick."

Again he looked surprised, then his face cleared and he smiled. "I didn't think you cared enough to worry."

Realizing how her reaction looked, she sat down abruptly. "Frankly, I thought maybe you'd taken the horses and gone on without me."

Now it was his turn to get angry. "What!" He strode across the room and stopped in front of her. "How could you think that? I gave you my word I'd take you with me."

"But I don't know you. How can I tell if your word is good?"

"Well, I'll be damned. After all we've been through together. I could have left you high and dry any time. You've slowed me down. I let the Raiders' trail get cold because of you." He inhaled sharply, and his voice lowered menacingly. "And now you get on your high horse and accuse me of—"

"I'm sorry." She stood up, her anger suddenly evaporating. "It's just that I thought . . . I was worried . . . after all . . . I'm sorry." She held out her hands, palms upward.

Clint jerked her against him, moving his hands up her arms. He encountered the shawl and jerked it off, tossing it to the floor so he could feel her skin. He handled her roughly, digging his fingers into her soft flesh as he moved up her arms to her shoulders. Then he slowly wrapped his hands around her neck.

144

She stood still, frozen with guilt and a growing fear.

"You amaze me. You're so damn vulnerable to me, to any man." He jerked his head back toward the door. "Out there you could be taken, held prisoner, used any way a man wanted to use you." His gray eyes suddenly turned to molten silver. "And yet you go on, acting like you have total control, like any man will bow to do your bidding. Damn, maybe they will. I sure have." His hands tightened around her neck.

"Clint, I—" He was really starting to scare her.

"But you're going to have to start paying me, Lacey. I think maybe you've learned how to get your way with men. You must have practiced your wiles on all those wounded soldiers, didn't you?"

"No. I told you—"

"Give me your wiles." He caressed her neck, smiling cruelly at her fear, her vulnerability. "Better yet, I'll take them." He lowered his head and pressed his lips to hers. Hard. Then harder.

She stood very still, totally unprepared for his assault. Perhaps if she did nothing, he would stop and go away. No man had ever made her react as he did. Still, he didn't know that, couldn't.

Shivering, she realized how hard it was going to be to remain calm, unresponding under his touch, for he spoke directly to her body, bypassing the control of her mind.

He released her neck to run his hands down her back and grasp her hips, pulling her against his hardness, his heat. Suddenly, she moaned and opened her mouth, wanting more of him. He thrust inside with his tongue, urgently exploring her, making her all his again. And she felt her body grow languid with passion as the kiss deepened and his hands caressed her body, feeling all her curves through the thin cotton gown.

As she responded, she ran her hands through his thick, dark hair, then pulled him closer, unable to feel him near enough, unable to get enough of him.

He left her mouth, red and swelling, and pressed kisses and quick nips down her throat to her breasts. Then he pulled the gown off her shoulders, exposing the tops of her breasts. Pressing heated kisses lower and lower, he suddenly pulled the garment to her waist, forcing her arms against her sides.

Her small, rosy nipples showed beneath the fine cotton chemise. He kissed them through the fabric, causing her to shudder, her body betraying her with each touch. Then he lowered the chemise, completely exposing her breasts and sucking one until she strained against him, clasping her hands around his waist. With both her nipples taut and her body pliant against him, he lifted her in his arms and started for the bed.

But there was a sharp knock on the door.

Clint looked around wildly. "Forget it," he muttered, then lowered his head to place soft, warm kisses over Lacey's face.

The knock came again. "Mr. McCullough, it's Kate. A telegram arrived for you."

He stilled, his eyes slowly turning the color of cold steel, and he set Lacey on the bed. "Business."

"What?" She pushed her hair back from her face, trying to make her mind work.

"Raiders. I'll take care of the telegram. Meet me downstairs as soon as you fix yourself up, and we'll have dinner." He strode toward the door, then turned back. "But don't think I'm done with you."

When he stepped outside, Lacey sat up. Her legs

were weak, her heart beat fast. What did this man do to her? In his arms, she could forget everything, even his anger, even his insults. When he kissed her, all she wanted was more of his heat, his scent, his nearness.

Shaking her head at her folly, she stood up. Pouring water into the bowl, she splashed it on her face, then brushed out her hair. Finally, she twined it into a chignon in back. Feeling better, she straightened her dress. She would not let this man get the better of her. And she would *never* believe her soul mate could treat her the way he did.

Calmer, she picked up her shawl and wrapped it around her shoulders. Then she left the room, her chin held high, realizing that once more she was doing as he bid.

In the lobby, a few people stood around talking and laughing. It was a pleasant scene, and in sharp contrast to the heated emotions that had so recently filled her room. The guests were simply, cleanly dressed, and most looked Southern.

Relaxing a little, she walked into the dining room. The light was soft, and a kerosene lantern with a red or green glass shade had been placed on each table. Red or green checked oilcloths covered sturdy oak tables, with matching chairs. A few diners were eating and the aroma of good food permeated the air. Lacey realized she was hungry all over again, especially for something hot and filling.

As she glanced around, Kate walked up to her. "Mrs. McCullough, how nice of you to join us."

Lacey nodded and followed Kate to a table for two near a dark window. Kate pulled out a chair and Lacey sat down, feeling uncomfortable.

"Mr. McCullough asked me to tell you he would be late. Perhaps you'd like something to drink? And we have an excellent bean soup tonight."

"That sounds good. Thank you."

After Kate left, Lacey gritted her teeth. Now Clint had the nerve to keep her waiting. She began to get mad again, then took a deep breath. No, there was no point in getting upset. She would eat a hot meal, forget Clint's games, then go upstairs and enjoy a good night's sleep. First thing in the morning she would pack up, get her horse, and start asking questions about the Raiders.

Satisfied with her decision, she smiled in appreciation when Kate brought the soup. A little surprised, she found it delicious. By the time she had finished, she was looking forward to the rest of the meal.

"Sorry I'm late," Clint said, coming up behind her and placing a quick kiss on her forehead.

Startled, she frowned, remembering how angry she was with him.

But he looked so pleased with himself, so boyish, that she almost relented. After all, it felt good to be with him. Nevertheless, she had to remember her plan and the fact that she couldn't trust him. Or could she?

Kate walked up and smiled. "We've got fresh pork chops tonight, fried okra, corn on the cob, cornbread and butter. And blackberry cobbler."

"Great!" Clint grinned. "Lacey?"

"That'll be fine." She spoke stiffly, hating the way she sounded but unable to stop it.

As Kate left, Clint leaned forward. "I gambled today."

"What!"

"And won."

She rolled her eyes, not knowing what to say.

"You know we were desperate for money and I

148

felt lucky after our little . . . well, after you kissed me."

"*I* kissed you?"

"We kissed each other." He rubbed the scar on his cheek. "So we've got some extra. I've already paid for Redbeard three nights. I'll buy you a new outfit."

"What I have is fine." He was making her feel like a child. And his happiness made her worry and anger seem petty. All in all, she was feeling worse by the moment.

"What's wrong, Lacey?" His voice was warm, his eyes concerned.

"You can't treat me like a child."

He hesitated as Kate set heaping plates of food on the table, then left. "I'm not. Maybe I'm being clumsy about it, but I'm trying to show you that . . . I care."

Jerking her head up in surprise, she looked at him warily. "You've a funny way of showing it."

"Here's your cornbread and butter," Kate interrupted as she set more plates on the table. "Enjoy."

Lacey watched Kate walk away, no longer feeling hungry.

Clint picked up a piece of steaming cornbread, then set it down. "Maybe we're all out of practice. Maybe the rules have changed since the war. I don't know. But, damn it, we're a team. And if we're going to work together, then we have to share. I got some money and I'm willing to give you some."

He was making her feel small and mean. She hated the feeling, hated the emotions she couldn't seem to control anymore. She took a deep breath. Perhaps she was overreacting. What she needed to do was relax and keep in mind her goal. Randolph's Raiders. Whatever it took to catch them was what

149

she had to do. And if Clint were willing to help her, then she should accept whatever he had to offer.

She smiled at him. "Sorry. I'm glad you got the money. I was just surprised you'd chance what little we had on gambling."

"Like I said, I felt lucky."

"And thanks for taking care of the captain."

"I figure we owe him."

She felt a little more like eating. "Did you hear anything about the Raiders?"

"Plenty. But wait a minute." He tackled his food with gusto.

Realizing she was going to have to wait for the news until he'd eaten some, she turned her attention to her own food. Cutting into a tender pork chop, she was delighted with the flavor. Soon her appetite had returned and she was eating with as much pleasure as Clint.

Finally, he wiped his mouth with a red checked napkin, took a long drink of water, then concentrated on her. "Seems the Raiders went up the Tennessee, then back down. They've been in this area for a while. Why, nobody knows. But they figure the Raiders are coming into town dressed like carpetbaggers and mixing with the crowd."

"And nobody's seen their faces because they kill their victims and burn their houses." Lacey looked thoughtful. "That way there's no trace left, is there?"

"Right. But we've seen them."

"And lived to tell about it." She finished a piece of cornbread. "Have you contacted the local law? Or is that what the telegram was about?"

He hesitated, his mind racing for a plausible answer. "First, I sent a telegram to a friend of mine in Tuscumbia. That's on the Tennessee River in eastern

150

Alabama. I was checking to make sure the Raiders hadn't been seen there in the last week or so."

"And?"

"The telegram he sent confirmed that. So I'm fairly sure they're in this area." He grimaced. "As far as local law, I don't know who to trust. Anybody from Northerners to local Southerners could be involved in payoff. And somebody's got to be handling the stolen goods."

Lacey felt chilled.

"Besides, I think we can do it on our own."

"I guess we'll have to. Where do we go from here?" She realized she was saying "we" again but knew it only made sense. With Clint on her side, she stood a much better chance of catching the outlaws.

"I know we could use some rest, but I want to hit the trail early tomorrow."

Kate walked up and smiled. "Blackberry cobbler?"

"Yes." Clint agreed. "And coffee."

"It was delicious." Lacey smiled with pleasure.

"Thank you." Kate picked up several plates, then left.

"First we'll go find that last burned house."

"But it rained." Lacey looked skeptical.

"I know. We might still find something. I'm betting the Raiders won't be around these parts much longer. It's bound to be getting hot for them."

"And if we can pick up a trail, we follow."

"Right. The horses will be well fed and we'll have fresh supplies. What do you say?"

Kate set down cobbler and coffee, picked up a few more dishes, then quietly left.

"I say I'm ready to go, but—"

"I won't promise I'll keep my hands off you."

Lacey raised a brow, then suddenly felt brave. "I'm not sure I want you to, anyway."

Clint grinned, a quick predatory movement of his lips. "I should get you to bargain your body for my help. I think by now you know you'd have a tough time making it without me. So, do I get your body?"

Lacey picked up her coffee and chuckled.

"I'm serious."

She looked into his eyes. They were molten silver. And she felt the heat clear to her core. "What if I say no?"

"Say yes."

She felt heat rise upward from her breasts to her face. "That seems so cold."

"Far from it."

"I don't think you'd make me."

"I'm still asking."

She stood up, desperate to get away from him, for she wanted to agree. Everything she'd ever been taught told her that response would be wrong, and yet every part of her cried out that it was right. Walking quickly from the room, she hurried through the lobby and stepped outside.

Taking in deep breaths, she looked upward. The moon was a silver crescent in the sky. Stars twinkled. And the air was scented with wildflowers. She heard Clint walk up behind her, but she didn't try to run away. And when he took her hand, she followed him into the alley beside the inn.

"We can't keep denying what's between us, Lacey, and still stay sane. We're going to be together a lot."

"I don't know what to say."

"Don't say anything right now." He took her in his arms, gently, tenderly, desperate to keep himself under control. "I want you. You can trust me."

She felt the strong beat of his heart under her cheek, then his hand turned her face upward. Their eyes met in acknowledgment of their desire. When his lips came down on hers, she knew she was lost and knew it was what she had wanted all along. With a sob, she opened her mouth to his, accepting his kiss. Then his body was hard and hot against her.

And there seemed to be nothing she could deny him.

Chapter Thirteen

Clint didn't give Lacey an opportunity to change her mind. Putting a hand firmly to the small of her back, he hurried her into the inn, up the stairs, then over the threshold to their room before either of them had much of a chance to think.

He lit the lamp on the dresser. It cast soft light over the room, bathing Lacey in a white glow. Angel or devil? He couldn't be sure. Sometimes she seemed so pure, so right in purpose, that he didn't think he should touch her. But then she would blaze with passion in his arms and he would realize she had to be experienced, had to have cut her teeth on Confederate soldiers.

Now he didn't care. He had let the beast surface to track the Raiders. And he'd picked up Lacey's scent as well. There was no turning back, not if they traveled together. He'd rather love than fight on the trip, and between the two of them it seemed there was no middle ground.

If there were to be guilt, he'd deal with it later. For now, he had to have Lacey. He unbuttoned the cuffs of his sleeves, then began at the collar, watching her watch him. As he exposed the thick, dark hair on his chest, he saw her eyes widen slightly and her lips part. He shrugged out of the shirt, then tossed it to the floor.

Her tongue flicked out to wet her lower lip. He smiled at her response, a feral movement of his lips. Yes, the beast was loose. And ready to seduce Lacey Whitmore. But what did it matter? He'd done a lot worse. And they had a right to as much pleasure as they could take after all they had been through, all they had yet to do.

He moved toward her, slowly, seductively, the light casting the muscled ridges of his body in sharp contour. And the scars, ranging in color from new to old, from small to large, told their own story of his prowess in battle.

Lacey reached out to him, slowly placing her hand against each scar, and he felt as if she drew out all the hurt and painful memories from the wounds with her touch. Suddenly, he felt a tightness in his chest, a desire that transcended the physical. But he had no experience with that feeling and cast it aside for the more immediate pleasures of the flesh.

She ran her fingers through the hair on his chest, teasing, exploring, then touched his nipples, felt them harden, and looked up at him in triumph.

Damn, but she was testing him, seeing how long he could stand her touch before crushing her beneath him. It was a test he was bound to fail. He wanted her too much to hold out long. Shuddering beneath her hands, he felt her explore the hard, smooth muscles of his arms, then move behind him, once more finding the scars, healing, exciting, teasing before coming back to stand in front of him.

Her blue eyes were dark, filled with the rising power of her sensuality. His nostrils flared as he caught her scent. He was so hard he felt as if he would rip right out of his trousers to get at her.

"Take off your clothes." His voice was low, rough with desire.

She smiled, a slight movement of one corner of her lips. Tossing her head, she pulled her hair out of the chignon and let it fall in a golden halo to her shoulders and down her back. Her eyes never left his, watching the molten silver grow hotter and hotter.

He took a deep breath, controlling himself with more difficulty all the time. "Your dress."

She hesitated, almost as if shy. And he suddenly wished she *were* a virgin, that he could make her completely his, a woman no other man would ever see or touch. Then he cursed himself for a fool. No woman with Lacey's looks and touch could have survived the war without at least one man, and most likely a whole company, at her beck and call.

As she began unbuttoning the tiny blue buttons on the bodice of her gown, her hands trembled. He watched her struggle for a moment, then impatience made him thrust away her hands so he could finish the job. But he suddenly found his own fingers weren't much more steady as he felt the heat and softness of her breasts against his hands.

Cursing, he finally finished and pushed her gown to the floor. She stood silently before him, her full, high breasts outlined by the sheer cotton of the chemise, the ruffled white petticoat concealing her hips and legs. In all white, she looked virginal, and his heart increased its pace.

"Take off the petticoat."

Again she did as he bid, but this time her hands moved more surely as she let the petticoat slip to the floor around her feet. Standing in her chemise and drawers, stockings held up with blue garters just above her knees, she was more enticing than he could ever have imagined.

When he stepped toward her, she blushed, the pale pink making her skin glow. He felt like a beast come to ravish her, and perhaps he was. For he could no longer control his passions.

He pulled her against him, feeling her heat, her softness, her satiny skin against his bare flesh, and he growled as he thrust his hands into her golden tresses to pull her head back. Looking into her eyes, the pupils enlarged, he pressed his lips to hers, then pushed inside.

As if the beast were finally released, he suddenly couldn't get enough of the taste of her, for he plunged with his tongue, then nipped with his teeth, teasing her lips with his own until she was moaning against him, twining her hands in his hair and her leg around his. Emboldened, he lifted her in his arms, pressing her body against his chest, and carried her to the bed.

He didn't lie her down gently. Rather, he jerked back the covers, then slid her into the center of the feather bed. And pounced. Holding her down with his heavy body, he grinned, a swift baring of his teeth, as he realized he finally had her where he wanted her. Now he would make her feel all the lust he had nursed for so long, make her think of nothing except him, make her beg for the pleasure only he could give her.

He wanted to rip the last of her clothes from her body, but he restrained himself. Instead, he slipped the chemise off her and tossed it to the floor. Her pale, round breasts with their perfect rosy centers beckoned him.

Running his hands down her breasts, he felt their tips harden. He was tempted to pause there but didn't. Instead, he slipped a hand inside her drawers and heard her inhale sharply in response. Then he felt the thick triangle of hair under his palm as he moved lower to her soft, hot entrance. She shivered under his touch and he stroked, calming her, before pushing two fingers inside. And then he almost lost control, for she was so wet, so tight, so exciting, and he felt so powerful that he growled, a low, rough sound as he fought to temper his reaction.

She moaned in excitement, reaching up to him, and he turned back to her, pulling his hand free. Eyes locked with hers, he put his fingers in his mouth and sucked. Now that he had the taste of her she could never get away. And she had to know it.

Leaning down, he kissed her lightly before dipping his tongue into her mouth. She clung to him, returning his kiss, her body feverish as his hands moved over her again. And his mouth followed his hands, kissing, stroking down to her breasts, where he kneaded and suckled until she writhed up against him in desperate desire. When he finally removed her drawers, she could only sigh in relief.

He looked at her, long and hard, seeing what he had been imagining for weeks. And he was not disappointed. Far from it. And then he looked at her face. Her color was heightened, her hair a wild mass around her face, her lips pouty from being kissed.

Smiling slightly, she raised a languid hand and pointed at his trousers.

Imperious to the end. But she was right. He stepped from the bed, jerked off his boots, then dropped his trousers. Naked, he stood before her. She raised herself on one elbow to examine him. Suddenly, he had the irrational, horrible fear she might reject him. Then the beast overrode that thought and he crawled in between her legs, raising her hips to receive him.

As he pressed his hard, swollen tip to her entrance, she seemed to recoil, as if surprised or afraid. But he was well past being able to reason. Feverish, he concentrated completely on controlling himself long enough to bring her pleasure. But when she wriggled against him, he could wait no longer. He pushed into her and was stopped. By a barrier. Even through the heat of his desire he knew what it meant. But he couldn't, wouldn't stop. Not now.

He thrust through to her depths and heard her cry out in pain, clutching at his shoulders. Suddenly, she was trying to get away. But he held her, knowing she would soon feel pleasure instead of pain if he could keep his own passion under control long enough.

Sweat beaded his forehead as he began to move deep inside her, the rhythm building faster and faster. Soon she no longer fought him but pulled him toward her, writhing up against him, moving with his rhythm, desperately seeking her own release. And in his fever, he realized he'd never reacted this strongly to a woman before, never felt such agony of need, such intensity.

159

Finally, Clint could hold back no longer and thrust fast and hard into her, and he was rewarded with her small cries of pleasure that built to a long moan as she reached the pinnacle of desire. Then he added his own groan of ecstasy as he found release deep within her.

In the aftermath of their passion, he rolled to his side and pulled her against him, pressing soft kisses to her face. When she shivered, he pulled the sheet up around her shoulders, although hating to cover her nudity.

Then he took a deep breath. "You should have told me you were a virgin."

"I wanted you. I didn't think it mattered." She was still breathing fast.

"It mattered." He squeezed her shoulder. "I'm glad I was the one." He felt an enormous pride in what she had given him, but he also knew she wouldn't have if she'd known he was a Northerner. He felt a slight sting of guilt in having seduced her, but it couldn't compare to his happiness in finally possessing her. "I'm sorry I accused you of having other men."

"It doesn't matter now."

"I knew better, but I was jealous."

She gently touched his face. Passion. Now she knew why women did what they did for men. But, soul mate or not, she couldn't think of a future with him, didn't even know if he wanted it, because they had yet to catch the Raiders and that must come first. And love? She sighed. Maybe it had become a luxury in the aftermath of the war and only a lucky few could afford it.

"Lacey, are you all right?"

She smiled and touched the tip of his nose with

her finger. "I'm happy. That was wonderful."

"It'll get even better."

Slapping his chest, she narrowed her eyes suggestively. "I don't know how."

"I do, and I'll teach you." Under the sheet, he touched her nipple, felt it harden, and laughed. "I take that back. Maybe you'll teach me." He hugged her against him, then groaned. "Damn, I'm hungry and the food's all downstairs."

"Not so." Lacey sat up. "There's some cheese, bread, and lemonade left."

He growled and grabbed her, nuzzling her neck. "Where are you hiding it?"

"What will you give me if I tell you?"

He jerked back the sheet, exposing his body. "Is that your price?"

"Yes." Laughing, she stepped off the bed.

He pinched her bottom.

"Ouch!" She gave him a hurt look, then laughed as she rubbed her hip. "Now I may eat this all myself."

"Only if I'm a gentleman."

"And are you?"

"Absolutely not!"

"That's right. You're a beast." She lifted the tray and started back for the bed.

But Clint was still. Beast. She was more right than she realized, but maybe that's what it took to survive, to take the woman you wanted, and to bring vicious criminals to justice. In that case, he was what he had to be, what he'd been made to be. Yet he regretted what he'd become and wondered if there would ever be any going back.

"Clint?"

He jerked his mind back to Lacey. Damn. The

161

last thing he needed right now was to think too much. Quickly, he fluffed the pillows and shoved them against the headboard.

She handed him the tray, then sat down beside him and pulled the covers up to their waists.

Balancing the tray on his legs for a moment, he frowned, then made a decision. Spreading a green checked napkin on the bed, he set the bread and cheese on it. Next he set the pitcher of lemonade and a glass on the floor. Last, he dropped the empty tray on the floor.

Looking at Lacey, he grinned. "Now we can eat in comfort." And he pulled her into the crook of his arm.

"This is comfort?"

"Yes." He tore off a hunk of bread and held it to her mouth.

Chuckling, she took a bite, then watched him do the same. Next he handed her the cheese. They ate together, back and forth, the pale light of the lamp casting their bodies in alabaster and shadow, their laughter low and intimate.

Finally, Lacey brushed at his chest. "Look, you've got crumbs all over you."

"Keep that up and I'll forget about food."

She looked into his eyes, saw the fire, and felt an answering response within herself. He kissed the tip of her nose, then reached down for the lemonade. He poured a glassful and handed it to her. She drank, but when she handed the glass to him, he turned it so he drank in the same place she had.

Suddenly, she began to feel warm all over, desire for him springing alive. She wanted to share so much with him, like they had shared the food. He offered the glass to her again, but she shook her head in denial. Finishing off the lemonade, he set the glass on the floor, then turned back to her.

She touched his face, wanting to make him happy, to show him how much he had come to mean to her. Yes, she wanted to share. Running a fingertip down the scar on his cheek, she wished she could heal it, make it go away forever. She leaned forward and kissed the old wound, feeling her nipples brush his chest. They were instantly hard and she felt a burning in her center.

But she restrained herself and pressed soft kisses to his forehead, his closed eyes, then the corners of his lips. Lightly, she stroked his mouth with the tip of her tongue, then pushed harder. He opened his mouth, and she teased the sensitive flesh of his inner lips before pushing deep inside, at the same time keeping her breasts lightly brushing his hairy chest.

Clint groaned but made no move to touch or hold her, wanting her to feel free to explore his body the way he had hers. She kissed him, not like a virgin but like a wanton, and he was hard pressed to restrain his growing passion.

Then she left his mouth and traveled down his neck, kissing, tasting, nipping, until she came to his shoulders, where she toyed with the sensitive places until he couldn't be still any longer. Groaning, he pulled her away from him and held her so he could look into her eyes. They were a bright, teasing blue, yet with intense heat in their depths.

She smiled, a seductive movement of her lips. "I'm not done, Clint."

Groaning again, he pulled her close and pressed hot kisses to her face and hair, running his hands over her naked body until he reached the blue garters still holding up her hose. He snapped one.

In retaliation, she playfully slapped his chest, then lowered her head and lightly bit each of his nipples.

"Lacey," he muttered, feeling himself grow impossibly hard. He took her hand and wrapped it around his arousal.

She inhaled sharply as he moved her hand up and down, teaching her the rhythm, what pleased him. "You're so big." She hesitated. "I don't know how you fit inside me."

He stopped her hand. "I'll show you."

"No. Wait. I wasn't done."

But he couldn't wait any longer and lifted her to straddle him. He slowly lowered her until his tip was pressed against her entrance. Fascinated, she grasped him again, then guided him inside. With a fierce movement, he plunged in deep, then stopped, willing himself to wait.

She moved experimentally. He groaned, shuddered, and dug his fingers into her hips. Sliding up and down on his shaft, Lacey could hardly believe the pleasure that flooded her or the building vortex of passion that she was sharing with him. How could it be so good? So right?

And then she shivered as he began to move her up and down with his hands, faster and faster, until she leaned over and braced her hands on his chest, her breasts dangling down close to his face. When he grasped one nipple with his mouth and sucked as he increased the pace, she suddenly reached her peak, cried out in passion, and dug her nails into his flesh. Soon his cry mingled with hers as they found ecstasy together.

Tears filling her eyes, she collapsed against him, wonderfully happy. He stroked her back, catching his breath, feeling his body relax. Never had he known a woman like Lacey. Never.

When he turned her on her side so he could face her, he looked into her eyes and was rewarded with a shy smile and a gaze filled with wonderment. He wiped away the moisture at the corners of her eyes. "Was I so bad?"

"You know better." She touched his lips with the tip of a finger. "You want a compliment, don't you?"

He grinned.

"You're wonderful. I had no idea what I was missing."

Suddenly, he frowned. "It's not that way with everybody."

She looked mischievous. "Does that mean I shouldn't go looking for comparisons?"

His gray eyes grew cold and hard. "I'd kill any man who touched you, Lacey."

She laughed softly, trying to lighten his seriousness. "Is that a threat?"

"The truth. Pure and simple. You're mine."

She sat up, suddenly disturbed. "Who knows what tomorrow will bring. You've been through the war. You know what it's like."

"Are you protecting yourself from hurt, or is it me?"

She pushed hair back from her face, suddenly cold. "I mean, we've got to catch the Raiders. Who knows if either one of us will come out alive."

Nodding, he drew her back to him. "I won't let anything harm you."

She shook her head, her eyes mutinous. "You can't protect me completely, Clint. If nothing else, the war taught us that." She pulled away, not wanting to feel so much for him, not wanting to be so close or see the possessive look in his eyes, because she didn't know if she could stand the pain if it were suddenly gone. "We'd better live each day as if it were the last."

"Then come here and I'll make you want to live forever."

She turned to him, having no doubt he could.

Chapter Fourteen

Heading south out of Guntersville the next morning, Lacey realized she felt a little uncomfortable with Clint. In fact, more than a little uncomfortable. For in the clear light of day her passion of the night before amazed her, slightly embarrassed her, and made her question her former control. How could she have felt so much, given so much, and yet still be herself today?

She had no answers, yet her mind wouldn't let it be. She kept reliving what they had shared and her body got hot with her thinking about it. She'd had no idea passion could be so overwhelming, so inspiring, so transcending.

Surprisingly, after being that intimately close to Clint the night before, today she felt stilted and strange, wanting to talk and yet not knowing what to say. Since getting up, there hadn't been much time for conversation because they'd been hurrying to start after the Raiders, and of course, they had spoken little during the night.

She didn't know what other women said after a night like she'd just had. Perhaps a polite thank you. But that didn't seem right, either. She was simply too inexperienced to know what was proper etiquette. But, then, how could she have been experienced for something like this?

Shaking her head, she decided to push thoughts of Clint to a far corner of her mind and think of something else.

She had hated to say good-bye to Manny, Kate, and Redbeard, having grown fond of them in a short time. Manny had cautioned them to be wary of strangers and not camp near the road. Kate had packed fresh food for the journey and reminded them to be careful where they ate when her food ran out. And Redbeard had promised to stay off his leg for two more days. Fortunately, his wound was healing well and Lacey knew he was enjoying his stay at the inn, especially since his merchandise had brought more money than he had expected.

Glancing around, she noticed that in the aftermath of the storm, the land was clean and the skies were a clear, bright blue. The road was still muddy and rutted from the storm, and they were the only travelers as far as she could see. Their horses were frisky from being well curried, fed, and rested, and they moved along at a good pace.

Then her gaze caught Clint's eye. He smiled and nodded. She felt her heart beat faster, then looked away. She still didn't know what to say.

Clint watched Lacey a moment, then glanced back at the road for any sign of Randolph. But his mind was brooding about her. He wished he could tell her the truth about himself but at the same time dreaded to reveal he was a Northerner.

He thought of the night before. A virgin. Maybe if he weren't so much a beast, he would regret having dirtied her, filling her with the filth of the war, taking her purity. But his life the past four years had taught him to take what pleasure he could get when and where he could get it.

Touching the scar on his face, he knew what he

had experienced with Lacey went well beyond a night's pleasure. And if not for Randolph, he'd take her to his lair and keep her safe and protected in his territory forever. But he couldn't do that, not now. Instead, he had to take her into danger and try to keep her safe. And away from other men's lusts.

He hated to have so many lies between them, but there was no way around it. And the lies were growing. He'd had to make up stories about the telegram and money to cover the truth. Actually, he had telegraphed his superior a coded report, and the reply had been to proceed with his plans. As for the money, he kept extra hidden in his belt, but he had to pretend they were short of funds as any former Confederate soldier would be. He had decided to use gambling as a cover every time they needed more money.

He needed to talk with Lacey about the night before . . . or thought he should, anyway, since she'd been a virgin. But there hadn't been time earlier, and now there was a tension between them. He didn't want to frighten her. He didn't want her to know how much a beast he was. So maybe it was best left alone.

As they rode on, the sun moved higher in the sky and Lacey was glad of the wide-brimmed straw hat tied with a red ribbon under her chin. Clint had bought it for her when he had picked up supplies. She also wore her kid leather gloves to protect her hands. Her gray dress was clean, although showing signs of wear, but she didn't care about that as long as she was comfortable. All in all, she was well protected from the sun and weather. Her mother would have been proud of her, and she knew enough not to want a sunburn or any more blisters.

Clint had bought himself a new shirt, and it was of a sensible gray and black plaid cotton. She knew the hat and shirt must have cost a lot, even if prices had gone down since the war. She hadn't told him, but the hat was the first brand new piece of clothing she'd had since before the war, for during those dark days clothes had become so scarce and expensive people would reuse, refit, and make garments from draperies or other large pieces of fabric. And as far as style, it had ceased to be of much importance.

Now she supposed things would go back to the way they were, but without much money she couldn't imagine Southerners living very differently than they had during the war. However, there would be plenty of Yankees and carpetbaggers around to sell and buy. And, of course, she enjoyed pretty clothes enough to wish she could afford new ones. But that wasn't for her now.

"This way, Lacey." Clint interrupted her thoughts as he turned his horse left down a rutted road.

"Do you think it's safe?" She paced alongside him, glancing constantly around for any sign or sound of the Raiders.

"Should be. From what Manny said, Randolph wouldn't have stayed around here after destroying that house several days ago."

But Lacey was still uneasy as they rode on down the road, trying to avoid potholes filled with water. Finally, they reached a clearing with a burned-out house in its center. A few stray chickens clucked and scratched in the yard. The smell of burned wood was still in the air. And the storm had blown down several trees.

Their horses pranced nervously. Clint jumped

down, handed Lacey his reins, and squeezed her hand. "Stay here. I'll scout around. You hear any shots, get the hell out of here."

"But, Clint—"

"If it comes to it, protect yourself." He gave her a hard stare, then walked toward the house.

More uneasy than ever, Lacey glanced around, straining to see or hear anything that might be creeping up on them. She also watched Clint as he wandered the area, bent down several times, then continued on around what was left of the cottage. She shivered, reminded of her own home. How many others had Randolph destroyed? And how many more would he burn before he was caught? Again she shivered, even though it was hot in the noonday sun.

Clint walked back to her, a frown creasing his forehead. "Not much left after the rain. But it looked like it was about the same size group as the Raiders."

Lacey handed him the reins, and he remounted. They started back down the road. Silent, Clint was lost in thought as they rode, and Lacey continued to watch for any sign of the outlaws.

As they reached the main road again, a wagon suddenly raced by, its mules walleyed, covered in sweat. A terrified family clutched the sides of the wildly rocking wagon.

Clint started after them, calling to halt.

The frightened driver saw Clint and tried to increase the mules' pace, but the animals were exhausted and could go no faster. Clint rode up beside them and pulled the lead mule to a stop. Then he approached the driver.

The man held up his hands in a defenseless position. "We got nothing more."

171

Lacey joined them and smiled encouragingly. "It's all right. We aren't going to hurt you."

At the sight of a woman, the driver relaxed, slumped, and turned toward his wife. Tears streaked her face as she clutched a baby to her breasts.

"What happened?" Clint moved his mount closer.

"Raiders!" The man pointed back in the direction he'd come. "We were going home after buying supplies. When we got close, we saw smoke. I turned right around and started back to town as fast as I could." He looked behind him again.

"Did they see you?" Clint clenched his hands around the reins.

"Don't know." The man was sweating and kept looking back, hardly paying attention to Clint. "No time to talk. They could be on us any minute. We're getting back to town. And you better, too."

"Where is your place?" Clint's voice was like steel.

The man looked at him in shock. "You don't want to go nowhere near there."

"Where?" Lacey moved closer.

The entire family looked at them as if they'd been in the sun too long, then the man shook his head. "Follow the road south. Third turn on your right near a pecan orchard. But you go back there, you're dead."

"Send the law." Clint turned his horse south.

The man shook his head, then clicked to his mules.

Lacey smiled in encouragement. "Kate's Place is clean and reasonable if you need a place to stay in Guntersville."

"Thanks." The man started the mules forward. When they wouldn't move fast enough, he called to them and snapped the reins. Finally, they broke into a trot.

"If it's the Raiders, we got a break." Clint looked grim as he watched the wagon head toward Guntersville.

"But that family didn't."

"They're alive."

She hesitated, thinking. "What do you mean, if it's the Raiders?"

"No proof. Not yet, anyway."

"But who else around here is burning houses?"

"Somebody could be learning Raider tricks." He took a deep breath. "But I think it's the Raiders."

"So do I."

He jerked his head back toward town. "You can go on in and come back with the law."

Her eyes narrowed. "No. This is my fight the same as yours. And by the time I got back, it'd all be over." She didn't say it, but she thought that by then he'd probably be dead and the Raiders gone. She wasn't going to abandon him now.

"All right. Let's go." He set his heels to his horse's flanks and took off at a gallop.

She followed, more anxious than ever to catch the Raiders.

They kept up the pace, wind whistling in their ears, the sun hot on their backs. The land was a green blur around them. And they were all alone on the road.

Suddenly, Clint saw the pecan orchard. He slowed his mount and Lacey followed his action. Off the road to the west, they could see smoke. And smell it, too.

When they came to the third narrow road, Clint

took it, but quickly guided his horse back into the trees. When he was satisfied they couldn't be seen, he dismounted. Lacey joined him. Without saying a word, he drew her into his arms and held her tight. Finally, he pressed warm lips to hers as if he might never get the chance to do it again.

"Lacey, I don't want you going in with me. I don't know what we'll find."

"I'm not being left behind." Her eyes blazed with determination.

"But—"

"No *but's*. Remember what they did to my family."

He relented, understanding her pain and determination, but still wanting to keep her safe, pure, untainted by death. Yet he couldn't stop her from taking revenge and he knew it.

Nodding, he pulled out his rifle, then took her hand. They began making their way toward the smoke, leading their horses through the trees, causing as little noise as possible.

When they came to the edge of the orchard, they were near a trampled vegetable garden. The house was crumbling in on itself. Intense heat radiated outward. Three dogs lay dead in the yard. Behind the house, the barn and several smaller buildings burned, thick smoke spiraling upward.

But there was no sight of the Raiders or any other human.

"We missed them," Lacey whispered.

"But we can track them." Clint's voice was full of determination. "Come on."

He led the way through the vegetable garden. When they neared the house, he started checking the ground for prints.

Keeping watch, Lacey realized how much this

174

burned farm looked like the one they had seen earlier. And how much they both looked like her own home. Renewed anger filled her.

"Lacey, over here."

She led her horse over to Clint.

"Look at that." He pointed at the ground, then kneeled and ran a finger over an indentation that showed an abnormal place on a horseshoe. "That print was left at your parents' house, too."

"Then we're after the right men." Her heart beat faster. They were close, very close.

"Come on. If it doesn't rain, we can track them."

Glancing upward, she was relieved to see the sky was still a clear, brilliant blue. There was not a threat of rain in sight.

They followed the Raiders trail down the road they had avoided when they'd ridden in. It led back to the main road, but then the tracks divided. Clint walked one direction, examining the trail, then the other way. Finally, he stopped and looked at her.

"Several Raiders went south. The others headed back toward Guntersville."

"Which way did the man who rides the horse with the marked horseshoe head?"

"South."

"Let's go after him, Clint. If the others went back to Guntersville, maybe we can catch them there."

"I don't like it. We could be walking into a trap."

"What choice do we have? This is the closest we've come."

"No choice."

They remounted. As they headed south, Clint

175

watched the trail, continually glancing all around. He didn't want to be taken by surprise. But so far they seemed to be behind the outlaws and there was no sign of the others having rejoined the band they followed.

Silently, they continued, watching, listening, and the tension increased. Lacey could hardly bear not having it over and done with. She wanted to race ahead and catch up with the outlaws. But she knew that would give away their location and perhaps put them in a position to be killed. So she remained quiet and tried to appreciate the beautiful day, the green forest around them, and Clint's company. But none of it took her mind off their danger or the Raiders.

At sunset, Clint left the road and guided them behind a rock outcropping. He got down, then lifted Lacey from her horse, letting her body slide down the length of him. He looked at her for a long moment, then gently pushed a strand of hair back from her face.

"Let's get some food while we can."

"Should we take the time?" She frowned in concern, although enjoying his touch.

"We've got to rest the horses. And us, too."

Reluctantly, she turned to take food out of her saddlebag. Clint was right, but she was so afraid of losing the Raiders' trail she didn't ever want to stop.

While the horses grazed, they spread out a picnic supper. The food looked delicious, but Lacey didn't feel hungry.

"Eat." Clint took a bite out of a large wedge of cheese.

She ate some bread but felt it lodge in her throat. Drinking warm water, she shook her head.

176

She was too tense to have any appetite.

"As I see it, we've got two choices. Go on after dark. If the Raiders feel safe and make a fire at their camp, we've got them."

"What if they keep going?"

"I'm betting they're arrogant enough to stop for the night, rest their horses, eat what they stole, maybe even get drunk if they got liquor."

"What's the other choice?"

"We rest and start out in the morning."

"If you're planning to stop on my account, don't."

Clint smiled. "I was thinking of the horses."

"No you weren't." She gave him an indignant stare, then returned his smile. It felt good not to be alone. Suddenly, she felt a little more like eating and picked up a piece of cheese.

"We're all tired, but we're close." He looked to the south. "I can almost smell them. And at night we can catch them off guard . . . I hope."

"It's been so long I can't wait any longer. If we can get them now, let's do it."

"I'm going to try to take them in alive."

"But what if they fight?"

"We'll do whatever it takes to stop them."

"Good." She picked up a fried pie, suddenly determined to eat as much as it took to be strong for the coming battle.

"And, Lacey, don't do anything dangerous. Stay behind me. I'm used to this type of thing."

She wanted revenge. She didn't want to be safe. But if she were to stay alive long enough to catch all the Raiders, she must protect herself. She nodded. "I hope Randolph's in this group."

"If we can get him, the others might disband on their own."

"Then let's go get him."

They repacked their food, remounted, then started out again. Dusk quickly turned to night, the heat lessened, and Lacey took off her hat. She tied it to the saddle, then checked her pistol, ready to use it if she must.

Clint watched for any sign of the Raiders, not knowing what to expect from moment to moment. Suddenly, he signaled for her to stop. He could smell a wood fire. Somebody had made camp up ahead.

Silently, he dismounted, and she did, too. He checked the trail again, making sure they were following the same horseshoe print. Satisfied, he led their horses off the trail and tied them out of sight. Finally, he pulled out his rifle, took extra ammunition, then nodded at Lacey.

Clutching her own pistol, she followed him when he headed back across the road. As they crept into the woods, she saw the light of a campfire nestled in amongst the trees bordering the road.

When they were close, he stopped and pulled her to him. "I'm going to get into position so I can pick them off with my rifle if I have to. I want you right behind me. Use your pistol if it looks like they're going to get away."

She squeezed his hand, then trailed him to the camp. They were so close she could smell food cooking and hear men's voices. Anger threatened to overcome her good sense, but she stood still, trembling with repressed emotions.

"Raiders," Clint called, "you're under arrest. Don't go for your guns and you can come out alive."

Chapter Fifteen

Clint's words were answered with gunfire.

And he returned in kind. Three men went down, while a fourth kicked dirt over the fire and grabbed a saddlebag. As the light went out, Lacey shot at the outlaw. He fired back, and she felt a bullet hit her left arm. Pain seared her, but she bit her lower lip to keep from crying out. She didn't think her wound was too bad, if treated soon and properly. But it would have to wait. What was more important now was to catch the Raider.

Clenching her teeth against the burning pain, she continued to fire at the outlaw, the noise of her pistol joining the sound of Clint's rifle. But the man slipped into the nearby underbrush and escaped.

"Damn!" Clint said, reloading. "Stay here. I'm going after him."

She grabbed his arm, suddenly afraid for him.

Covering her hand, he squeezed. "Keep down."

Then he was gone, running through the camp. He knew he made enough noise to cover the sound of the fleeing Raider, but he couldn't do a thing about it. As soon as he was in the concealing darkness and cover on the other side, he stopped and listened.

Nothing.

Too silent. He knew the outlaw was experienced, wary, and maybe wounded. All of that made him very dangerous and very cautious. But now Clint was the hunter. The tables had been turned and the man had to know it. The Raider was alone and vulnerable, but still a tough opponent.

Looking for anything that might lead him to the outlaw, Clint took several more steps. Twigs snapped. Several shots were fired at him and he hit the ground, lucky he hadn't been shot. Then the ground shook as horses were sent thundering toward him. He fired into the air, not wanting to wound the animals but not wanting to be trampled to death either.

The animals parted around him, and more bullets were shot in his direction as the horses ran past. He looked up, dust churned up by the animals' hooves stinging his eyes. But it didn't keep him from seeing the dark shape of a man riding one of the horses. And then they were gone.

Suddenly, shots rang out from the road and the horses stampeded, going in all directions. Clint stood up wearily, dusted himself off, and started back to the camp. The outlaw had been clever. At night, with the horses scattered, it would be impossible to pick up the right tracks. By day, they should be able to find the trail of the horse carrying extra weight. But by then, the man would be well away.

Disgusted, he walked into the Raiders' camp. Three Union soldiers lay dead. He hated the sight. Would the war never be over? Would his hands never be clean? He ran a hand through his hair. But he'd done what he had to do. Now he had to think about Lacey.

He went to where he'd left her, but she wasn't

there. Suddenly, he was afraid he'd been misled by the Raiders and she'd been captured. His heart beat fast as he glanced around.

"Lacey?" he called softly.

"Here." She'd heard him approach, but she'd waited to reveal herself until she was sure it was safe.

Relieved, he found her and knelt by her side. Grabbing her shoulders, he started to pull her close. But she winced and twisted away.

"What happened?" There was wetness on his hand where he'd touched her left shoulder.

"Gunshot wound." Her words were clipped through clenched teeth.

"Don't worry. I'll take care of you." He picked her up and started walking back toward the road. "How are you feeling?"

"Not so bad. Only a little weak."

"Did the bullet go through?"

"I think so."

He hesitated by the side of the road, all his senses strained to detect danger. When he decided it was safe, he hurried across. Reaching the horses, he set her feet on the ground.

"I don't want to stay here, Lacey." He untied their mounts. "That outlaw probably won't stop running till he rejoins the Raiders, but we can't take the chance he might double back."

"It's okay." She took a deep breath. "I tied my handkerchief around the wound. Let's get out of here."

He helped her to the back of her horse. "We won't go far."

She nodded, feeling weak, feeling pain, and hating to admit she might slow them down.

Quickly remounting, he headed back to the road

and she followed. They turned south, moving slowly, quietly, listening for the Raiders. But the only sounds they heard were the usual ones of the forest after dark.

When Clint thought it was safe, he led them off the road and back into underbrush, until he found a place he thought would make a good, defendable camp. Helping Lacey from her horse, he led her to a tree. She sat down and leaned back against the rough wood. Deciding it wasn't safe to unsaddle the horses, he led them to an area where they could graze and still be accessible. He carried the saddlebags back to Lacey, then knelt and started building a fire.

"Are you sure that's safe?"

"I've got to have a look at your arm."

"As soon as we treat the wound, let's put it out."

He stopped and looked at her.

"I don't want what we did to them to happen to us."

"Neither do I." But he struck a match anyway. When he could see well enough, he tore the fabric away from her wound and took a good look.

"How is it?"

"Not bad. More of a graze than anything."

"Good," she said in relief, then opened her medicine bag. She handed him astringent, cream, and a clean cloth that could be wrapped around her arm to serve as a bandage.

His hands were gentle as he worked on her, and she relaxed, soothed by his presence and the comforting flicker of the fire. Her mind wandered. Three Raiders dead. How many more? Nine? Or less? It didn't matter. They would hunt down all of them. But revenge wasn't as sweet as she had expected. In the end, the outlaws were men like any others and they'd died just like so many had during the war. What she wanted more than anything was for the killing to stop. But that couldn't be. Not yet.

As Clint tied the bandage around her upper arm, she winced, unable to hold back her reaction any longer.

"Sorry. I'm almost done."

"I guess I'm not used to being a patient."

He finished, then pressed a quick kiss to the tip of her nose.

"Thanks." She replaced her medicine and closed the bag.

"Now for something to eat." He opened a saddlebag and took out more of Kate's food. The aroma of fried chicken made Lacey hurry to help him. Soon bread, cheese, chicken, and fried pies lay on a red checkered napkin.

As she bit into a chicken leg, Lacey murmured in contentment, and Clint chuckled as he picked one up, too. They were silent as they ate, quickly consuming the food, then drinking water.

Finally, she leaned back against the tree and groaned. "I can't tell you how good that was or how tired I am."

"Why don't you lie down and get some sleep? I'll put out the fire and keep watch."

"I'm not going to argue. But don't let me sleep too long. I'll take the second watch."

He shook out a blanket, and when she lay down, Clint tucked one half of it over her. Placing a kiss on her forehead, he tucked the blanket under her chin, hoping she wouldn't get too warm or develop a fever from the wound.

She was asleep almost instantly. He kicked dirt

into the fire to extinguish it, then sat still, listening to the sounds of the night. Nothing unusual stirred. He began to feel every ache and pain in his body. And tiredness crept over him. But he couldn't sleep much. It wasn't safe and he knew it. He had to keep watch over Lacey.

Stretching his legs, he looked down at her. She was so still he was afraid for a moment she'd died in her sleep. He put a hand on her, felt her breathe, and relaxed. It wasn't a bad wound. She would be fine. They'd simply have to be more careful. If that were possible.

But they'd gotten three Raiders. And maybe the fourth would lead them to the others.

Lacey stirred and instinctively moved closer to him. He felt a new tenderness steal into his heart. She had seemed so competent, so independent before, that he'd thought she'd never really need anybody. Today she'd needed him. He'd brought her through and it made him feel good. And protective. But he couldn't let her get hurt again.

He looked out into the darkness, feeling the tiredness catch up with him. The night was so calm, so still, so peaceful after the brief deadly, bloody gunfire. And that's how it went. You'd prepare, practice, hunt, then the moment would come and go in a blur. And you rarely got a second chance.

He was too exhausted to let his mind wander and tried not to give in to the deep sleep that was threatening him. He had to stay alert, except for quick naps. He'd used that technique to get through days, even weeks, during the war.

And as the night wore on, he dozed, woke, checked the darkness for danger, then repeated the process until finally birds chirping woke him completely. The early light of dawn was creeping through the trees.

Glancing down at Lacey, he touched her forehead. Good. She was cool, having failed to develop a fever during the night. If they kept the wound clean, she'd be all right. Relieved, he stood up, stretched, and went to get the horses.

Leading them back, he smiled as he saw her sit up and look around sleepily. When she saw him, she returned his smile, then frowned as she moved her arm.

"How do you feel?" he asked as he began rolling up the blankets.

"Better, but my arm's sore."

"You're lucky it wasn't worse." He picked up the saddlebags. "Ready to move on?"

"Give me a piece of bread and cheese, and I'm ready to pick up that trail."

"Something else." He handed her the food and took some for himself. "I want to get the Raiders' bodies and take them to the nearest town."

Lacey frowned.

"The law needs to know we got three of them."

"I suppose you're right. But I hate to go back there."

"Come on. I'll take care of it."

They mounted and started back down the road, the sun rising to reveal another warm, cloudless day. Lacey put on her hat, careful not to hurt her arm. At the rate she was going, she was afraid she'd be injured in some way the whole time she was hunting the Raiders. But as long as they were stopped, she didn't care what she suffered.

It didn't take them long to get back to the Raiders' camp, and while Lacey waited with the horses, Clint walked in alone. When he stepped into the clearing, he thought he was in the wrong place for a moment because it was empty. There were no bodies in sight. He checked around, found the cold campfire, then noticed the ground churned up by so many boots there was no way to distinguish how many men had been there.

Puzzled, but growing more concerned by the moment, he went back to Lacey.

"Let's get out of here," he said as he mounted his horse.

"But—"

"I'll explain later."

They hurried back to the road, and he dismounted to check the ground for prints.

"Clint, what's wrong?" She was feeling more nervous by the moment.

"The bodies are gone."

"What!" She glanced around in alarm. "Raiders?"

"I don't know. Wasn't animals, anyway. There've been a lot of men here. Not long ago. But the tracks are so churned up there's no way to tell anything."

"I'll bet it was the Raiders. Can you find that special horseshoe print?"

"No. Can't tell a damn thing. But it'd be like former soldiers to come back for their dead. That's the way we did it in the war."

Lacey felt chills run up her spine. "Let's go, Clint. I'm afraid. The two of us can't stand up against the whole band."

He nodded. His unease had turned to dread. Something was very wrong. "Let's put some distance between us and this place, then we can make new plans." He touched heels to his horse's flanks and took off toward the south.

Lacey kept pace, but she continued to look back for fear the Raiders would suddenly appear behind them. If the outlaws had come in the night or that morning to pick up their dead, they couldn't be far away. They also had to be looking for the ones who had killed three of their gang. And one of them had seen Clint, even if only by moonlight.

When no one appeared behind them, Clint slowed. The horses couldn't keep up the pace. They needed water. And he didn't want to push Lacey for fear her arm would get worse. Still, he felt the battle edge, heightened senses, and a need to fight or flee.

He had to find out what the hell was going on before they could ease up much. His main concern was that they had suddenly become the hunted. It wasn't a position he wanted to be in. And worse, he couldn't stand the idea of Lacey falling into Raider hands.

Jaws clamped tight, Clint rode on, waiting, watching, wondering. When he finally saw a stream, he knew they had to take a chance and stop. Lacey was looking pale and the horses needed water. Besides, the Raiders had left no tracks going south. Maybe they'd buried their dead, then headed back to Guntersville. But he doubted it, since the outlaws had already worked that area of Alabama. He suspected they'd be heading south. Somewhere near them.

But they rode down to the stream, anyway. He helped Lacey off her horse, then left both of the animals drinking water. While she sat down under a tree to rest, he scouted around the area. Tree limbs spread out over the stream in places, shading the water and turning it a dark green. Elsewhere, bright sunlight dappled the water so that it looked blue and gold. Wildflowers grew in a meadow close by, and a breeze carried their scent to him.

As he walked back toward her, he thought he didn't know when he'd seen such a beautiful day or countryside. If not for the nagging feeling of danger, he could have relaxed and rested there for days. As it was, he didn't want to leave her alone for long.

When he could see her again, he stopped by the stream, still looking, listening for any sign of the Raiders. The horses were drinking near a large boulder that had somehow come to rest in the middle of the creek. Water ran around it, creating gurgling whirlpools on the other side.

Insects buzzed around his face, and he brushed them aside as he walked over to Lacey and sat down. "How're you feeling?"

Fanning her face with her hat, she smiled. "Don't worry about me. I'm fine. It's the Raiders I want to talk about."

"I'd like to take you someplace safe and leave you there till you heal."

She threw down the hat and turned to face him. "How can you suggest that? You know my wound's little more than a scratch."

"In the heat, it could get worse fast."

"I'm a doctor. I can take care of it."

"Lacey, I'm worried about you. I don't want you hurt."

She relented slightly. Touching the scar on his face, she smiled. "When you got this, you didn't stop, did you?"

He shook his head, his gaze traveling down to her lips and back again.

Feeling the heat of him, seeing his eyes suddenly grow dark, she felt an answering response in her-

188

self. Passion. She wanted him, wanted to touch him, to be close to him like she had in Guntersville. Leaning nearer, she rested a hand on his chest and felt the fast beat of his heart. She was glad to know he felt as she did.

Suddenly, her vision tunneled, and she could hear gunshots and see brief flashes as rifles were fired from the shadows of trees. Although she couldn't see him, she knew that somewhere in the trees Clint was in danger. She wanted to go to him, to help him. But the vision abruptly passed as quickly as it had come.

Shivering, she clutched Clint's shirt. They were in even more danger than she had realized.

But before she had a chance to warn him, he lowered his head and captured her mouth with his lips. She moaned as his arms went around her and pulled her against his chest. He felt hot and hard, so ready for her as his tongue plunged into her. Responding, in spite of the approaching danger, she ran her hands through his thick hair, feeling her body twist inside with need. She returned his kiss, tasting him, feeling him, wanting to be joined with him completely. At this moment, she never wanted to be separated from him again.

He left her lips to press soft kisses over her face, briefly touching her eyelids, her forehead, the tip of her nose, then going back to her mouth, which he nibbled until she groaned and shuddered in his arms.

"Clint, I wish—"

"No more than me." He inhaled sharply. "But the time's all wrong. There's too much danger around us."

"The Raiders. I think they're near. We should move on. Oh, how I wish it was all over and done with."

"It will be soon."

Suddenly, she realized he could be taken from her by the Raiders. Her vision had been so very real. She mustn't let that happen. They must go at once. Yet she couldn't stand to be parted from him. She pressed hot kisses to the scar on his face, willing to take it upon herself to rid him of the old wound, the old pain, the old memories.

This time he groaned and placed a hand on each side of her face. Then, watching her eyes, he slowly brought her face closer and closer until their lips met. He thrust his tongue into her, joining them once more, as his arms pulled her close. Unable to get near enough, he suddenly pushed her toward the ground, covering her body with his own as he sought to unite them.

Suddenly, a shot rang out nearby, then a bullet whistled overhead to sink into the bark of the tree above them.

Chapter Sixteen

Clint muttered a string of words Lacey hadn't heard since the operating table at Whitmore cottage. She was horrified she hadn't had her vision in time to help. Now there was nothing she could do to change their situation. She had no doubt it was the Raiders who had found them, and the only good thing she could think of was that they finally had the outlaws in one place.

Bullets whizzed around them while Clint cussed a steady stream. He was so mad at himself he could hardly see straight. He'd known they were being followed. He'd felt it like during the war. But he'd dismissed his own instincts to take care of Lacey. And he'd known better than to bring her along in the first place. It'd serve him right if he ended up dead for being so damn dumb.

But he didn't want to die, because if he didn't make it, the Raiders would take Lacey. And that was a thought he couldn't tolerate. Dead or alive.

Fortunately, he had his rifle with him, but the Raiders were shooting from concealed places in the trees and brush around them. If their horses hadn't been in the stream, they'd have stood a chance of getting away. As it was, the animals were easy targets, and if they hadn't been used to gunfire from the war, they'd probably have already been long gone.

He knew they couldn't stay where they were. The Raiders were going to close in. As luck would have it, the outlaws hadn't been able to circle them. The stream was their only way out, but across it was an open meadow. No cover there and no way to get to the trees beyond without a bullet in the back.

Cussing again, he felt Lacey stir under him. He pressed her to the ground. No way in hell was he going to let her get her head up and get it shot off. They were damned lucky to be alive, and somehow he was going to keep it that way. But how?

The Raiders stopped firing all at once. Clint knew they were moving in closer. He had to stop it. Raising himself, he fired in an arc around them, then flattened himself against Lacey. His gunfire was returned. And from the sound, the outlaws were closer.

But he had a better fix on their location now. As he reloaded, he thought about the situation. If he went into the woods, he might be able to pick off the Raiders one at a time. If he were still good enough. And if he didn't have Lacey to worry about.

Again the firing stopped. He repeated his earlier action to make them hold their line. But it couldn't work forever because he was going to run out of ammunition soon. Then they'd be at the Raiders' mercy, and the outlaws obviously had none. They were going to have to take chances. There was no way around it.

When the Raiders started firing again, they were

closer. Clint quickly made up his mind as he reloaded.

"Lacey, we don't have much choice."

"Do you think you hit any of them?"

"No. I'm only trying to keep them backed off till we can do something."

"I'll help. I've got my pistol."

"It'll take more than that. We're boxed in here. And you're wounded."

"Don't worry about me. I can take care of myself."

"But I am worried about you. I see only one way out and it's a long shot. I want you to run to that boulder in the stream. Get on the other side of it and hold the outlaws off for as long as you can with the rifle. When you run out of bullets, use your pistol."

"What about you?" Suddenly, she was deeply frightened. And she hated the idea of being separated from him.

"I've got my knife. And pistol. I'm going into the woods and try to get them."

"But what if I hit you?"

"I'll be low. You shoot high."

"No. You could get hurt." She clutched his arm, knowing she was being unreasonable and not caring.

"You're going. It's our only chance." He shook her lightly. "Next break in the firing, you make a run for that rock. And stay low. Bent over. I'll cover you from here." He swallowed hard. "And if you get hit, keep going even if you've got to drag a leg."

"Clint, please." She pleaded silently with her dark blue eyes. "Let's go together. We can get to the horses."

He thrust the rifle in her hands and pushed her toward the river.

Exposed, she had no choice except to scramble as fast as she could. Bullets whizzed around her, then slowed as she heard Clint return fire. Still, she felt several stings as she hit the water. Slowed down, she held the rifle and ammunition above the stream to keep them dry. The water was waist-high by the time she reached the rock, and as she rounded it, she felt another bullet hit her left shoulder.

But she didn't stop. She got behind the chunk of rock, her wet skirts weighing her down, and took a deep breath. The firing had stopped. Was Clint alive? Had he gotten all the Raiders? He'd been a soldier, but so had the outlaws.

She looked at the horses. They had moved out of the water to the bank away from the noise. If Clint didn't come back, if she were still alive by nightfall, and if the animals waited, she'd try to make it to them. But dusk was a long time away and the ammunition was low. She had her pistol, and she'd save the bullets in it to shoot as many of the Raiders as she could before they took her.

But that was the worst case. What she wanted was for Clint to get the outlaws, one by one, as he'd said. She wished she was helping him more, but she'd probably be a hindrance so she was hopefully best off where she was. Yet she was still determined to help him some way. If she could keep the outlaws' attention on her, keep them firing at her, then Clint would stand a better chance of success.

Moving to the side of the boulder, she knelt in the water, feeling the current tug at her. But she ignored the distraction and concentrated on getting a view of the tree line without being seen. She watched the fire, realizing she could see where the individual Raiders were located from their gunshots.

Good. She might be able to pick off at least one, for she was an accurate shot, especially with a rifle. Aiming, she squeezed the trigger, then ducked back behind the boulder. Several bullets immediately knocked pieces of rock out of the area where she had been. There was no doubt they were good and experienced marksmen.

She waited, thinking about Clint. Was he safe? Had he been able to sneak up on any of the Raiders and kill them? Or was he already lying dead somewhere in the trees? No, she wouldn't believe that. She had to hold firm, hold to the belief that they would triumph, that somebody would finally stop the Raiders for good.

And she had to help. She moved to the other side of the boulder, staying as low in the water as she could get and still use the rifle. She watched the gunfire. If she was judging right, she'd hit an outlaw, for there were no shots from that area. And maybe Clint had taken out a man, too, because there were fewer areas of gunfire now. She felt better. Maybe they had a chance after all.

But she'd killed a man. That thought disturbed her. She'd wanted revenge, had come seeking it. Yet she had always healed people, not hurt them. Now she had no choice but to see men die by her own hand if she could possibly do it.

She aimed and shot again, then ducked behind the boulder, waiting for the return fire that would sprays bits of rock into the air. She stayed still, listening. The gunfire continued, and she realized they weren't going to give her another chance to get at them.

Leaning back against the rock, she took deep breaths to calm herself. She would have to wait, listen, and be ready. If they came after her, she would get as many as she could and hope that Clint had somehow gotten away.

But the gunfire grew less and less, until it finally stopped. Surprised, she waited, not daring to move until finally she looked around the boulder. Still nothing. She shot into the air. No sound.

Suddenly, Clint walked out of the trees, carrying a limp man in his arms.

Tears stung her eyes. Clint was still alive. They'd won. She could hardly believe it. Starting to rush out of the water, she found she could only move slowly. Fighting her heavy skirts, she finally reached the bank and hurried to Clint.

But his attention was completely on the man he'd carried from the woods. He'd laid the man on his back and was bent over him, talking.

She knelt beside them, wondering if she could help.

"Talk, damn it," Clint said to the Raider.

Blood trickled from the Raider's mouth, but he refused to reply.

"He's wounded," Lacey said. "Let me take care of him."

"No." Clint's voice was hard. "Wait till he talks."

"Won't talk, you murdering, thieving Confederate," the Raider finally said. "And get your whore of a woman away from me."

Clint clenched his fists to control his anger, then glanced at Lacey. "Get the horses. You'll need your medicine bag. Maybe we can save him long enough to answer some questions."

Lacey hated to leave, but she did. She went back into the water, crossed the stream, and walked to the horses. She spoke soothingly to them, for they were skittish after all the gunfire, and soon they allowed her to take their reins.

As she started back toward Clint, she realized she was willing to save the outlaw's life if she could, despite the fact that he had killed so many people, including her family. She could never forgive him for what he'd done, but she was still a doctor and she couldn't turn away from the sick or hurt. Besides, the law would deal with him if he lived, and he would hurt no one else.

Clint watched her a moment, glad he had sent her away. There were things he had to say she was best off not hearing, not now, anyway. He turned back, and the expression on his face was totally ruthless.

"Listen, you lowlife"—and suddenly Clint's voice held the clipped accent of the North—"I'm a Yankee same as you. I was sent after you to take you in, one way or the other. I'll save you if I can. The woman with me is a doctor. But first you've got to answer some questions."

The man looked confused for a moment, then frowned. "I ain't saying nothing. Randolph'd kill me if I did."

"You're going to die if you don't talk."

"You got us all. Ain't that enough?"

"No. Where's Randolph? Nothing's over till I get him."

"You'll never get him." His eyes looked wild. "Don't you know? That man's got more than God on his side. He does what he wants, when and where he wants." He coughed and blood rushed from his mouth. "Hell, I'm never gonna make it."

"Hang on. She's coming back with her medicine bag." Clint clutched the Raider's shirt. "Where's Randolph? Tell me for your country's sake if nothing else."

The man hesitated, as if remembering why he'd started fighting in the first place. "We did what was right." He coughed again, then closed his eyes. His voice was weak when he continued. "Dirty Rebel bastards had to be taught a lesson. We did it, didn't we?"

Clint leaned closer to hear him. "Yes. We won. But the war's over now."

"Can't ever let 'em off their knees. Remember that."

"Where is Randolph?"

The man shook his head in denial, then looked up.

Lacey stood close by. She dropped the reins of the horses, then carried her medicine bag over to the Raider and knelt.

"Tell us where Randolph's gone and she'll do what she can to heal you." Clint's clipped Northern accent abruptly changed to a slow Southern drawl.

"You ain't never gonna catch him. He's gone south to the cities. He's rich now." He coughed again, the blood bright red. "And he'll see the war never stops till every last dirty Rebel is dead."

Furious, Clint raised the man and shook him hard. "Where? What city?"

The Raider smiled. "Montgomery." Then his eyes rolled back in his head.

"Clint put him down." Lacey tugged at his sleeve. "Let me see what can do."

"No use. He's dead."

"What!" She put an ear to the outlaw's chest.

198

No breath. Sitting back on her heels, she looked at Clint in concern. "Killing was a lot easier to think about than to do."

"It always is." He glanced around. "If what he said is true, we got them all."

"Except Randolph. And now we know where to look."

"Not Montgomery."

"But that's what he said." She stared at Clint in surprise.

"He protected his leader to the last. He said Montgomery, so we'd better head in the opposite direction."

"Up north?" She felt confused, trying to understand but not doing a good job of it.

"I bet Randolph headed south just like this Raider said. There's not much other choice for him. If he's rich enough now, he can carry on his war without the Raiders and he'd want to disappear into a city and change his image."

"If not Montgomery, then where?"

"Mobile. I think that's where he'll head. It's a port and it'd give him easy access to all the Gulf states. It's also big enough that it'd be hard as hell to find him once he gets there."

"Then we've got to stop him fast." She felt renewed anger rush through her.

"Right. We'll head for Birmingham, and if we don't catch his trail there, we'll go on to Tuscaloosa. Chances are he's heading there to take the Tombigbee River right into Mobile."

"Clint, I'm scared. How much of a head start does he have on us?"

"No way to know. He must have left the Raiders here to cover his trail. While everybody was looking for him in northern Alabama, trying to stop his outlaws, he'd fled south. Smart man."

"But we can't let him get away with it."

"We won't." Clint glanced at the horses. "But first things first. We've got to get to a town, contact some officials about the Raiders, then let them get out here and clean up this mess."

"Clint, I just had a thought. What if this outlaw lied? What if Randolph is already dead? What if he was simply stringing us along? What if—"

"I know." He ran a hand through his hair, looking tired. "But we got the band. I don't know what happened to Randolph. Maybe somebody else shot him. Even his own men. Or maybe he's holed up somewhere back in the Appalachians. We may be planning a wild-goose chase."

"But we have to go, don't we?"

"Yes." He took her hands and held them gently.

"He might really have gone to Montgomery."

"If he's alive, yes. But all my instincts say he's alive and headed for Mobile."

"But you could be wrong."

"Yes." He smiled, a crooked twist of his lips. "But that's where I'm headed. Do you want to go on with me, or do you want to go home now?"

She stood up. "Randolph's the man we must catch or find proof of his death. Otherwise, I'm afraid he'll continue his killing spree."

Clint stood and pulled her close. He winced, then stilled his features. "I'm not going to tell you to go home where it's safe because Randolph burned your home. I'm not even going to tell you to go stay with friends." He took a deep breath. "I want you with me, Lacey. We make a good team."

Suddenly, his face whitened, pain twisted his features, and he slumped against her.

"Oh, no, you're hurt!"

Helping him to the ground, she ripped open his shirt, furious with herself for not having noticed his pain earlier. There was a knife wound several inches long in his side. It was bleeding freely and appeared deep. He was losing blood fast and would probably need stitches. But first she must stop the loss of blood.

She grabbed her medicine bag, then quickly disinfected the wound and applied a temporary bandage. She wanted to get Clint out of there and to a safe place, where she could get him hot food and tend him better. And she especially felt a need to take him away from the scene of the battle. There must be a small town nearby or even a farmhouse. But if she didn't find something soon, she'd stop, make camp, and care for his wounds.

But he wasn't the only one who needed healing now. She looked down at her shoulder where another bullet had torn through her bandage. The padding had helped protect her arm, but she was bleeding again. Jerking off the old bandage, she disinfected the cuts, then applied a new cloth. She had received other nicks and scratches, but she would deal with them later.

Glancing down at the Raider, Lacey decided not to leave him in the open. She pulled his body into the trees and left it there. As soon as she reached a town or a house, she would see that the law came out and dealt with the dead outlaws. Until then, she could do no more.

From now on everything she did had to be fast, because if Randolph lived—and she felt deep in her bones that he did—they had to pick up his trail before it was lost forever. And that was a thought she couldn't abide.

Hurrying back to Clint, she helped him to his saddle, then mounted her own horse. Soon they were back on the road and headed south, a new urgency driving them.

Part Four

Moonlight Madness

Chapter Seventeen

"Surprise!" Clint kicked the door shut behind him as he juggled boxes and bags in both arms.

Lacey raised up on one elbow to look at him. She lay nude under a soft cotton sheet on the feather bed in room 43 at the Planters' Plaza in Tuscaloosa. She'd been shamelessly napping in the late afternoon, enjoying more luxury and rest than she'd had in over four years. Maybe ever.

But now she was worried about Clint. She'd tried to keep him from going out, but he'd insisted in order to see if he could learn anything about Randolph. Now his eyes were fever bright, and carrying so much had to be putting a strain on his wound. Yet there was no stopping him when he'd set his mind on something.

They'd been over a week getting to the central Alabama town of Tuscaloosa, and the destruction they'd seen along the way had made her feel sick. Nothing could ever be worth the kind of loss the Confederacy had suffered during the war, and now it continued as Northerners moved south, taking what little was left.

Watching Clint walk across the room and drop his purchases on the bed, she thought about the money he was spending. It worried her and made her wonder about him. How could any former

Rebel spend as he did? Perhaps since he seemed to be so good at gambling he considered it easy come, easy go, especially if it was Yankee money he was winning.

Maybe that should be her attitude, too. Was it time she learned to play again? Or was it even possible anymore? Yet how could she possibly think about having fun with Randolph still loose?

"Don't frown." Clint touched a fingertip to the end of her nose. "It's not so bad. We took care of the Raiders. We even saw Union soldiers leave to take care of the bodies."

"I know, but Randolph's still out there somewhere."

Clint tossed a newspaper toward her. "Look at that headline."

She picked it up and read aloud, "Union Soldiers Catch Raiders. Randolph Believed Dead." Glancing up, she frowned again. "I'm glad you persuaded that Yankee officer to keep our names out of it."

"He was more than willing to take the credit." But Clint remembered how he'd had to take the major aside and explain that he was an undercover Union officer and didn't want the publicity. After that, they'd gotten all the help they needed, even if Lacey had grumbled about accepting aid from Yankees. But they'd both been in bad shape and there'd been little other choice.

"Why do they think Randolph's dead?" She scanned the article.

"From the gossip I heard on Tuscaloosa's streets, nobody's seen or heard anything of Randolph in a while, so they figure he's dead. More than anything, it's wishful thinking."

"But you don't believe that, do you?"

"I wish I did. Randolph's smart and I still think he's gone underground, heading for Mobile."

"So do I." She pushed her hair back from her face, thinking about Randolph, wanting him to be out of their lives but knowing they couldn't give up yet. "I just wish I knew how we were going to find him."

"We're going to prowl this town till we find some sign of him or decide he's already gone."

She sighed. "I'm so tired I don't want to go on. If only he'd been with the others."

"That's why I bought you some things to make you feel better." He hesitated, looking thoughtful. "We're going to get him."

"You're right. It's just that once I slowed down, I can't seem to get up any energy again."

"You will. Give it some time. After you've had a few good meals in you, more rest, then you'll feel like your old self again."

"But why aren't you tired, too? Your wound is worse."

"I'm used to being wounded, dog tired, and on the run. There was little chance to rest during the war." His eyes looked haunted a moment, then he shook his head. "Besides, in my outfit we worked as a unit. We all had to keep each other going. It was the only way to limit the losses. Right now, I don't know much of any other way to be."

She squeezed his hand, finally understanding what he was doing. She'd worked those kind of weeks, trying to save lives. To him, she was a downed horse or a wounded soldier. He thought he had to get her back on her feet or lose her completely. And maybe he was right.

Glancing at the packages, she accepted his decision to spend money. It was a way of keeping

207

them both going. Even a way of helping them find Randolph. They did need a good place to rest, hot nourishing food, and probably whatever the packages contained.

"You want to see your presents now?"

"Yes. And I'm sorry I've been so—"

"Don't apologize. You've pulled your own load all the way. And you're right to rest now while you can." He picked up a package. "But for the moment, let's forget the past."

She nodded, agreeing but knowing later she would have to find some way to get him to rest so his wound would heal properly.

"Yankees must be the worst gamblers in the world, because I cleaned up again today." He grinned, trying to raise her spirits. Actually, he'd wired a report about subduing the Raiders, that he intended to continue after Randolph, and he'd asked for more money. His job was close to being over if they could catch Randolph or get proof of his death.

"I hope you weren't extravagant, Clint."

"No. I got us what we needed." After he'd picked up the money wired to him, he'd decided clothes were a top priority. "You know as well as I do that our clothes were about shredded catching the Raiders."

"I won't argue about new clothes."

He smiled at her, glad to see a sparkle back in her eyes. He hated like hell to push her any farther and felt like a beast for having already put her through so much. But she'd never have stood for being left behind. Anyway, she wasn't the only one who was tired. He felt like he could sleep a solid week. And he would if Randolph weren't free.

As he opened a package, Lacey watched, feeling excited. He was right about their need. Her gray dress was so thin and torn it was impossible to mend. She had ended up with only the cotton print Sarah had given her, but it was not a day dress. Due to the fire, she had so little left of her own and that bothered her.

Pulling out something in a dark blue and pale blue bold stripe, he tossed it to her. As she caught it, she raised herself up completely, letting the sheet fall around her waist. But she didn't notice, since she was so absorbed in feeling the soft silk of a beautiful blouse. Glancing at Clint, she started to thank him, but he was looking downward. She suddenly realized her nudity and jerked up the sheet.

"It's a little late for modesty, Lacey." He stroked the scar on his cheek.

"How can you even think about—"

"With you around, there's not much I can do about it."

She blushed lightly as she quickly slipped into the blouse. It felt wonderfully cool and luxurious against her skin.

"It looks good on you." He smiled. "I thought it would."

"I need a corset."

"That's the last thing you need."

She shook her head at him. Men! They never understood proper dressing. But as she looked at him, she began to feel heat build in her. It'd been a long time since he'd touched her intimately and her body suddenly remembered his caresses, craving them once more. But she was not going to let that stop her from seeing her new clothes. "Thanks, Clint. This is beautiful."

209

"It wasn't easy to surprise you. There's a dress-maker in town who had a few things ready-made which she thought would fit. But I promised to send you in for a special dress when you're feeling better."

"Thank you, but—"

"No *but's*. Open this." He pushed a garment box toward her.

Opening it, she laughed in delight. A dark blue skirt of satin to match the blouse lay folded in-side. She pulled it out, examining the fine work, the small stitches, wanting to try it on. But she was completely naked. "Turn your back."

Clint shook his head negatively. "Don't I get some reward for my effort?"

She smiled and stood up, letting the cover fall away from her body. Surprising herself, she found she enjoyed Clint looking at her, his gaze suddenly dark and hungry. Then she pulled on the skirt, pleased with the wide pleats and narrow waist-band. Tucking the blouse inside, she walked over to the full-length pedestal mirror in one corner of the room.

Looking at herself from every angle, she decided he'd made a good choice in clothing. And it would be comfortable for traveling.

"There's more, but if I give it to you now, you'll want to put it on and cover yourself up."

Laughing, she walked over and hugged him. But when she started to step away, he pulled her close, running his hands up her skirt to her waist.

"You're not getting away that easy," he growled, then tugged her down to sit on his lap. He quickly placed a hot kiss on her lips, then pushed inside with his tongue.

She moaned with the sudden heat and power of

him, then felt an answering flame within herself.

Abruptly, he ended the kiss. "You'd better get to the other side of the bed, Lacey, or we'll never get these packages unwrapped."

Suddenly, she no longer cared. All she wanted was Clint. She'd missed him more than she'd realized. Instead of moving, she pressed closer, ran her hands through his thick dark hair, and smiled seductively. "I think I'd rather see you than the new clothes."

"They'll keep." He slipped the blouse off her shoulders, then lowered his head and took the tip of one breast between his lips. Just as he sucked, she felt the sensation spread to her center and the heat in her body grew more intense. When she thought she could stand no more, he moved to the other breast and began teasing that nipple.

Moaning, she clutched at his shoulders, feeling the hard muscles tense under her touch.

"Keep that up, Lacey, and I'm not going to be able to wait." He unhooked her skirt and slipped his hand inside. His fingers were rough against the smooth skin of her stomach, and when he slid his hand downward to cup her, she moaned. As he kneaded the center of her desire, she murmured his name over and over.

Lifting her off his lap, he let the skirt drop to the floor and feasted his gaze on her nude body. Then he pushed all the packages to the floor. Jerking back the sheets, he picked her up and placed her on the soft feather bed. Never taking his eyes from her body, he quickly undressed, jerking off his clothes and throwing them down.

When he stood naked before her, she felt her own need for him twist out of control. She held out her arms, and he quickly sat down on the bed

211

and pulled her against him. He was hot and hard and so ready she hardly dared touch him, and yet she was as driven as he was. Slowly, tentatively, she ran a hand down through the thick mat of dark hair on his chest, then closed her fingers around his thick column of passion.

He groaned, forced himself to remain still, then covered her hand with his, showing her the rhythm, feeling the softness of her hand around him until he could stand no more. Then he abruptly pushed her onto her back, spread her legs, and quickly pushed inside.

A soft cry escaped her at the sudden rough entry, but soon she was moving in time with him, her hips rotating to meet his every thrust. She felt on fire, scorched by his heat. When his lips came down on hers, she eagerly met the kiss, thrusting her tongue inside him, tasting, teasing, wanting desperately to be one with him.

When he cupped her breasts, kneading the tips into hard, sensitive peaks, she felt so much emotion and feeling rush through her that she shivered in anticipation of their coming union. Then he left her lips to press hard kisses over her face, repeating her name as if in a litany.

Suddenly, he groaned, and his body began to shudder as he stroked into her hard and fast. She felt an answering flame explode as they climaxed together, then held their union as long as they could.

When he lay back and pulled her against him, he was breathing hard, sweat dampened his body, and she could hear his heart beating fast. She clung to him, thinking back to her mother and all she had said about a soul mate. Could Clint be any less? Their passion, her visions, what more did she want to convince her?

And yet it was not time. Randolph still roamed free, threatening to resume his slaughter of innocent Southerners. Her life was not her own until Randolph was stopped. And neither was Clint's. Besides, how could she explain to Clint about a soul mate, about visions? What would he think? No, she must say nothing yet. Nothing about love, about the rest of their lives, children, a home. Yet she felt such an urge to do exactly that that she had to bite her lower lip to keep from speaking.

Then there was no need, for he slept, exhausted, wounded, overextended. She raised herself slightly and checked the bandage covering his wound. He wasn't bleeding, which meant he hadn't torn out the stitches. Good. She was grateful for that. She should have known better than to let him make love to her until he was healed. Yet she hadn't been able to wait, and neither had he.

Rising, she slipped from the bed, then pulled the covers up around his chest. As exhausted as he was, she knew he would sleep deeply and for a long time if he wasn't disturbed. And she planned to see that he wasn't.

She walked over to the washstand and poured water from the pitcher into the bowl. Then she carefully washed herself, almost hating to rinse away Clint's touch. When she was clean and dry, she began picking up the packages and carrying them to the settee near the door to their room.

Finally, she sat down to see what else Clint had bought her. She discovered a pale blue petticoat of fine cotton, with dark blue lace around the hem. There was a matching chemise to wear with it. But he hadn't included a corset. There was also silk stockings, blue garters, and a pair of navy kid boots with elastic sides. All in all, he had chosen perfectly, and comfortably as well.

Putting on the chemise and petticoat, she looked inside the final packages and found a man's suit in dark gray, with a white shirt and black tie. He had also bought himself a new pair of black Wellington boots, black socks, and a black leather belt. He would look very fine in his new clothes.

Suddenly, she thought of the expense. How had he possibly gambled enough to make the kind of money it would take to buy their new clothing? She frowned. Of course, she knew little about gambling, so she supposed it was possible to have done it quickly. Still, she was concerned. And what if they needed the money later?

But there was no denying they had to have clothes, and to ask questions and get answers all over town they would need to be properly dressed. Clint had chosen well for a lot of reasons and yet she still worried.

"You look good enough to eat." Clint watched her from the bed.

"Oh!" She turned around in surprise. "I thought you were asleep."

"Couldn't wait?"

She smiled sheepishly. "No. And, Clint, it's all perfect. Including yours."

"Thanks." He sat up. "I feel a lot more rested."

"Your wound isn't hurting, is it?"

"No. Can't think of anything that'd heal me faster than a beautiful woman in my arms."

She blushed lightly again, every inch of her aware of his body, of their previous closeness.

"But I'll tell you one thing." He stood up.

Heat rushed through her. Shocked at herself, she realized she wanted him all over again. "What?"

214

But her mind was following his body's movement, not his words.

"I'm starved. How about you?"

Now that she thought about it, she was hungry. "Yes."

"Then put on your new clothes and let's go find a good restaurant."

"Are you sure we can afford it? I mean —" and she looked down at all the new clothing — "after buying so much."

"I was lucky at gambling. Real lucky. Besides, we can look for Randolph while we're out. Maybe take a tour of the town. What do you say?"

She smiled, feeling more lighthearted and happy than she had in a long time. If Clint had won plenty of money gambling, then they might as well enjoy it and look for Randolph at the same time. Besides, she was famished and it'd been a long, long time since she eaten out in a nice restaurant. Laughing, she began getting dressed.

"I'm going to take that for a yes."

"Right." She stopped, suddenly serious. "And, Clint, thanks."

"It's no more than you deserve, Lacey. We got those Raiders, and we're going out now and celebrate." He walked over and began pulling his new clothes out of their packages, then stopped and took her hand. He touched the spidery birthmark in her left palm. "The Whitmore women deserve a lot of thanks and I've just begun to see you get it."

Tears suddenly stung her eyes and she looked away, pulling her hand free. "Come on, let's hurry."

Chapter Eighteen

As they walked down one of Tuscaloosa's main streets, Lacey thought about what she knew of the town. Right off, she remembered it had gotten its name from the Choctaws, for in their language *tusko* meant "warrior" and *loosa* meant "black." And that referred to the fact that the town was situated on a high plateau at the fall line of the Black Warrior River. Southward, Tuscaloosa connected with the Tombigbee River, which ran all the way to Mobile on the Gulf of Mexico.

Because of its locale in the center of surrounding cotton farms and its connections to the Black Warrior and the Tombigbee, Tuscaloosa had long been a center for merchants and planters. But now Lacey saw very little of the activity she had seen when her parents had taken her there as a child.

Long rows of water oaks had been planted along the wide streets, and in some areas huge columned mansions were nestled behind them. Tuscaloosa was also known as the City of Oaks or Druid City, because of the oak trees. And Lacey remembered the beautiful trees from her childhood as well.

As they walked eastward, she saw a great difference in the once bustling town. Union soldiers were apparent, as well as carpetbaggers and other

Yankees. As far as Southerners, she saw two kinds: a few who were making money off the outcome of the war, and those who were struggling to survive. Free blacks lounged here and there, some offering their services for hire. But she knew few Southerners would have the money to pay them.

She was anxious to see the University of Alabama, now not far away. It was the seat of one of the best and oldest universities in the South, and its architecture was well known for its stately beauty. A great deal of planter money had gone into making the university one of the best, and she hoped with the war over students would be able to resume their studies. If any Southerners could still afford it.

They rounded a corner and Lacey caught her breath, suddenly feeling sick at her stomach. She clutched Clint's arm. Instead of the huge columned stone structures of the university, she saw instead burned-out shells of buildings. Yet even as she looked, she could hardly believe her eyes. It was too horrible for words.

Suddenly, fury consumed her. There could be no excuse for the Union Army burning the University of Alabama, for it was no military stronghold, no meeting place for Confederate generals. It was simply a place to educate Southerners. Spite. Pure, mean spite could have been the only reason Yankees would have burned a university.

"Lacey?" Clint pulled her close in concern as he looked in horror at the burned buildings. It wasn't the worst he'd seen during the war, but it came close.

"The university. How could they have burned it? How will we ever be able to build it back?" Lacey felt tears sting her eyes.

Not for the first time, Clint wished he was anywhere but where he was. How would Lacey ever forgive him for being a Union soldier? He felt sick at heart, for the university, for the South and the North. "There were a lot of bad things done during the war, and this is one of them."

"Those damn yankees." She clinched her fists, then turned her back on what was left of the university and started walking rapidly away. "Heartless. Cruel. How I hate Yankees."

Clint kept up. "The North didn't do all the wrong things, Lacey. A lot of Union soldiers died, too."

She stopped and glared at him. "How can you say that?"

"Well, they did."

"But the South carried the brunt of the war. You, of all people, know that. Yes, the North lost men, but many of their soldiers were European-hired mercenaries. And we did not destroy their land, burn their crops, their houses, their universities, their towns. We fought a fair fight the best we could."

"It doesn't much matter now. The South lost."

"I can't believe my ears. Doesn't matter? You just looked at what's left of the University of Alabama and you can say that? I'm beginning to wonder what side you fought on?" She took off again, as if she could outrun the horrors of the past.

He kept up with her for a moment, then pulled her to a stop.

She jerked her arm away, glaring at him. Anger made her breathe fast.

"Listen, Lacey, the war's over. We've got to put our lives back together. Somehow we'll rebuild the

218

university."

"I don't know if it'll all ever be over." Her eyes took on a faraway look. "You can't do to a people and land what was done in the South and simply have it go away. We're broken." She sighed. "In many ways."

"But not down. Never that."

"I know what you're saying. I know we have to go on. You're right. Yet so many people have been hurt."

"But the slaves are free now."

"To do what? How are they going to live? How are any of us going to live? Do you think the North will feed us all? Not likely. Do you really think Yankees will treat the freed blacks any better?" She rubbed her hands together in agitation. "I just don't know. We never owned slaves. A great many Southerners didn't. Slavery is wrong, but it was coming to an end in the South. We all saw that. And surely it could have been stopped without a war."

He took her hand and squeezed, very afraid he was going to lose her when she finally learned the truth concerning him. "The war was about a lot more than freeing the blacks. It was about power and economics, Lacey, about who was going to control the destiny of our country. Blacks were caught in the middle, the common people were caught in the middle. And the North won. You have to accept that."

"Yes, Northerners will finally get what they wanted, control of Congress. But it took a war for them to get it. The South was too strong before."

"But not now. There's nobody to fight for laissez-faire anymore. Northern businesses will get the government subsidies they've wanted for so long, and the South won't be able to object."

"But there should always be an alternative to war, Clint, always a way to settle differences without bloodshed."

"I agree, but the world's not a perfect place. And now that the war's finally over, we have to go on. We'll catch Randolph and you can—"

"What? Go back to my burned-out house? My dead family and friends? Tell me, Clint, what have I got now that the war is over? What do you have, for that matter?"

He rubbed the scar on his cheek, knowing he was going to lose her and feeling sick. "We have the future. We have our lives. Isn't that enough?"

Suddenly, she flung herself against his chest, tears rolling down her cheeks.

He held her close, feeling the sobs shake her body. He wished he could do something, ease her pain someway. But nothing could take away her loss, all their losses. Yet maybe there was still hope for them, just like there was hope for the North and South to work together again as one nation. But it was going to take a while and a lot of understanding on both sides.

As she continued to cry, he stroked her back. Maybe her tears were for the best. They'd been a long time coming. She'd held back her emotions for so long that they had come out hard and all at once. Perhaps now she would be able to forgive and go on. But at least she was finally mourning her loss and that was the first step in healing. He knew that only too well. For, despite Lacey's view, the South had not suffered alone.

When her crying finally slowed, then ceased, he gave her his handkerchief. Her eyes were red as was the tip of her nose, but she'd never been more beautiful to him, for she finally seemed human, not an ice queen or legendary healer. Now she was simply Lacey, the woman he wanted to keep with him forever. But he didn't let his mind go down that path, for too much stood between him and a future with her.

They began walking back toward their hotel, the university behind them. Lacey was quiet, occasionally dabbing at the corners of her eyes with the handkerchief. Trying not to obviously watch her, Clint was still concerned. She'd been through so much, lost so much, and now she had finally felt it all. He didn't know how much more she could stand.

But finally, she glanced at him and smiled, tentatively. "I guess I made a spectacle of myself."

"No. You're mourning and no wonder."

"But I have to be strong. I have to keep going. We haven't found Randolph."

He stopped and pulled her close, not in the least concerned at the people walking around them. "Listen to me. You're strong. Look what you've been through. You're owed a few tears. And we'll get Randolph."

She smiled, her eyes not quite so bruised-looking now, then nodded. "Yes, we will." She hesitated, glancing around. "But what I mean is I don't feel so strong inside anymore."

"You've let go of a lot of tension, anger, and pain, that's all. You'll be fine." He tucked her hand in the crook of his arm and started down the street. "What we both need is a good meal."

"I'd love that."

He glanced into her dark blue eyes and found a warmth there he'd seldom seen before. And he couldn't help thinking what she would be like in

221

the big feather bed at the Planters' Plaza now that her emotions were released. That thought made his trousers suddenly too tight, and he hurried them toward a good but not lavish restaurant he'd been told about at the hotel.

When he hesitated outside the Red Oak Inn, Lacey read the fine print about the restaurant, which claimed it had been serving satisfied customers for over fifty years. Still feeling a little shaky, she allowed Clint to open the heavy oak door and show her inside.

She immediately warmed to the place, because it had a tasteful decor of oak tables and chairs, with crisp white linen tablecloths and napkins. Dark green damask draperies were tied back at the windows, which let in late afternoon sunlight. The walls were unadorned, but dark squares on the faded wallpaper showed where paintings had once hung. Lacey had no doubt the original oils had been sold to help finance the Confederacy, or on second thought, perhaps they had been stolen by the Union soldiers who had burned the university.

She pushed that unpleasant thought aside as she glanced around the Red Oak Inn. Several obvious former Rebels dined in the comfortable surroundings of the restaurant, and she was relieved Clint hadn't taken her to a place only Yankees could afford. Suddenly, she realized he would never have done that and was surprised at her train of thought. Did she no longer trust him? Had his earlier words caused her to question his loyalties?

But there was no time to ponder that thought as a waitress with gray hair and a sorrowful face led them to a table. Lacey was seated near a window, and she gazed out at the spreading oak trees, imagining the town as it had been years ago.

"Do you like the restaurant?" Clint asked, concerned with her faraway look.

"Yes. Thank you." She smiled at him and took a sip of water. "I was just thinking of the past."

He nodded, understanding. She looked better and he relaxed somewhat. There was no point in worrying. They would have a good dinner, then go back to their room. His gray eyes darkened with passion as he looked at her. He wanted to touch her now, not wait. Yet he had to be sensitive, gentle. But his body didn't understand. He glanced away, hot and uncomfortable.

When their meals were brought, plates heaped with roast beef, mashed potatoes, green beans, and sweet white corn, with fresh bread, butter, and honey on the side, Lacey wasn't sure she could eat. But as soon as one mouthful passed her lips, she realized she was starving. She didn't know when food had tasted so good.

By the time the waitress brought fresh apple pie, Lacey felt sated, relaxed, and happy despite all she'd been through. And she realized she still trusted Clint, for earlier he had only spoken the truth, no matter how unpleasant. Looking into his gray eyes, she thought of the room at the Planters' Plaza and of being alone with him. Suddenly, she was anxious to touch him all over again, to feel them joined as one.

Surprised and slightly embarrassed at her sudden desire, she glanced away and locked eyes with a stranger at another table. The man's hard black eyes bored into her and she caught her breath, looking away as quickly as possible. Her appetite was gone and she felt unaccountably nervous. Then she chided herself. After all she'd been through, there was no need to let a man's gaze

223

disturb her. She glanced back to prove she could do it, and he still watched her. Enough. She turned to her pie, but felt the man's hot look still on her.

Then something teased at the back of her mind. Something familiar. About the man. She paused, thinking back to how he had looked. Black eyes. Clean shaven. Black hair neatly trimmed. Very fine clothes. Suddenly, she saw him another way, with wild black hair, a full beard and mustache, cold, menacing black eyes, and astride a horse. Randolph!

Shocked, she glanced back. And met his stare again. He nodded slightly. She looked away. Suddenly, her palm itched and she absently rubbed the spidery birthmark.

"Lacey, are you all right?" Clint had stopped eating and was watching her closely.

She took a deep breath. "Would you recognize Randolph if he looked like a successful businessman?"

"You think you've seen him?" Clint tensed in his chair.

"Don't look, but at a table behind you a man just reminded me of Randolph. I think Randolph is right here in Tuscaloosa where you said he'd be."

"But you aren't sure?"

"No. How can I be? He looks so different. Yet, there's something about him. I could swear it's the same man. But how can we find out?"

"Relax, Lacey. Don't look at him. Is he watching you?"

"Yes."

"How? I mean, in what way?" He gave her a meaningful look.

She appeared embarrassed. "Lust, I think."

"Good."

"Good!" She frowned, offended.

"If he's interested, it means he's vulnerable to us. Understand?"

"I see."

"I'd never let him touch you. Don't think that."

"I didn't. It's just that—"

"Notice anything you can about him, but don't be obvious." Clint casually finished his pie but had obviously lost his taste for it.

"Should I appear interested?"

"No. Just notice him. That's enough for now."

"Okay." She followed his instructions. "He's with a very large man who's tall, broad-shouldered, heavily muscled, quite dangerous-looking, and dressed in all black. Randolph—or whoever he is— isn't small, but this man with him is huge."

"Bodyguard?"

"I don't know. Maybe, now that you mention it."

"Raider?"

"He could have been." Her heart was beating fast. She tried not to look directly at Randolph, but he was like a magnet drawing her to him. She resisted the impulse to stare into his eyes.

"All right." Clint took a sip of water. "We're going to order coffee and outwait them. When they leave, they'll have to walk by us and I'll get a look at them."

"Then what?"

"If I agree it could be Randolph, we'll follow."

She felt a little nauseous with sudden fear. "Won't they notice?"

"It'll be dusk soon and harder to see outside. Also, nothing says our path doesn't follow theirs

225

once we're out of the restaurant."

"We've got to be careful."

He reached across the table and squeezed her hand. "We will be."

Soon they were drinking coffee and attempting to keep up a conversation, but all Lacey could think about was dragging Randolph into the law. But what if he were the wrong man? No, she had to find out the truth first, but she could hardly stand to play the game. Just when she thought she couldn't wait any longer, the two men got up and headed toward her table. She glanced up.

Randolph slowed, nodded at her with an intense look, then glanced at Clint. A moment later he strode on, the large man following.

Clint beckoned the waitress over, paid their bill, then escorted Lacey outside. The two men were heading down the street, seemingly unconcerned with anything except the sights of the early evening. Clint didn't move until he'd decided the direction the men were taking, then he smiled at Lacey. "Nice evening for a walk, don't you think, my dear?"

"Oh, yes, so lovely." She returned the smile, but it didn't reach her eyes.

Following the opposite side of the street, they looked in store windows, stopped to examine a particular oak tree, and in general tried to appear nonchalant while burning up with curiosity inside. When the two men stopped outside the Planters' Plaza, then walked inside, Clint squeezed Lacey's hand.

"Could he have been so close all this time?" Lacey asked, amazed they could have been staying at the same hotel.

"Yes. And we might have missed them if not for

dinner tonight."

She started across the street, but Clint pulled her back. "Wait. They might be back out and we don't want to run into them."

They walked on down the street, but Clint kept watching the main entrance to the Planters' Plaza, worried the men might have gone out a back door or slipped away from them some other way. When he thought they'd waited long enough, they crossed the street and walked back to the hotel. Leisurely climbing the stairs, they stepped inside.

"I'll get our key and some answers at the same time," Clint said as he left Lacey to sit on a red velvet settee near the door.

Smiling, he walked to the reception desk and looked innocently at the clerk. "The key to room 43, please."

As the clerk slid it across the desk, Clint added, "By the way, I thought I saw a couple of men I knew from the war. A dark-haired, slim, well-dressed man with a tall, large man wearing black. I saw them earlier this evening. Do you know if they're staying here?"

"Don't know if it's the same ones, but two men who fit those descriptions have been staying here a few days."

"And their names?" The clerk was looking suspicious, so Clint added, "You know how easy it was to lose track of friends during the war."

"Sure do." He checked the register. "Name's Rand Scanlon and Mr. Oakes. That them?"

"No, I don't think so."

"Not surprised. They're gamblers. Going out on the *Alabama Queen* when she sets out for Mobile." He nodded. "Didn't think they were your type."

227

"How do you know so much—"

The clerk looked proud. "My kin helped found this town. We're still here and we're going to stay here, no matter what them damnyankees do. If it goes on in Tuscaloosa, my family knows about it."

"Thanks. And good luck." Clint walked as casually back to Lacey as he could.

She stood up, put her hand on his arm, and leaned close. "Is it him?"

"Not now. Smile at the clerk as we walk past."

Smiling, she nodded at the clerk, then hurried Clint up the stairs to their room. Once inside, with the door closed, she pounced on him. "Now, before I can't stand it any longer, what did you find out?"

"Do I get a reward if I tell?" His eyes were like molten silver.

She raised her chin. "And what did you have in mind, stranger?"

"I'm hungry."

"I thought you'd just eaten."

He pulled the pins from her hair and let it fall in a wild honey-colored mass to her hips. "I'm not thinking about food."

Her eyes darkened with need, and she moistened her lips with the tip of her tongue. Then she frowned and flounced away. "Tell me quick, Clint, before I forget about everything except you."

He walked away from her, then turned back. "The man's name is Rand Scanlon."

"Rand. Short for Randolph." She hurried over to Clint.

He held up a hand. "Not enough proof. The other one calls himself Mr. Oakes. But their names are meaningless if they're changed."

Biting her lower lip in agreement, she frowned.

"They're supposed to be gamblers headed out on the *Alabama Queen* when she sails."

"When's that?"

"I don't know. Soon, I imagine." Clint looked worried but fierce at the same time.

"What are we going to do? We can't let them get away."

"But what if that man's not Randolph?"

"I think he is, Clint. Rand. Randolph."

"What if we follow and leave the real Randolph behind?"

Lacey felt chilled. "Do we have a choice? It's the best lead we've had."

He paced the room. "I got a good look at Rand Scanlon when he passed our table and I watched him move on the street. I think he's our man, too."

"Good." She felt a deep sense of relief and at the same time a worry that they might be making a mistake.

"If we're in agreement, then we've got to follow Rand and Oakes onto the *Alabama Queen*. But we'll have to go undercover." He hesitated, thinking. "I believe it'd work if I go as a gambler. You'll be my woman and good luck charm. And you can pull in Rand like a fish on a line. You'll get in close to him, but not too close."

She shivered. "He gives me the creeps. I don't know if—"

"I'll be with you." He took her in his arms. "I'd never let him touch you, Lacey. I'd kill him first."

She nodded but felt even colder inside. "Then we'll do what we have to do. But I'm scared."

"Think about all the harm Randolph's done. Nobody but the two of us would have recognized him. We've got to get him, and a little fear is a good thing. The man's dangerous."

She touched the scar on Clint's face. "But we're more dangerous."

"We better be."

Chapter Nineteen

In her cabin on the *Alabama Queen,* Lacey giggled, tried to stop herself, then fell onto her bed in peals of laughter. Tears sprang into her eyes as she laughed, and finally she was forced to sit up, hiccuping. As the laughter trailed away and she tried to control the hiccups with deep breaths, she suddenly grabbed a handkerchief, held it to her nose, sneezed twice, giggled, then leaned back against a pillow, weak.

While Clint gambled, she'd just been given a grand tour of the steamboat by Josh, a very precocious ten-year-old. His father was a Yankee who had moved south after the war to make his fortune. The aging *Alabama Queen* had seen service in the war and Josh's father had bought it for a little of nothing, or so Josh had explained, then his dad had spent four times as much on outfitting the riverboat in grand style.

The *Alabama Queen* was one of the stern-wheelers that had plied the Tombigbee during better days, carrying cargo and passengers from Mobile to Tuscaloosa and back. Lacey didn't know what it had looked like before, but Josh's father had completely refinished it in elaborately decorated scrollwork and gilding. The passenger accommodations were adorned with oil paintings, intricately carved woodwork, velvet curtains, and chandeliers. It was a combination of ostentation and vulgarity that Lacey had decided was hilarious.

As she gazed around her room, she realized she seemed to be alone in her viewpoint, for the steamboat was crowded with Yankees looking for the luxury and gentility of the old South. Perhaps they thought they could buy their way into the Southern world.

Actually, when Lacey thought about it, the situation was sad. And terrible. For the things Northerners had professed to loathe were the very things they seemed determined to now confiscate for themselves, as if they had the slightest idea of what being Southern was all about.

Her parents had often told her the South was a state of mind, as well as place, and it had nurtured generations of people who had worked hard to carve it out of a wilderness. One thing she knew for sure was that the soul of the South could not be bought, although outsiders might possess some of its trappings.

Glancing out the window, she watched the wide Tombigbee glide by. It would have been a peaceful time, relaxing, if not for the job that lay ahead. Rand Scanlon and Oakes were onboard and soon she must begin wheedling her way into their confidence. And it wasn't a pretty thought.

But that wasn't something she wanted to muse about yet. Instead, she turned her mind back to the *Alabama Queen,* which flew a Union flag where once a Confederate flag had flown. The boat had been painted white, with red and blue stripes below the railing on the promenade of each of its three levels. The enormous stern paddle was painted red, and twin stovepipe funnels poured out thick black smoke. There was nothing now to show it had ever been a Rebel riverboat.

As she looked out her window, Northerners dressed in ostentatious finery strolled along the promenade deck. Blacks in crisp white uniforms served them with deference, and Lacey frowned, hoping the former slaves' lives were now better, but for the moment their jobs didn't seem to have changed.

And yet for all the vultures swarming over the South, there was a boy like Josh, and probably many more. He would grow up in the South, have children, and then would his Northern blood matter? Perhaps they must look to their children to heal the wounds, to make a place of peace for everyone and let their innocent souls take root in the rich Southern soil, cleansing it of past atrocities.

Sighing, she stood up and pulled shut the drapes of gold satin trimmed with royal-blue dyed fur. She must think about the job ahead, not the larger problems of the South or even of the money poured into the decor of a riverboat.

It would soon be time to join Clint, and she had to be dressed and ready to go. She could still hardly believe it, but she now possessed a new evening gown. Clint had insisted she must have something that fit the image of a gambler's woman, especially for nighttime.

They'd only had a day to get ready to board the *Alabama Queen,* but the dressmaker had altered a deep violet silk gown to fit her. Self-color piping and lavender fringe trimmed the décolletage, waist, and hem. It was simply and elegantly designed, and Clint had thought it suited her perfectly. For her, the dress was wonderfully rich and beautiful. She had felt guilty about spending the money on it, but Clint had insisted that in order to catch

Randolph they must fit into their new roles perfectly. And she'd had to agree with him.

So that evening she was donning the violet gown for the first time. The dress would take her into Rand Scanlon's world and hopefully help to lure him into her snare. And that would be worth the price of it.

But she would not forget to wear the matching kid leather gloves, for she and Clint had decided that if Rand Scanlon were truly Randolph, then he was probably aware of the birthmark on the Whitmore women's hands. So, above all, she must not take the chance of letting Rand see her left hand bare.

Walking over to the beveled mirror above the washstand, she poured water from a hand-painted china pitcher into a matching bowl with peacock feather designs. Splashing cool water over her face, she felt refreshed. Now she would fashion her hair a little more stylishly than usual, allowing a few curls to frame her face as the dressmaker had shown her. Looking at herself critically in the mirror, Lacey began preparing herself for the evening ahead.

After a while, when she was satisfied with her hair, she applied rouge lightly to her cheeks, then turned to her clothes. Again, Clint had insisted on buying more than she felt was necessary. She put on a corset, but as she slipped on the lavender drawers and matching camisole, she could not help but enjoy the luxury of sheer silk. She pulled on silk stockings and violet garters, a petticoat, then slipped into the evening gown.

When she looked into the mirror, she was surprised to see a very different woman gazing back at her. She could now, in fact, be a gambler's fancy lady. Amused at the idea everyone would

234

think that of her, she was still sure nobody would try to buy her for the night. Actually, the elegance of the gown made her look like a wealthy lady, enjoying a trip down the Tombigbee River.

And that was what she needed Rand Scanlon to think of her. A lady. Otherwise, he would think he could buy her attentions, and he must be made to believe it took much more than money to win her. That would be her defense as well as her offense, for it would serve to keep him at arm's length while challenging him to woo her.

She just hoped she could act well enough to convince him that she was interested in him as well. Then she frowned at her reflection in the mirror. Visons of Whitmore cottage, as well as other houses burned by Randolph's Raiders, ran through her mind. No, there was no hope about this. She *must* make Rand believe her, want her, then reveal the truth of his identity to her.

Picking up the dark blue silk shawl Sarah had given her, Lacey slipped it around her shoulders to hide the still-pink and sensitive gunshot wounds on her left arm. Last, she put on slippers, then stepped from the stateroom onto the promenade outside. The sun was setting, casting a reddish orange hue over the landscape as well as the *Alabama Queen*. She closed the door behind her, then walked over to lean against the railing. Tall trees along the bank were silhouetted against the colorful sky, and the scent of wildflowers came to her on a soft breeze.

It would be a beautiful night. A night made for lovers. For her and Clint. But, no, that couldn't be. Not now. Sighing, she turned her back to the countryside and looked down the promenade. People were walking, some holding hands, some talking, many moving toward the dining room.

Near it was an area where a small orchestra played, drinks were served, and people gambled and gossiped. There she would begin her seduction of Rand Scanlon.

As she started walking, Josh suddenly darted around several people and came to a stop in front of her. He was all dressed up from boots to suit to hat. Raising his hat, he smiled.

"Evenin', Miss Lacey." He was affecting a Southern gentleman's drawl to impress her.

"Good evening, Josh." She tried to look serious, although she was more amused than anything. In fact, he simply looked cute, but she knew that wasn't the image he wanted to project.

He offered his arm. "Might I escort you to dinner or perhaps for music?"

"Music, I think." She put a hand on his arm.

As they walked down the promenade, other people turned to watch, then smiled, stepping aside to allow them plenty of room.

"A lady like you gets respect," Josh commented, his chin held high, his face straight ahead, but his eyes moving back and forth to catch everyone's reaction.

"I think, possibly, it's your presence, Josh."

"You think so?" For a moment he forgot his haughty demeanor as he looked around, then remembering himself, he quickly regained his earlier composure.

"Undoubtedly."

"I want you to know somethin'." He led her to the railing, then fixed intent brown eyes on her.

She smiled, knowing she couldn't spend much longer with him but not wanting to hurt his feelings, either. "Yes?"

"I'm gonna inherit all this." He waved a hand around the steamboat. "And this is just the beginnin'. My dad's gonna buy us one of those big ole Southern mansions. Says we can get one cheap."

Lacey's smile faded. "No doubt that could be arranged." Her words were cold. Obviously, the child had no conception of the pain his words could cause a Southerner.

"We're gonna build an empire right here, me and him."

"Perhaps, Josh, but you will *never* have the legacy or heritage of a true Southern family."

He looked puzzled a moment, then his face cleared. "Sure we will. I'm gonna marry myself a Southern lady. Like you. In fact, if you'll wait, I'll marry you."

She felt chilled to the bone. "So you buy the estate and the woman who goes with it as well?"

Josh cocked his head, considering. "Good idea. If she suits me. Like you. You're the finest lady I ever met, and my dad agrees."

"I'm so glad." Her words were sarcastic, but she honestly didn't know what else to say. He was a child repeating what his father had told him, what he had learned during the war. But still he could very easily grow up to be a man with those same beliefs in his head. He could very well always believe that the South and Southerners were simply toys to be moved here and there to satisfy his whims.

"I knew you would be. Now, shall I escort you, fair lady?"

"Josh, I want you to promise me something."

"Anything, lovely damsel." He was enjoying his role enormously.

"Always remember I'm much more than a lady. I'm a person. I love the South, the land, the people." She took a deep breath, hating to shatter his illusions and yet knowing she must try. "My parents and friends were murdered by Northern soldiers."

Josh paled. "I'm sorry, ma'am. You don't have any kin left?"

"No. I'm alone. My home burned, my possessions stolen or destroyed by Yankees." She was desperate to make him see Southerners as real people. "Your father and men like him did this to me and mine."

Stepping back, Josh shook his head. "No. My dad didn't do nothin' like that. He was a good soldier. He helped to free the slaves. And we're down here now to see they get a fair shake."

"Why are you really in the South, Josh?" She wanted very much for him to be able to sort out the truth.

He frowned. "Like I said, we're here to help."

Smiling sadly, she leaned down and placed a soft kiss on his cheek, then walked away. People would believe what they wanted to believe or what they had been taught. She only hoped that as Josh spent time in the South, he would come to see it and its people as something besides the spoils of war.

By the time she reached Clint, she was depressed, upset, and not feeling in the least like dealing with Rand Scanlon and Oakes. But as she stepped into the room, she put a smile on her face and a twinkle in her eyes.

And she was rewarded with the attention of a number of gentlemen. As they started to approach her, she quickly moved to Clint's side. The men stepped back but still watched her from a distance. Clint was playing cards with Rand and three other men. Oakes stood near Rand's back and gave her a cold stare as she glanced around the group.

Quietly, she watched them finish the hand of

poker, then Clint turned to her and smiled. He put his winnings in his pocket and stood up. "Gentlemen, if you'll excuse me."

"You aren't giving us a chance to rewin our losses?" Rand asked, his eyes flicking around the table.

"Later." Clint chuckled. "But at the moment I have a greater pleasure awaiting me." He took Lacey's hand. "This is my good luck charm, Miss Lacey Wh—White."

"Gentlemen." She smiled, glancing at each man in turn but letting her gaze linger on Rand Scanlon.

Rand stood up, quickly pocketing his winnings, then walked around the table. He bowed slightly to Lacey. "My name's Rand Scanlon." With a jerk of his head, he added, "And my friend's Mr. Oakes."

"How nice to make your acquaintance." Lacey inclined her head regally. "Would you care to join us for drinks, Mr. Scanlon?"

"My pleasure. But call me Rand."

She fluttered her eyelashes slightly, as if in dismay at the impropriety. "I'm not sure—"

"You'd call a friend by his first name, wouldn't you? And as Clint'll tell you, we're all in the same profession."

"I see." She glanced at Clint and when he nodded positively, she looked back at Rand. "In that case, Rand, I think that'll be just fine."

Rand held out his arm. "Then, lovely lady, let me escort you to a table." He glanced at Clint to make sure he didn't object, then smiled at Lacey.

Clenching her jaws, she raised her hand. Rand took it, lifted it to his lips, and pressed a kiss to the back of her hand. She shivered, hating his touch, and was glad she was wearing gloves.

Tucking her hand into the crook of his arm, he led her to a round table near a window. There they had a good view of the orchestra as well as of the Tombigbee, and she allowed him to seat her near the window. Soft music floated around them.

Rand sat down next to her while Clint took the chair on her other side. Oakes eased his large bulk into the last chair and looked uncomfortable, although his face showed no emotion whatsoever.

"What would you care to drink?" Rand used the question to get Lacey's attention. Although he spoke of food, his eyes clearly sent a message of more intimate ways of slaking a thirst.

She held his black gaze as long as she could, then looked out the window. "Lemonade would be nice."

Beckoning a waiter, Rand was obviously determined to a show his skill as a gentleman. "The lady will have lemonade. Whiskey for me, Oakes here, and Clint—"

"Another whiskey."

When the waiter left, Rand leaned forward. "I don't know about you, Clint, but with the South opening up and carpetbaggers running thick down here, people like you and me stand to clean up."

"I agree." Clint gave Rand a considering look.

"And with a lady like Lacey, you could do even better."

"How do you mean?" Clint's eyes narrowed.

"A man naturally wants to impress a woman like her. They might not normally gamble, but if she lured them to you and you suggested a little game, they'd be hard pressed to turn you down. If they did, they'd feel weak in her eyes. See what I mean?"

Clint nodded. "In other words, you're looking at drawing in men who might not gamble otherwise."

"Right. It's good in a place like this riverboat, but you can set up a card game in a hotel room, too. Like I said, Lacey's a fine jewel." Rand smiled possessively at her.

"I'd have to agree with you." Clint squeezed Lacey's hand, then looked at Rand, a strong message in his steely gray eyes. "And she's all mine."

Rand raised a black brow. "A woman like Lacey could have her choice of men."

"And she chose me."

"For now." Rand chuckled. "Bet she keeps you on your toes, right?"

Clint nodded as the waiter set their drinks on the table.

Lacey took a sip of lemonade, then frowned at the men. "Gentlemen, I'm getting mighty tired of being talked about as if I'm not even here. I don't know when I've seen such bad manners." She rolled her eyes in feigned dismay, letting her words sound like flirting.

Rand grinned. "Southern Belles. There's nothing like them. They can insult you straight to your face and make you beg for more. Never seen nothing like it."

Lacey fluttered her eyelashes. "If you're trying to flatter me, Rand, it won't work because I know there are beautiful, gracious women up North as well."

"Beautiful, yes, but mighty different." Rand let his gaze roam over her face, then down to the décolletage of her gown, which exposed her smooth, pale skin.

"But don't forget they can be Iron Magnolias when crossed," Clint added, deciding he hated the game they were playing. If Lacey didn't find out Rand's true identity soon, he didn't know if he could control himself. He was so damn jealous of

241

her flirting with the outlaw that he was about ready to lock her out of sight of any other man.

"Frankly, I'm thinking I'd take a Southern Belle any way I could get her, Iron Magnolia and all." Rand took a quick drink.

Lacey smiled as if in satisfaction at the compliment, then looked at Oakes. "Is your friend shy, Rand?"

"No. But he doesn't say much. He prefers to observe." Something about Rand's words suggested that Oakes observed all that went on in his life, even to his liaisons with women.

Suddenly feeling chilled, Lacey glanced at Clint for support.

He nodded and raised his drink to her in a small salute, then said, "Can't blame a man for not talking unless he's got something to say."

Oakes still remained silent but took a sip of his whiskey. For such a large man, his movements were very precise, and he gave the impression of being well aware of everything going on around him.

"If you're interested," Rand said, drawing the conversation back to him, "I think the three of us would make a good team. Lacey could lure men to us, then Clint and I could play off each other, one being good while the other bad. It'd keep the other players off balance and under control. What do you think?"

"It's not a bad idea." Clint examined his whiskey glass. "But we're doing all right by ourselves."

"I'm doing good, too, but as a team I think we could make more faster. And have fun, too."

Clint frowned. "What kind of fun?"

Rand cast a glance at Lacey. "Whatever kind of fun we wanted. I'm not a man limited by other people's morals."

Lacey smiled coyly, trying to give Rand a smoldering look from under her lashes and hoping she didn't just appear sick. But it seemed to work well, for Rand suddenly reached under the table and squeezed her hand. Shocked, she froze until he took it away. Then she took several quick, deep breaths. She didn't know if she could keep up the charade, for she could hardly stand to be touched by Rand Scanlon.

"But I'm a man who's damned possessive about what's mine." Clint was having no trouble playing his part because Rand's barely veiled suggestions of a sexual relationship with Lacey or with all of them at the same time made him furious. If the man weren't Randolph, he might as well be. And Clint was going to get him now, one way or another.

"Don't blame you." Rand smiled. "But sometimes it's more advantageous to share." He stood up. "Tell you what. Why don't we all go in to dinner and discuss this matter further. My treat."

"How nice. There're some delicacies on the menu I've been wanting to try." Lacey stood up, leaning slightly toward Rand so more of her cleavage would show. She was pleased when his look dropped to below her chin. He was definitely interested. Now if she could get him to reveal his real identity before she had to carry the game any farther, all would be well.

"Whatever you desire, my dear." Rand held out his arm, and as she placed a hand on it, he covered it with his own hand. "A lovely lady like you should always have what she wants."

"My sentiments exactly." She smiled, then glanced at Clint. "Coming?"

He unclenched his fists and stood up, not knowing whether he should tag along or knock Rand down and take Lacey, damning the whole mess to hell. But he held his temper, and as they walked from the room, he realized his real fear was that Lacey might somehow start to want this other man and that Rand Scanlon wouldn't be Randolph at all.

And that was a thought he couldn't take.

Chapter Twenty

Clouds scudded across the nighttime sky, allowing only occasional silvery moonlight to shine down on the Tombigbee River. Sounds aboard the *Alabama Queen* were muted by fog that left a trace of moisture everywhere. A slight breeze brought the scent of river water aboard the steamboat, and pale yellow light spilled from the boat's open doors and windows to cast shifting patterns over the water below.

Leaning against the fore railing on the second deck, Lacey thought the eeriness of the evening suited her mood, for the past two nights she had woken with a sharp vision of Clint in dark, swirling water struggling to survive. She knew he was in danger, but she didn't know how to keep him safe except to watch out for him.

And that hadn't proved easy, since he was determined to keep her as far away from Rand as he could, even though he knew the necessity of her getting close to the outlaw. But that was the problem. Rand wanted to get close, very close, and Lacey was having trouble keeping him at arm's length. Worse, she hadn't been able to find out anything about his past.

Now worried about Clint, especially since his wounds weren't completely healed, and also worried about Rand, she simply wished it was all over. Her nerves felt stretched to the breaking point and still she had no clue as to Rand's true identity. Another time she might have been pleased about Clint's jealousy, for it proved he cared, but now it was dangerous to them and threatened their mission. Yet he was doing his best, trying to go along with the plan. But it was taking its toll on him and she couldn't help but be worried.

That was why she was out on the promenade rather than inside watching them gamble. If she stayed away, Clint didn't get so angry or Rand so lecherous. But it meant she couldn't watch Clint as closely, either. However, since he was inside away from the river, she felt he was reasonably safe. And it gave her a chance to relax.

They would arrive in Mobile soon, and if she could keep Clint out of harm's way till then, she thought the danger would be over once he was on dry land. Trying to feel calmer, she took a deep breath, and suddenly her vision tunneled. She could see Clint in dark water, struggling upward toward the surface. Then the vision was over, and she slumped against the railing.

Shaking her head, she tried to clear it. Fear made her heart beat fast. The danger was closer, greater than she'd realized. She mustn't let Clint out of her sight again till Mobile. She started toward the gambling room.

But Josh suddenly appeared out of the fog and gave her a quick bow. "Good evenin', Miss Lacey."

"Josh, how are you?" She was surprised to see him, for he'd kept his distance since their last encounter.

"I wanted to tell you I talked to my dad. He said a lot of bad things happened during the war but he wasn't a part of them."

"I'm glad to hear that."

"And he said we weren't gonna steal nothin' from nobody." Josh took a deep breath. "But he said I ought to apologize for bragging to a lady, mostly 'bout being better than her folks."

Lacey couldn't help but feel touched, even though she realized Josh had mostly missed her point. Still, something about her words had disturbed him, so maybe he would remember and understand them better when he was older.

"I'm sorry, Miss Lacey."

"Thanks for the apology, Josh."

"Does this mean we can be friends again?"

"Yes."

"Great!" He grinned. "In that case, the cook's made us a special pie. Let's go get it before I've got to go to bed."

He held out his arm, but as she took it, there was a loud splash over the side of the boat below them.

Josh froze, then hollered, "Man overboard." He stepped back from her. "Ma'am, I'm going after my dad and the captain. Don't you worry. I'll take care of it." Then he was gone, running down the promenade, shouting for his father.

Wasting not a moment, Lacey hurried to the stairs and made her way to the lower deck. Clint. She could think of nothing but the vision of him in dark, swirling water. If necessary, she'd rid herself of her petticoats and dive overboard to find him.

But it was difficult to see much of anything with the swirling fog, dark water, and lights and shadows from the riverboat. "Clint," she called, not knowing for sure if he had gone overboard but feeling deep inside that he had. Suddenly, she heard the engines stop and quiet descended over the river.

A moment later, Josh ran up with his father, the captain, and some other men. They wasted not a second as several pulled off their boots and dove over the side. The lapping of the water against the hull of the boat seemed loud as no one spoke, all straining to hear from the men in the river.

The minutes stretched by like hours as Lacey waited, wondering if she should run up and see if Clint were safely gambling. But she was afraid if she did, she might miss whoever was brought out of the river, for that person might need medical assistance. On the other hand, perhaps they would be lucky and only some piece of equipment or other object had fallen overboard. But the captain ran a tight ship and she doubted it.

For that matter, how could anyone have fallen over the side, for the railings that completely encircled the promenades were waist-high? She grew more suspicious and worried all the time. And with no cooling breeze, she became more and more warm. Soon her hands itched inside her gloves, and although she wanted to pull off the leather, Lacey knew she didn't dare in case Rand abruptly appeared.

Suddenly, aft, one of the men called, "Over here. Got 'em."

En masse, they hurried to the other side of the riverboat, Josh leading the way. A rope was thrown over the side, and soon a limp body was hauled up to the deck. As the wet man was laid out gently on the promenade and the rope removed, Lacey stepped forward, her heart beating fast.

"I've had some experience with the sick and wounded," she said, hoping neither Rand nor Oakes were within hearing but realizing anybody could be standing in the shadows. "Let me see him."

The group stepped back to give her room, and several turned to help the men overboard back onto the steamboat. But Lacey was unaware of that as she focused completely on the inert body before her. Light filtered through open windows and she couldn't restrain a gasp when she saw it was Clint, a bleeding gash on the side of his head.

"Quickly, I need something to stop the flow of blood." She knelt to check Clint. Pulling off her right glove, she tucked it in a pocket. His forehead was cool to the touch, but his heartbeat was strong. Relieved, she looked around.

Josh jerked off his shirt and handed it to her. "Who is it?"

"Clint McCullough. And thanks." She took the small shirt and wrapped it around Clint's head, using the sleeves to tie it tight.

"Is he going to be all right?" Josh persisted.

"Yes, I think so. If some of you men will carry him to our cabin, I'll take care of him there."

"We're real sorry about this, ma'am," Josh's father said, placing his hands on his son's shoulders.

"As long as he's okay, Mr. Samson, that's all that matters." She glanced around the group of men. "And thanks for saving him."

"If there's anything we can do—" Mr. Samson said.

"Just get him to the room." Lacey stood up.

Two men picked up Clint. He groaned. Lacey inhaled sharply, then quickly led the way up the stairs to the second promenade. Josh joined her as they walked rapidly down the deck.

"I'm gonna stand right outside your door all night in case you need me to run get something." Josh looked very worried.

"But I don't think—"

"This is my boat, too, and me and my dad don't want accidents."

Lacey nodded, understanding. "I'd appreciate it, Josh, but maybe one of the other men could relieve

249

you later." He was so young to be so earnest, so determined to make a better place for himself in the world. And so protective of his father. She'd never thought to ask about his mother. Perhaps she had, somehow, been another casualty of the war. And maybe this drive to build a safe, secure life for his father and himself was his legacy of the war.

"No, it's my job to watch out for you, Miss Lacey. A fine lady like you should never be hurt, 'specially on my boat. And we want to know what happened."

"Certainly." She stopped outside her stateroom, opened the door, then gestured the two men carrying Clint inside. When they had laid him on the bed, she felt relieved. "Thank you, gentlemen," she said as she ushered them outside.

At the door, Josh's father stuck in his head. "You want anything, tell Josh. He's going to keep watch."

"If you'll send up brandy now and some broth later it'll help."

"We'll get right on it."

"I'll get it, Miss Lacey," Josh called, then darted down the promenade.

Mr. Samson cleared his throat. "We'll want to talk with Mr. McCullough when he wakes up."

"I'll let you know as soon as he's well enough."

When the door shut, Lacey jerked off her left glove and shoved it in a pocket of her gown. Walking quickly across the room, she poured water from the pitcher into the bowl, wet a cloth, then removed Josh's shirt from around Clint's head. Washing away the blood, she examined the wound more closely. Superficial. She felt relief flood her, knowing head wounds bleed freely and usually looked worse than they were.

Hurrying to rinse out the cloth, she wiped Clint's face clean. For the moment there was nothing she could do about his wet clothes, for she didn't dare move him anymore until he regained consciousness.

Setting the cloth in the bowl, she picked up her medicine bag and returned to Clint's side. As she worked, disinfecting the wound, putting a salve on it, then winding a long white bandage around his head, she thought that the last thing he needed was another injury. If they both came through this ordeal in one piece, they were going to be lucky.

Opening each of his eyelids, she checked his eyes. They appeared normal, and again she was relieved. Stunned by the blow, the fall, and the water, his body was simply giving itself a chance to recuperate before waking. Or, at least, that's what she hoped was going on. If he didn't awaken soon, though, she would begin to worry.

There was a knock on the door and Lacey crossed the room to open it.

Josh held up a small bottle of brandy. "How is he?"

"Better."

"I'll be right here." He sat down in front of her door, as if protecting them.

"Thank you." Shutting the door, she turned back to Clint. If she could get a few sips of brandy down him, it should help to revive and warm him.

As she poured some brandy into a glass, she tried to be professional and detached, but everything inside her was screaming that this was Clint McCullough, her lover, her companion, and almost surely her soul mate. Nothing must stop him from getting well. Nothing must stop them from completing their goal so they would finally have time for themselves.

And yet she fought back tears, for she could suddenly imagine how very alone she would be without him. No, she couldn't lose Clint. The thought was

251

unacceptable. Raising his head, she tilted the glass to his lips, then poured a small amount of brandy into his mouth. He swallowed reflexively. It was a good sign. She tried again. He drank more brandy, then groaned.

Suddenly, he flung out his arms, as if warding off an attack. He tried to rise, but she held him down.

"Clint, it's me. It's all right. You're safe."

Groaning, he tossed his head and opened his eyes. "Lacey?" His voice was weak, confused.

"Yes. Right here." She stroked his face. "Relax. It's just a bump on the head."

"I'm seeing double." But his voice already sounded stronger.

"Close your eyes. Give your body a chance to adjust."

"Where's the brandy?"

She chuckled, pleased he was already making demands. As she poured more brandy into the glass, her hands suddenly shook. She stopped, realizing just how worried she'd been about him. When she felt more stable, she finished pouring the liquor, then lifted his head and held the glass to his lips again.

He drank greedily, then leaned back against the pillow. "Did anybody see who did it?"

"Did what?" She suddenly felt alarmed.

"Hit me and shoved me overboard."

She stood up, horrified. "Somebody tried to kill you?"

"Damn sure gave it a good try."

"But, Clint . . ."

"He had to be a big man."

"Oakes?" Lacey paced the room.

"You've done a good job on Rand Scanlon. He's willing to kill me to get you."

"We don't know that." She sat down on the bed

252

again and took his hand.

"Don't we?"

"But, Clint, it's what we planned to do."

He grasped her shoulders and pulled her close to him. "I know. But I don't want that man even *thinking* about putting his hands on you."

Pressing herself against his chest, she hugged him close. "I was so worried. If anything'd happened to you, I don't know what I'd have done."

"Well, you wouldn't have had to look far. Rand'd have been there to support the grieving lady . . . if you were grieving at all."

She sat up. "How can you say that? I don't want Rand Scanlon. I think he killed my parents." Her voice held pain.

Clint immediately looked concerned. "I'm sorry. He makes me mad. I think he's our man, too. But don't let him touch you, Lacey. I'd have to kill him, Randolph or not."

She put a fingertip to his lips. "He's not going to touch me. Remember, it's a game to get him to admit who he is. But it's getting too dangerous. Nothing is worth losing you."

His eyes turned dark silver. "Not even revenge for your family?"

She hesitated, then shook her head. "No. You're more important now."

Jerking her to him, he set his lips to hers, then pushed deep into her mouth with his tongue. She shivered from the heat of him, the driving need, the desire to possess her entirely, and quickly felt an answering flame deep within. Returning his kiss, she tasted brandy and triumph and passion. Alive. The near disaster made their caresses that much sweeter, that much more urgent, and she moaned softly as his hands drifted down her back to cup her hips. Pulling her hard against him, he seemed determined to join them in a way that nothing could ever separate them again.

But there came another knock at the door.

Clint cursed but held onto Lacey.

Confused for a moment at the sudden interruption, Lacey's head finally cleared. "Broth. That must be Josh."

"Broth! Damn, but that's what I really need right now."

Lacey pushed him back down on the bed. "Yes, you do. Remember, you're the patient and I'm the doctor."

He scowled.

She walked over to the door and opened it.

Josh held up a tray of food covered by crisp white napkins. "Soup, bread, and water."

"Thank you." She took the tray.

"How is he?"

"Awake. Would you like to get your father?"

Josh nodded, then raced off.

Again, she shut the door. She set the tray on a table, then went to Clint. "Why don't you sit up and I'll feed you the soup."

Clint grimaced. "I'm not sick. I'll eat at the table, but I'd rather have a juicy steak. And some dry clothes."

"No doubt. But first you're going nowhere till you've eaten and are stronger. Then we'll get you out of those wet things."

He tried to rise, felt his head swim, then leaned back, furious at his weakness.

She quickly fluffed the pillows behind him, then helped him sit up in bed. Next, she set the tray on his lap and sat down on the edge of the mattress. Tucking an edge of a napkin in the front of his shirt, she began feeding him.

"I feel like a damn baby."

"Please, Clint, we'll have you stronger soon. We must. Right now Josh is bringing his father, who's going to want to know what happened."

Clint frowned, but he picked up a slice of bread and took several big bites. When he swallowed, he said, "We don't want the truth to get out. If I point a finger at Oakes or Rand, we might lose them."

Lacey nodded, continuing to feed him.

Another knock came at the door.

"Follow my lead." Clint finished off the slice of bread and motioned for her to take the tray away.

She set the tray on the table, then let Josh and his father inside.

"I'm sorry about your accident, Mr. McCullough," Mr. Samson said. "How're you feeling?"

"Much better. And sorry for all the trouble."

"Do you know what happened?" Mr. Samson stepped closer, Josh right beside him.

Clint shook his head. "I'd gone for a walk. You know, to clear out my head from the gambling. I was leaning over the railing when the next thing I know I'm in the water being dragged up to the deck."

Mr. Samson frowned suspiciously. "You don't know if you slipped, or dropped something and leaned over to get it, or—"

"Sorry, but I don't know a damn thing." Clint looked uncomfortable. "I'll be damned if I can remember how it came about."

"We don't want to frighten the other passengers," Mr. Samson added.

"Less said about it, the better with me."

"Good." Mr. Samson looked relieved. "Now, anything you need—food, whatever—will be at our expense."

"I think you need something besides that broth," Josh said, looking at what was left of the soup in disgust.

"I think he's well enough to eat whatever he wants now," Lacey agreed. Picking up Josh's bloody shirt, she handed it to him. "Thanks for your quick thinking."

Josh bowed his head. "It's my job to see to the passengers, ma'am." He hesitated, taking a quick look at his father, then back at Lacey, his eyes suddenly holding a mixture of awe and amazement. "I've never met a lady doctor before."

"I have a few skills, that's all." She played down her experience, not wanting a lot of dangerous attention.

Josh nodded conspiratorially. "I understand, Miss Lacey. You're on holiday."

"Well, glad to know you're all right," Mr. Samson interrupted. "We'll let you rest now."

"Wait." Clint looked ravenous. "Josh, if you'll bring me up a big steak, barely browned, and all the fixin's, I'll be a lot more hearty in the morning."

"Yes, sir, and I'll send up a special pie the cook made today." Josh looked at Lacey, letting her know he was giving their pie away to a better cause.

"I'd like some of that pie," Lacey said. "It's been a long night."

"I'll say." Mr. Samson put a hand on Josh's shoulder, led him outside, and quietly shut the door.

Clint reached out, snagged Lacey's hand, and pulled her to the bed. "How long do you think it'll take them to get that food up here?"

"Long enough for what you've got in mind." Laughing, she smiled with pleasure as he pulled her into his arms and pressed hot kisses to her face.

Part Five

Defy the Storm

Chapter Twenty-one

Sitting on a bench in Bienville Square, Lacey glanced around Mobile's beautiful park. It was shaded with live oaks, gray moss hanging from the limbs, and planted with azaleas. Gray squirrels played in the trees, chasing each other through the thick branches, while sparrows sang from the tree-tops.

Although it was morning, the day was already warm, so she cooled herself with the fan Captain Redbeard had given her. She smiled, thinking back to the people who had befriended her on the quest for Randolph. She would never forget them or allow their friendship to lapse.

Through the trees she could see the Bienville Hotel where she was staying with Clint. Yesterday, the *Alabama Queen* had docked on the Mobile River. A few blocks east of her the river flowed into Mobile Bay, then into the Gulf of Mexico. But hopefully they would have to go no farther. Rand Scanlon was staying at the Bienville, too, and she was determined to get the truth from him as quickly as possible. There had already been too much delay.

And too much danger. Clint was doing well after a good night's sleep in the hotel, but he had insisted on going out early to scout around the city. She had wanted to go with him, but he had insisted she enjoy breakfast in bed. Acquiescing to him, she'd been glad she did, because she had been exhausted from the trip as well as from so much worry.

After a delicious breakfast, she had leisurely dressed in the blue striped blouse and matching skirt Clint had bought her, put on her straw hat and white gloves, then ventured into the lush park. From where she was sitting she could see Clint when he returned, and it gave her a chance to see a little more of the city before he took her on the tour he'd promised.

She thought of Josh, so mature for his years, and the life he planned to build in the South. Perhaps it would go well. When they'd parted, he had insisted she would always have a place on the *Alabama Queen,* and she thought she'd keep up with him. He had impressed her with his willingness to learn and to help others. And she'd found she couldn't help but like him, even though he was a Yankee.

There was no doubt about it, the trip had changed her. The pain over the loss of her parents and friends had lessened, although she knew it would always be there. But she had found she could make new, wonderful friends. In fact, life could go on after all her sorrow, even though it would never be the same.

And, of course, there was Clint McCullough. She hardly dared think of a future with him for fear something would keep it from coming to pass. But with all she had felt, all they had shared, her visions, how could she not think in terms of love and soul mates? Yet, until Randolph was caught, she still didn't feel free to follow a life of her own and neither did Clint.

Looking at the painting on the fan, she mused about Rand Scanlon, then glanced up. Walking toward her was the man of her thoughts.

"Good morning, Lacey." Wearing an expensive blue suit and brocade vest, he sat down beside her, then motioned Oakes away. The large man took a position under a nearby tree.

She forced herself to smile and look happy to see him.

He handed her a single white rose. "A beautiful flower for a beautiful lady."

"Thank you." She sniffed the rose, appreciating its beauty but wishing she could reject it and the man who'd given it to her. Instead, she smiled coyly and looked up at him from beneath slightly lowered lids.

"Did you sleep well?" Rand leaned toward her.

"Yes. And you?"

"Not at all."

"I'm sorry." She toyed with the rose. "Why ever not?"

"You should know." His black eyes sparkled with deep meaning.

"I'm afraid I don't."

He took her hand, turned it over, and stroked her palm through the glove. "You plague my dreams as well as my waking hours, Lacey. You know that." He sighed dramatically. "Why are you so cold to me?"

She forced a husky laugh from her throat. "Do you think me cold?"

Squeezing her hand, he leaned even closer. "Oh, no, you're not a cold woman, Lacey White, but a clever lady used to getting what she wants."

She looked away, trying to get rid of his scent, a cloying musky smell. She fanned herself briskly. "You think me devious?"

"You're like me, that's what I think. But right now I'm going to be honest. In fact, I don't think I can be anything else with you." He planted a hot

261

kiss on her cheek. "I want you."

She shivered, then slapped his shoulder playfully yet meaningfully. "You seem so sure of yourself."

"You're a tease, a real Southern Belle, but you're more, much more, or I wouldn't be trailing you around like a lost puppy."

She laughed and gave him a direct look. "Puppy? You!" She fluttered her eyelashes, wishing she was far away. "A man like you could never be a lost puppy."

"Only you can turn me into one."

"You're trying to catch me off guard. You're a gambler and I'm simply a new prize to be won." She tried to slow her racing pulse, wondering how far she dared push him. "Or are you something else? I know so little about you."

He smiled mysteriously. "You're a dangerous woman, aren't you? And you like strong men. Maybe men who've been outlaws, pirates, highwaymen. Is that it, tell me?"

Moving a little closer to him, she tried to look excited. "Yes, I like strong, dangerous men."

"A woman like you would." He put a hand on her shoulder, letting the heat from their bodies mingle. "And I'm just the man for you. I want you, and I intend to have you." He put his hand around her shoulder and drew her against his chest, then tilted her chin upward so she had to stare into his eyes. "Name your price." Then he pressed hot lips to hers, grinding against her, trying to force her mouth open to receive him.

Disgusted, she didn't know what to do, how to play the game. She put a hand on his shoulder to push him away, but he simply drew her closer, running a hand down her back.

Suddenly, a foot crunched some leaves near them. "You just gambled and lost," Clint said, his voice cold and menacing.

Rand raised his head, gave Lacey a light kiss on the tip of her nose, and stood up. "I never lose." He smiled smugly, beckoned for Oakes to follow him, then turned his back and walked away.

Clint started after him, but Lacey grabbed his arm and pulled him back. He looked into her eyes, saw the fear and worry, and backed down. Gritting his teeth, he pulled her hand through the crook of his arm and led her from the park to a waiting carriage.

Only after he had helped her to the seat of the open coach and started the horse forward did he dare speak. "Next time I'm going to break Rand's neck."

"Clint, we're close. I'm going to get him to confess soon. He wants me. He's willing to pay a price."

"And he thinks you want him enough to keep me in line. Damn!" He clenched his fists. "I hate being in this position."

"I know, but it's not for much longer. I know I can bargain with him and find out who he truly is. He almost told me today. Just a little more and I think I can push him into bragging to me."

"Maybe. Or he can simply kidnap you sometime when I'm not around."

"We must take some chances if we're going to catch him, Clint. I'm willing to put myself on the line."

"But I'm not."

"We've got no choice." She looked at him in determination, her blue eyes intense.

"I'm going to think of something else."

"That's fine with me if you can, but in the meantime, let's forget about Rand Scanlon for a while. Let's just enjoy the day. I've never seen Mobile before."

Gripping the reins, he forced the anger down.

She didn't need the added problem of a jealous man. He had to start acting like the professional he was. Slowly relaxing, he smiled at her. "You're right. I brought a picnic lunch we can share. Let's forget about Rand for a few hours."

"Good. I'd like that."

"But first, get rid of that damn rose he gave you."

She'd almost forgotten about the flower. Not wanting to destroy it, she tossed it to a young man walking beside his lady down the nearby walkway.

"There. Someone else can enjoy it." She settled back against the cushioned seat and looked out over the city.

Clint made a good guide as they drove down residential and business streets, because when he was younger he had spent time in the city. Lacey could soon see the influence of French, Spanish, and English, whom Clint explained had all at one time ruled Mobile until Alabama became part of the United States.

Ornamental ironwork fences enclosed houses that bore the imprint of Spain in their facades and flat roofs. From France came sharply hipped roofs and green-shuttered windows. Azaleas, camellias, and crape myrtles bloomed profusely, and roses cloaked walls and picket fences.

Clint pointed out the Federal Building, a massive three-story granite structure of Italian Renaissance design that had been completed in the fifties.

Next they drove past City Hall, another building of 1850's construction. It was a two-story white structure of brick covered with smooth stucco, occupying half a city block. Arched openings with wrought ironwork, decorated brackets under the wide eaves, and a cupola showed Spanish influences in the design. Clint explained it was originally used as a market, but a Confederate soup kitchen had been established on the ground floor to feed thousands impoverished by the war.

Driving through residential streets with beautiful homes lined with huge trees and blooming shrubs, Clint continued to point out landmarks.

He stopped in front of Barton Academy, the oldest public school in Alabama. It was a three-story structure of white stucco over brick. In the center of the front facade, which extended almost the length of the block, were six massive columns. An impressive column-supported dome surmounted the building.

But Lacey was most impressed when he drove to the City Hospital. He knew it had been built as early as 1825. It was a two-story and basement brick and stucco structure of Greek Revival design. Over a dozen Doric columns across the front facade supported the roof and the balconies were enclosed by green-painted balustrades. Next to the City Hospital was the Marine Hospital, erected in the forties.

As they drove on, she cast a last glance at the hospitals and made a personal vow to visit both of them before leaving the city.

Having seen much of Mobile, Lacey was quite impressed, although she saw many Yankees and Union soldiers. But she was finally realizing that Northerners had become part of the South and she might as well get used to it, if she ever could.

When Clint drove south out of Mobile, she began to enjoy the beauty of nature, as before she had taken pleasure in the beautifully designed city.

The narrow dirt road took them along Mobile Bay, where small boats to large ships plied its deep blue waters. Fluffy clouds hung overhead in a brilliant blue sky. A breeze blew off the Gulf, bringing with it the scent of the sea. A wide variety of green shrubs, wildflowers, and trees grew in abundance along the road, and Lacey leaned back, feeling deeply relaxed.

Clint smiled at her as they left Mobile behind, and not long after he turned the carriage down an overgrown road into lush vegetation. Lacey sat up and looked around, surprised as he drove them back into denser growth, where the scent of plants was strong. Finally, he turned the carriage south again, urged the horse through what appeared to be dense thicket, and stopped beside a secluded cove.

Water birds took off, complaining with loud cries. And then they were all alone, the small bay protected on all sides by trees and shrubs, except for a narrow outlet to Mobile Bay. Water lapped gently against a sandy shore and the sun shone down warmly, making the sand and water sparkle like jewels.

"It's beautiful," Lacey said on a sigh.

Clint placed a quick kiss on her lips. "And it's all ours. For the moment."

"You mean nobody knows about this place?"

"Didn't you see the road into it?"

"Yes, but—"

"We're really alone, Lacey. At least for a few hours. Let's enjoy it." He stepped down, then tugged off his jacket. Next he unbuttoned his shirt and tossed it into the carriage beside the jacket.

Shocked, she simply stared at him. "But what if someone comes by?"

"Anybody comes this way, we're going to hear them long before they see us."

She listened. It was so quiet, so peaceful, except for the water lapping against the shoreline, that she couldn't doubt his words. Still, she hesitated until he walked around and held out his arms. Leaning down, she let him lift her from the carriage so that her body trailed down the length of his until she stood on the soft sand. He felt hot from the sun, and the healing scars on his body looked much better. Yes, the sunlight could be good for him.

He kissed her, quick nibbling bites to her lips, then down to her neck. She shivered, suddenly too warm in her silk and satin.

Stepping back, he grinned, then shucked off the last of his clothes and left them in the carriage. The horse waited patiently in the shade of a tree, nibbling tall grass. Clint waded out into the water, the sunlight casting his body in hard planes and angles. His dark hair took on a reddish tint as he threw back his head and laughed.

"Come on in, the water's fine," he called, then waded out until he could dive into its depths.

As he struck out toward the narrow inlet, she became concerned. He wasn't completely well and there could be danger in the deeper waters of the bay. Again, she stopped her thoughts. He was well enough now and the swim would do him good. She mustn't be overly protective. But the thought of him being in any more danger was something she could hardly stand. Still, she'd had no vision so all must be well.

Standing in the direct sunlight, she suddenly realized just how warm it was and how inviting the water looked. Glancing around, she thought of strangers coming upon them swimming in the sea. Yet Clint was right in that it was a very secluded spot and they could hear anyone approach.

She hesitated a moment longer, but when Clint turned back and beckoned her toward him, she quickly made up her mind. Stepping back into the shade, she began undressing, amazed at her boldness. But she was not the same woman who had left Georgia, and she was not going to miss out on this chance at pleasure.

When she had stripped down to her chemise and drawers, again she hesitated. She could wear her underclothes into the water, but she wanted to be with Clint, as he was, with nothing between them. She quickly took off the last of her clothes.

She stepped into the sunlight, felt the warmness of the sun and the coolness of a sea breeze against her skin, then moved into the water. It was cool and wet, inviting her deeper. Glancing up, she saw Clint had come back closer and was now standing waist-deep in blue water. He watched her, apparently spellbound as she moved toward him, the water lapping higher and higher.

When she neared him, the sea now around her thighs, he said, "Don't come any closer."

She stopped, afraid of some underwater danger. "What's wrong?"

"I don't want to lose sight of you."

Laughing, she continued toward him, feeling rough sand under her feet. The water was wonderful. She felt so free, almost naughty to be enjoying herself so completely. Suddenly, she dipped her hands into the sea and brought them up, splashing water into Clint's face.

"Now you've done it," he growled in a mock menace. And grabbed for her.

But she evaded him, splashing more water, then diving into the sea and swimming away. He came right after her and caught her foot, dragging her under and toward him. When she came up she was sputtering, water dripping from her hair. But she was laughing, too.

Her amusement stopped as he pulled her up against his chest. His skin felt hot against her, with the coolness of the water around them. And he was hard, so ready for her. Suddenly, she could think of nothing except him, how he excited her, pleased her, made her want only him in her life.

"Oh, Clint." Her body trembled as she put her arms around his neck and hugged him, her breasts flattening against his hard chest.

"You don't have to say anything else." He lifted her into his arms, water cascading from her body, and walked to the edge of the bay in the shade of trees. Kneeling, he laid her at the edge of the water.

On her back, with the sand soft under her, she felt his shadow cover her as he looked down, his eyes worshipping her body, water sparkling over her like jewels. And all around her, the sea lapped against her skin, heightening her senses, making her aware of every inch of her body. "I want you."

Leaning down, he placed quick kisses over her face, then licked water off her skin until her face was dry. "You're so beautiful, Lacey. So perfect. You make me feel like a beast for touching you, needing you, wanting to make you mine completely."

"A beast?" She raised up on one elbow.

He sat down. "You don't see me that way?"

"Never. You've been unfailingly kind, considerate, helpful. You've never pushed me to do more than I wanted."

"Fortunately, you can't read minds." He picked up her left hand and rubbed a thumb across the spidery birthmark on the palm. "Although sometimes it seems as if you can."

"No, not that. But I've dealt with a lot of sick people and it's made me attuned to others."

"Lacey, there's something I need to tell you."

"Please, if it's anything that'll spoil the moment, don't. We need this time away from our troubles with Randolph."

Looking into her deep blue eyes, he took a breath, knowing she was right. It wasn't the time

269

to tell her about his past. He wanted her badly and he was beast enough to continue the deception to get what he wanted. Growling, he pulled her against him and covered her lips with his.

Thrusting deep into her mouth, he ran his hands over her body, feeling all the curves and valleys, reveling in the sounds of her growing excitement. He shuddered, hardly able to control his own building excitement. Leaving her lips, he trailed kisses down her neck to her breasts. Massaging her nipples with sensitive fingers, he soon replaced them with the heat of his mouth, letting his hands move lower, pushing into the soft, moist heat of her center.

When she groaned, digging her nails into his shoulders, repeatedly whispering his name, he could hardly keep from entering her and blazing his way to fulfillment. But he wanted this time to be memorable for her. In fact, he never wanted her to forget how a Yankee soldier had brought her to perfect bliss on the banks of Mobile Bay. Later, they would catch Randolph and it would all be over between them, for she would have to know the truth. Then she would hate him for his birthright.

As he lowered his head, needing to taste her inner depths, needing to know he had touched her so intimately this final time, needing it to last a lifetime, he knelt between her legs, raised her to him, then thrust his tongue deep inside her, tasting, teasing, taunting, and was rewarded with small moans as she twisted up toward him, burying her hands in his hair.

But it was bittersweet for him. It was probably the last time he would ever make love to her, for soon she would know him for a beast and he didn't think he could stand the look in her eyes when she saw him for what he was. But for now he would love her, and the past and future be hanged.

Raising his head, he moved her legs over his shoulders, then pressed the tip of his manhood against the seat of her burning need. Then he plunged, in one swift movement, deep into her. She cried out, clinging to him as he began moving, faster and faster, the primitive rhythm driving them relentlessly until finally he covered her mouth with his and plunged his tongue into her, filling her completely with himself as the spasms started and he let passion wipe out everything except the emotions that made them one.

When they were spent, he raised his head and looked into her eyes. She was crying, softly, quietly. He caught a tear with the tip of his finger and raised it to his lips. Catching it on his tongue, he drank it, knowing she had finally entered him, as he had her. There would not be a day for the rest of his life that he would not think of her, whether they were together or apart.

And there was nothing he could do about it but be glad he had known this great a love, despite the pain, despite his betrayal, despite the gulf that separated them.

Then he pulled her against his chest and held her so hard that he knew she couldn't breathe. When he finally let her go, she looked at him in wonder. But he couldn't explain himself, and for now there was no need.

He walked away from her, then dove into the water and swam toward Mobile Bay.

Chapter Twenty-two

Driving back to Mobile, Lacey felt closer to Clint than she ever had. In fact, for the first time she was able to look beyond catching Randolph to a new life. She wanted that life to include Clint, but would he agree or did he have secrets, too?

For she had withheld from him the knowledge of a very important part of her. The Whitmore legacy. But the legacy was so new to her own experience that she'd waited to see if it rang true. Now that they had been through so much and the danger warnings about Clint had been unfailingly accurate, she felt sure that, like her mother, she carried the trait.

But what would Clint think about it? Would he laugh, scoff, or simply disbelieve? Could he accept that it was a part of her and would be a part of her life with her soul mate? She felt chilled, believing she needed to discuss it with him before they went any further. Yet she was afraid of his reaction.

He'd been quiet since they'd made love, as if his mind were somewhere else, and that made her reluctant to discuss something so personal with him. After all, they hadn't known each other very long. Still, she felt driven to share with him the last part of herself that was so vital to her.

Taking a deep breath, she turned to him. "I want to talk with you about something."

He froze, thinking she had found out the truth about him. Now it would all be over, sooner than he had expected. He didn't look at her, couldn't. "What is it?"

"From the first, there's something I haven't told you. About me. And my family."

Surprised but relieved, he glanced at her. She looked very worried, almost afraid. He squeezed her hand. "You can trust me, Lacey."

"It's about the Whitmore legacy."

"Legacy? You mean Whitmore cottage and taking care of the wounded?"

"No. It's not that." Watching Mobile Bay, she drew courage from deep within. "The birthmark on my hand usually goes along with something else." She rushed on. "There's a legend in my family that the women will always recognize their soul mate, the man they are destined to love, because they have premonitions of when he is in danger."

Clint frowned, looking at her, then back at the road. This was so far from his personal worry that he hardly knew what to say. "What do you mean?"

"Visions. That's what I was doing at the train wreck. Mother always knew when Father was in danger. She saw the train blowing up in a vision. It was just before she died. I tried to get there in time to stop the train and get him to safety. But I got there too late and you—"

"I wouldn't believe you." He felt a little sick. "And that's why you thought I'd killed him and the others."

"If you'd listened to me—"

"There was still no time." He clenched the reins.

"I realize that now. Anyway, I couldn't tell you that was the real reason I was there, not when I

273

didn't know you."

"Why are you telling me now?" He was more suspicious and worried than ever. "If you don't want to see me again after we catch Randolph, you don't have to make up some outrageous story about a former soldier you've been having visions about. You can just say it's over."

She smiled. "It isn't a story, but I have been having visions when a certain former soldier is in danger."

"Damn!" He stopped the horse, turned to her, and took her hands, holding them hard. "Listen, Lacey, I don't care about the legacy, true or not, but don't walk away from me. We can work this out."

She put a fingertip to his lips. "You're the soldier I've been having visions about, Clint."

He shook his head, as if he hadn't heard right. "Me?"

"Yes."

"Soul mate?"

"Yes."

He lifted her into the air and set her down on his lap. Hugging her close, he kissed her face until she laughed and pushed at his chest.

"Does this mean you don't mind about the legacy?"

"Mind?" He kissed her again. "Lacey, anything that makes you want to stay with me forever is all right by me. Just so long as it's me in your visions, I don't give a damn how many you have."

She laughed and hugged him to her. Then she grew sober and leaned back. "There's another thing. It's rare. My father didn't have it. But it's been handed down in the family that in some cases the legacy is sort of catching. I mean, if the soul mates are exceptionally close, the man will sometimes have visions of his love being in danger."

Clint looked disappointed. "It's never happened to me. And I love you, Lacey, with all my heart."

Tears sprang into her eyes. "I love you, too, but—"

"There's still Randolph to be caught." He frowned.

"But there's afterwards."

He sat her down on her side of the carriage, then clicked to the horse. "The sooner we get back to Mobile, the sooner we can get that outlaw behind bars. And the sooner we can get on with our life. Together."

"Right." She snuggled close, her heart soaring in a way she would not have believed possible. He loved her. He really, truly did. Just like her father had loved her mother. Soul mates. Now she would never be alone again.

But Clint was silently cussing himself. He'd forgotten in the excitement of learning she loved him that his past could kill all their dreams, all their hopes, even such a thing as the Whitmore legacy. Could she really be having visions, or was she simply worried about the man she had come to love? It didn't matter. All he cared about was that somehow she returned his love, but when he told her the truth, that love would turn to hate. And there wasn't a damn thing he could do about it.

Furious with his fate, he snapped the reins over the horse's back. Now he just wanted it all over and done with, for every moment he spent in her company was another moment of pain.

When they got back to Mobile, Clint drove straight to the hotel and left the carriage with the doorman. They walked into the lobby, and he led Lacey to a chair.

"I'll be right back. I want to get you something."

Surprised, she sat down, watching him, but when he headed for a flower vendor, she smiled in understanding.

Clint bought a bouquet of gardenias, their fragrance reminding him of Marsden cottage and the time he'd kissed Lacey. But he pushed the thought from his mind. He had business that couldn't wait. He walked to the reception desk, then glanced back at Lacey and smiled before turning around.

"McCullough. I need my key, and do you have a message for me?"

The desk clerk handed over the key and a telegram. Keeping his back to Lacey, Clint quickly scanned the message, then crumpled it in his fist. He resisted the impulse to throw it on the floor and instead tucked it in his pocket.

Trying to keep a scowl from his face, he headed back to Lacey, his grip on the bouquet of gardenias crushing their stems. But his mind was far away.

He'd contacted his superior officer, asking for more time and more funds. But the reply had been negative. Since catching the Raiders, there had been no new reports of their activity and the department believed Randolph was dead. Clint had watched the newspapers for reports, too, and he'd asked around Mobile for news of Randolph. True, there had been no new Raider attacks or reports about their leader, but that didn't mean Randolph was dead.

Frustrated, he wasn't quite sure what to do. They were so close to catching Randolph that if Rand Scanlon turned out to be their man, they couldn't stop now. And if Rand were innocent, then Randolph was still out there and had to be brought to justice. But Clint had been given an order. Stop. Report to headquarters.

Reaching Lacey, he gave her the flowers, hardly registering her expression of pleasure. When she squeezed his hand, he looked at her in distraction and saw the look of concern and puzzlement on her face. That brought him back. He couldn't let her know the truth, not when they were so close to catching Randolph.

He figured he had a day, maybe two, to find out Rand Scanlon's true identity, because it might have taken him that long to pick up the message. That meant there was no time to lose. He had to get answers quick, and the only way he knew to do it was out on the street, asking questions of the right people. In addition to that, he needed money. He was going to have to gamble in earnest, or the Bienville would have them out on their ear.

"Clint?"

"Sorry." He forced himself to focus on her. "Listen, I realized our money's getting low. I've got to go out and gamble for a while."

"I was afraid of this, Clint."

"Don't worry. I want you to go back up to the room and relax."

"How can I? Let me help."

"No." He said it more strongly than he'd meant to and immediately regretted the hurt look on her face. But he had to keep her out of this. He had to protect her at all costs.

But she persisted. "We've got to find out about Rand, then we wouldn't have to worry about keeping up this image. I simply must get him to confess to me."

"Don't push it, Lacey. He's dangerous. I couldn't stand it if he hurt you."

She smiled, but she was feeling cold inside. Clint was trying to cover up his worry, but their situation must be perilous for him to be so tense.

And it made her nervous. "Go on and gamble. I'll be all right." She squeezed his hand again. "And thanks for the day. It was wonderful."

He raised her hand to his lips and kissed the back of her fingers. "Don't forget what we talked about."

"I never could."

Inside he winced, knowing how much harder it was going to be to tell her the truth. "Everything will be fine. I'll be back as soon as I can and we'll have dinner."

"Go ahead, and good luck."

He handed her the key to their room, and she watched him take long strides out of the hotel, as if he could hardly wait to be outside. As she turned to walk to their room, she was suddenly struck with a thought. Could he have lost interest now that he was assured of her love? Could he be rushing off to a new conquest?

Frowning in dismay, she shook her head. No. Clint had said he loved her and she believed him. The Whitmore legacy couldn't be wrong. She must have faith in their future. But first she had to deal with Rand Scanlon. It was time for the last act of their play.

Turning around, she walked to the desk clerk, knowing she was going to have to endure his disapproval.

"I'd like to leave a message for Rand Scanlon."

He raised a brow but made no move to help her.

"I'd like a pen and paper, please," she said in her most commanding voice.

Sliding it across the desk to her, his expression was censorious.

But she ignored him and wrote a message to Rand, asking him to meet her in the lobby at six so he could take her to dinner. Folding the piece

278

of paper, she tucked it in an envelope and wrote Rand's name on the outside. Handing it back to the desk clerk, she made sure he put it in the right slot, then turned on her heel.

As she ascended the stairs, her heart beat fast, for she knew how dangerous Randolph could be. However, she wouldn't be foolish. They could dine in the hotel, where there were plenty of people around and where she was known. When Clint returned, she'd have proof from Rand's lips one way or another. In fact, she might even have the outlaw in custody all by herself. Then they could get on with their lives, one way or another.

Unlocking the door to her room, she stepped inside and shut the door behind her. Locking it, she sighed. Safe, for the moment. She glanced around at the tasteful decor of the room, decorated in beige and blue, with delicate Louis XVI furniture. A blue canopied bed dominated the room, and there was also a desk and chair, a settee, an armoire, and a dresser. She put the gardenias in water and placed the blue vase on the desk.

Enjoying the luxury, she decided to take full advantage of the room before they had to leave. There was time before six to take a hot bath and wash off the seawater. When she met with Rand, she wanted to look her best and be as relaxed as possible.

Ringing for service, Lacey began to undress. By the time she stepped into the steaming bath, she felt even more determined. Enjoying the luxury of fragrant oil and bath bubbles, she soaked, then washed her hair. Later, she sat by the window, drying her hair until finally it was time to dress. But by now, she no longer felt relaxed.

As she put on the deep violet evening gown, she tried not to think, but troubling thoughts pounded through her head. There was always the possibility that Rand hadn't gotten her message, or that Clint would get back too soon, or that she simply wouldn't be able to get Rand to confess even if he did meet her for dinner.

But those were ideas she didn't want in her head and so she drove them out, concentrating instead on the change she was undergoing as she transformed herself into a lovely lady. Finally, satisfied she was as well dressed as she could be, she picked up the small derringer Clint had bought for her. She checked to make sure it was loaded, then pushed it into her reticule, a small drawstring bag Clint had bought for her in Mobile.

Now she was armed not only with a pistol, but with fashionable clothes as well. The wounds on her shoulder were now simply pale pink lines, but she wrapped Sarah's shawl around herself, anyway, as much for moral support as for cover. Finally, she pulled on the matching lavender kid gloves to cover the spidery birthmark on her left palm.

At last it was time to go downstairs. She didn't want to be late. Feeling her heart beat fast, she stepped out of her room, locked the door, then made sure she had the key in her reticule. Now there was no turning back.

As she descended the staircase toward the lobby, she glanced around. She didn't see Rand and felt acute disappointment. But perhaps he hadn't arrived yet. As a last recourse, she'd check to see if he'd picked up his message.

Walking across the lobby, someone caught her arm. Surprised, she turned around.

"Good evening." Rand smiled, his expression possessive and triumphant.

"I'm glad you got my message."

"So am I." He presented her with another white rose.

"Thank you. This is lovely."

"I thought you'd like it. Did you have in mind a particular restaurant? Mobile has several fine ones."

"Here. I mean, the Bienville has good food."

Rand raised a brow. "You can have whatever you want."

"My time is limited. Clint may be back soon."

Nodding in understanding, Rand steered her toward the hotel restaurant. "You're right, this restaurant's quite good."

Lacey noticed Oakes followed them at a discreet distance, and she felt an added anxiety. Until now she'd forgotten about Rand's bodyguard. But Oakes shouldn't matter if he kept his distance, and that was exactly what he seemed to be doing.

Rand had obviously quickly gained the respect of the hotel's staff, for the maitre d' quickly seated them at a table near a window overlooking Bienville Square. Oakes was placed alone at a nearby table. Lacey tried to push away the uneasy feeling of being constantly watched but it didn't help, so she decided to simply ignore Oakes and concentrate on Rand.

"I'm going to order a bottle of champagne to celebrate." Rand was clearly pleased with the turn of events.

"Are you so sure we have something to celebrate?" She had to remember to be coy.

"I'm very sure." He grinned, then motioned for the waiter. "A bottle of your finest champagne." He tipped the waiter, who hurried away. Glancing back at Lacey, he added, "Life runs very smoothly on well-greased palms."

She smiled, making sure her eyes twinkled in admiration. "You do seem to have a way of getting what you want."

"Yes. And I'm a man who knows my mind. I see something I want and I take it or buy it or—"

"Steal it?" She caressed the words.

"I was going to say gamble for it. But stealing is not beyond my abilities, either."

She smiled, raising a brow. Now she had him moving in the right direction.

The waiter returned and made a great production of presenting the champagne. By the time they lifted glasses of sparkling liquid, she decided ten minutes must have passed and Rand didn't look in the least like talking about robbery.

"Now, for a toast to us." Rand touched his glass to hers, then took a sip, watching to make sure she drank, too.

Taking a quick drink, she wondered how the potent brew would affect her. She hadn't drunk much liquor in a long time, and she had to remain completely sober. But she also couldn't upset Rand by refusing to celebrate. Caught in a difficult position, she took another sip, enjoyed the taste, then took another.

"You should always drink champagne, my dear." Rand was watching her closely, his glass already half empty. "And eat the finest food. Wear the best of clothing. And live in the most lovely of homes."

"I couldn't have said it better." She laughed a low, seductive sound.

"Champagne agrees with you, I see. Good. We'll eat in a while. I spoke with the maitre d' and the chef is preparing the finest of French meals for us."

"That's sounds wonderful." She took another sip, tried to ignore Oakes, and suddenly wondered what Clint would think if he returned and saw her sitting with Rand. But it was something else she didn't want to think about and Lacey forced it from her mind to concentrate on the man across from her.

"More champagne?"

The waiter appeared and their glasses were refilled as if by magic.

Feeling a little light-headed, she knew she had to push Rand, had to get some facts. "You appear to be a wealthy man, Rand. That's not very common in the South just now."

"No, it's not. But I believe you're a smart enough woman to want to hook up with a man who can help her lead the kind of life she was born to live."

She smiled, thinking back to Whitmore cottage. A grand lady she was not, but then he was no gentleman so he had little idea how to tell the difference. However, she had been raised a lady, if not in the grand sense of the term. "I have to admit I've been wanting a change in my life."

"Then I'm the man for you, Lacey. In fact, unlike Clint McCullough, I'll marry you."

She looked surprised.

"You don't realize your own worth. With your looks and style and my abilities, we could make a fortune in the South. Marry me, and I'll see you're always happy."

"This is so sudden."

"No. You know I've wanted you from the first. I'm a jealous man and I don't want other men to have a chance at you." He reached into his jacket pocket. "And to prove my intentions, I want to give you this." He pulled out a forest green silk handkerchief and handed it toward her.

She took it, feeling a heavy weight in its center. She hesitated, concerned the dinner wasn't going anywhere near where she had planned to lead it. But she must keep up the game or all would be lost for sure.

As she slowly opened the handkerchief, one corner after another, she become more and more worried about its contents for it felt like a ring. An engagement ring? She wanted to stop, to give it back, but there was nothing to do but continue or lose the game. Finally, she revealed the ring. It was a large marquise emerald nestled in glittering gold, a beautiful ring, a valuable ring, a ring to touch the heart of almost any woman.

And it touched her deeply, for it was a piece of Whitmore heirloom jewelry. She clutched the ring, her eyes burning with fire as she looked up at Rand.

"I don't feel hungry anymore."

Chapter Twenty-three

"I've pleased you?" Rand looked very satisfied with himself.

"Oh, yes." Lacey's voice was deceptively smooth as she slipped the ring on the third finger of her right hand and easily over the snugly fitting glove.

"But that's the wrong finger, since we're now engaged."

"It's exactly where it belongs."

"We can have it sized later." He completely misinterpreted her actions. "I promise to make you very happy, Lacey."

"And I'm going to hold you to that promise." Her eyes were like blue fire as she touched the derringer through her reticule. He was going to make her happy, all right, but not the way he had in mind. She was going to smile when she took him into the law, if she didn't put a bullet in his heart before. Then she realized he could have bought the ring off a Raider. She still needed more proof and he was the only way to get it.

"Are you ready for dinner now?" He looked expectant, his dark eyes possessively watching her.

"I'm so sorry, but I seem to have lost my appetite what with all the excitement."

His face fell in disappointment. "But the chef's preparing a special feast for us."

Leaning forward, she tapped his hand with her finger. "I want to talk with you now in a more private place."

He no longer looked disappointed. Glancing at the waiter, he said, "Keep it warm. We'll be back later."

Barely holding her anger under control, Lacey was so mad she was beyond thinking in terms of danger to herself. Besides, her fury made her feel invulnerable. She had to get Rand some place alone and question him. Now that they were supposedly engaged she felt sure he would tell her the truth, but she didn't think she'd ever get it out of him in public.

As he helped her up, he whispered, "My room?"

Fluttering her eyelashes, she shook her head negatively. "I must still think of Clint."

"But—"

She tucked her hand into the crook of his arm, deliberating leaving the rose behind. "Let's go to the square. It'll be beautiful by moonlight."

Eagerly leading her from the restaurant, he motioned for Oakes to follow them just as the bodyguard's meal was set on his table. Lacey was delighted to see she was ruining the outlaws' plans, and it was only the beginning.

They left through a side door. Outside, the air was cooled by a strong breeze off the bay, clouds were gathering overhead, and lightning flashed in the distance. But in the square, flowers scented the air and lightning bugs made bursts of tiny illumination here and there. They strolled through the park, with Oakes a comfortable distance behind.

Selecting a bench not too far from the hotel, Lacey sat down and beckoned for Rand to join her. When he sat down, she said sweetly, "Why don't you send Oakes a little farther away? I'm

286

afraid I'm somewhat shy."

"Certainly, my dear." He gestured at Oakes, and the bodyguard walked away.

"Now, Rand, darling, this big ring says we're engaged and you've said we're going to live a wonderful life, but I still don't know much about you or how we're going to do that."

He put an arm around her waist and began working his fingers up toward her breasts. "What do you want to know?"

"Well, have you always been a gambler?"

"No."

"Then what?" She pulled his hand around her stomach and held on, hardly able to stand his touch. "Oh, you want me to guess." Standing up to get away from him, she leaned down so he would concentrate on her cleavage. "Randolph?"

"Yes," he replied, then frowned as he realized he'd responded to something besides Rand.

"Rand Scanlon." She inhaled sharply, her eyes wide. "You wouldn't . . . no, you didn't . . . oh, surely not!"

He lost the angry look on his face, then grinned, suddenly focusing on her face. "What do you think I've done that's so impressed you?"

"You wouldn't be *that* Randolph, would you? You know, Randolph's Raiders?"

"And what if I was?" He was obviously testing her.

"No. I don't believe it. That'd be too exciting. Why if you were that man, we could have anything we wanted, do anything we wanted, and you'd be so dangerous." She put her hands behind her back and pulled the derringer out of her reticule. Holding it out of sight in the folds of her skirt, she watched him.

"You like dangerous men, don't you?" He

snagged her around the waist. "Now come back here and keep me company." He pulled her down to his lap, then began nuzzling her neck. "This dangerous enough for you?"

But she couldn't let him get too distracted. "Better, but tell me true, are you Randolph of Randolph's Raiders fame?"

"I confess." His beard stubble scratched her skin where it was exposed by the décolletage of her gown.

"Oh!" She wiggled in his arms, wanting him to think he was exciting her. "You're just saying that because you know it's what I want to hear." But she knew his name was Randolph because she'd caught him off guard on that one. Now if she could only get him to prove he was the Raider leader. "How would I know for sure? You'd know all about him from the newspapers."

"You'll have to take my word." He lifted his head and grinned.

And she believed him. It was there in his eyes, the look she'd seen when he'd ridden around Whitmore cottage as it burned. "Tell me something the newspapers didn't mention."

"I could, but you wouldn't know if it were true."

"Let me think. What would convince me?" While he ran his hands up and down her back, then began pulling her face close to his, she realized that their underground network would have kept the news of Whitmore cottage's demise out of the papers to protect those left.

She leaned away from his searching lips, holding out her hand to look at the ring on her finger. "Where did you get this emerald, Rand?" She made her voice sound excited, all the while wondering how much longer she could stand his hands on her body. "Did you get it on one of your raids?"

Narrowing his eyes, he smiled. "As a matter of fact I did, and I've been saving it for the perfect lady." His voice took on pride. "In Georgia, me and my men got a place called Whitmore cottage. They'd helped wounded Rebels during the war and still were. That ring's about the best thing we got."

Lacey bit her lip and tasted blood. Now she had her proof and she wanted to kill him on the spot. But she forced herself to remember that she healed people rather than hurt them. Even now. She stood up, pulled the derringer from the folds of her skirt, and pointed it at Rand's chest. "I'm taking you into the law."

He looked at the pistol in disbelief, then at her face, then back at the gun as reality finally penetrated through his fantasies. "Well, I'll be damned. What the hell's going on?" Suddenly, he was no longer the unsure lover but the deadly Raider, and it showed clearly in his eyes.

"Like I said, I'm taking you to the law. Stand up and keep your distance."

He laughed. "Honey, you've just made the biggest mistake of your life. I was willing to marry you, take care of you, *love* you."

"I didn't want any of that. Now get up."

"That's a mighty little gun and Oakes isn't far away."

"But he won't want me to shoot you."

"No." Rand grinned, a sudden feral movement of lips drawn back over teeth. "Now I'll tell you what we're going to do here. And it has nothing to do with the law."

"I insist you stand up or I'll be forced to shoot."

"What's that thing got, one shot, two if you're

lucky?" He shook his head. "Like I said, you've made a bad mistake, Lacey White or whoever you are. If I cared I'd ask why, but there'll be plenty of time for that later."

Lacey felt hot and suddenly very afraid. Rand was not acting like he should and she was becoming sure she *would* have to shoot him, and she didn't want to do it. "There'll be time for nothing, since you'll be in jail. Now, move."

"What I'm going to do is take you for my mistress, no marriage now, and I'll treat you rough, any way I want. As for Clint, I'll have Oakes make sure he has an accident, permanent this time."

"Then it was Oakes who pushed him overboard?"

"Sure."

"Oh!" Furious, she really wanted to shoot him and struggled to restrain herself. But the emotions distracted her.

Rand lunged for the pistol, not believing she would dare shoot him, and got his hands around hers. She held on tight, realizing the gun was all that stood between her and Rand's viciousness. They struggled, each trying to gain control, and suddenly the gun went off, the shot loud in the square yet muffled by the trees.

Slumping, Rand fell to the bench. Horrified, Lacey checked his pulse. Alive. But wounded. She couldn't move him because he was too heavy. Suddenly hearing someone running toward her, she looked up and saw Oakes coming at her.

Horrified, she ran toward the hotel. But she heard Oakes behind her, moving much more quickly than she would have thought possible. If she didn't reach an entrance in time, he would drag her back to Rand and that fate would be

290

worse than death. Her breathing was loud in her ears, for with the corset she couldn't inhale deeply and she was terrified the exertion would cause her to faint.

Glancing around, she looked for other people, but for some reason the square seemed to be empty. Hadn't anyone heard the shot? Why weren't people running toward her? But her questions didn't help matters, for the fact was she was alone, terribly alone. And now she was beginning to see black spots before her eyes and flashes of light. She knew that soon, very soon, if she didn't stop running, she would simply black out. And she cursed the corset and the long, heavy skirts that were slowing her down.

From behind, she felt Oakes grab her shawl. She was pulled back just as she reached out for a side door to the hotel. She let go of the shawl, jerked open the door, and stepped inside. Glancing back, she saw Oakes face filled with fury, holding her empty shawl. Then she rushed toward the lobby, desperately afraid he would still come after her.

She walked as quickly as she dared to the lobby, stuffing her derringer back into her reticule. She weren't at all sure she could count on anyone here to help her. After all, Rand was a customer, too, and obviously had ingratiated himself with the staff. No, she didn't dare depend on anyone to save her. Besides, who among them, now that the war was over, would be carrying a gun?

Trying to appear normal so no one would stop her, she forced a smile on her face as she walked through the lobby. Hurrying up the staircase, she hoped desperately that Clint was back from gambling. She needed him now more than ever. But if he weren't, she would get her father's pistol, then go to the law. Unfortunately, that gave Oakes a chance to get Rand into hiding. But Rand would have to have a doctor's care, so they would be able to catch them when he sought help, if not before.

But first she had to stay alive to see Randolph was brought to justice, and that meant getting her pistol. Glancing back over her shoulder at the top of the stairs, she searched the lobby. She didn't see Oakes, but that didn't mean much except she should be able to reach the safety of her room.

Hurrying down the hall, she stopped at the door to her room, looked both ways, then inserted the key. Slipping quietly inside, she shut and locked the door, then leaned back against it.

And saw Clint.

Relief flooded her and she hurried toward him.

"Where were you?" His words were like pistol shots.

Surprised, her steps faltered. "I went—"

"I told you to come back here and wait."

"But I—"

"You know how dangerous it is. What if . . . you look like you've been running. What happened to your hair?" Suddenly, he stood up. "Lacey?" The tone of his voice changed completely. "Are you all right?"

At his sudden kindness, she felt ready to burst into tears. Forgotten were his earlier harsh words. Now there was no time for her own emotions or any differences with Clint. Gasping for breath, she wanted desperately to take in deep gulps of air, but there was no time to undress and loosen the corset.

"Lacey?" He walked to her and gently touched her hair.

"It's Rand. I shot him."

"What!"

"In the square. Oakes chased me." She panted, then continued, "I came to get my gun. And you. Then the law." She turned from him, fumbled through a drawer, and pulled out her father's pistol. Checking to make sure it was loaded, she traded it for the derringer.

"Lacey, tell me exactly what's happened."

"No time. I left Rand alone. Oakes'll go back and move him." She grabbed Clint's arm and started tugging him toward the door. But he resisted, and she looked up at him in surprise. "What's wrong?"

"We can't get the local law."

"What!"

He clenched his fists. Finally, he had to tell her the truth. There was no time to do it right, but he didn't dare do it wrong, either. At the moment, she was more important than Rand or Oakes or even the United States Army. She came first, but he didn't know how to tell her he was a damnyankee. "Lacey, sit down."

"Sit? They're getting away." She looked wild, then confused, then concerned.

"I've got something to tell you."

"Tell me later. We've got to get the law and they'll warn the doctors in town. That way he can't escape, don't you see? Or maybe Oakes hasn't moved him yet. Or maybe somebody heard the shot and sent for—"

"Sit down, please."

She had a sudden sinking feeling in the pit of her stomach. "You're one of them, aren't you?"

"Yes."

"Oh, no! A Raider. I was right at the train. Why did you trick me? I don't understand. Yes, I do. This has all been to keep me out of the way, off Randolph's back. But the shoot-out with the

293

Raiders? No, I don't understand. Wait, maybe Rand wanted us to get rid of his outlaws. Yes, that makes sense." She paused to catch her breath.

"Lacey, stop it! I'm not a Raider."

"No?" She frowned, looked even more confused, and finally sat down, setting her reticule and her father's pistol on the desk. "I think I'm going to be sick. I think I don't understand anything. All I ever wanted to do was catch Randolph." She took quick, shallow breaths. "So, who are you, Clint? I take it I'm not going to like the answer."

"We can't go to the local law because I'm overseeing this case for people who want it handled quickly and quietly. In fact, Randolph is their problem and they want to deal with him themselves."

"You're working for underground Rebels? Why would you think I'd hate that? Even if you're outside Union law, you're still helping Southerners."

"I'm helping Southerners, but Randolph is a soldier, still a member of the United States Army, and they want him brought to trial in their own court."

"In that case, I can understand." She spoke cautiously, with great control, as if waiting for the next blow. "But local law would turn him over to Union forces, wouldn't they?"

"If a lynch mob didn't get him first. Former Rebels, Southerners in general, will want Randolph's head. Here, now. Not back East. Besides, the Union wants to show it can clean up its own messes."

"But, Clint, what does this have to do with you? Why are you working for the Union Army?" She felt sicker by the moment. "Did they force you to work for them when you were held captive? Are they holding some of your relatives hostage?" She stood up and walked over to him. Touching the scar on his face with a gentle finger, she added, "We've all done things we aren't proud of to get through the bad times. I'll understand and help."

Almost unable to stand her tenderness, her sympathy, her understanding, he jerked away. "No, Lacey, none of those are my problem. The fact is" —and he slanted a glance at her—"I'm a Northerner, born and bred."

Silence reigned absolute over the room. Lacey's eyes widened, her eyebrows rose, but other than that she simply stared at him in shock. Slowly, her speech returned.

"You . . . you're a Yankee?"

"Yes."

"But your accent?"

"Remember, I have relatives in southern Alabama. I spent a lot of summers there when I was growing up."

"Still you fought for the Union?"

"Yes. My father's land was up North."

"Even now you're working for them?"

"Yes, I'm part of the United States Army."

Suddenly, tears brimmed her eyes. "You're hateful! How could you betray me so? You're the enemy. You helped kill the Confederacy. Men like you murdered my parents, my friends, destroyed my home. And you're down here now, just like the carpetbaggers, to feed off what little is left."

"That's not true, and I didn't mean to hurt you."

"Oh, no! Certainly not. That's why you never told me. That's why you led me on. Well, I won't count on you for anything else. You . . . you damnyankee! I'll finish getting Rand and Oakes on my own. Traitor!"

Flinging a look of pure hate and fury at him,

she ran across the room. As she fumbled with the lock, he grabbed her arm to stop her. But she jerked free, then opened the door and slammed it shut behind her.

Lacey heard him open the door and start after her. But she didn't look back. Retracing her earlier steps, this time she ran, heedless of what anyone thought, for she was driven now more than ever before by the need to get Randolph behind bars. She would see that he went to a Southern jail and got Rebel justice, not some Northern hand slapping for being a naughty boy.

And as for Clint McCullough being a damn-yankee, she couldn't think about that at all. Wouldn't think about it. There had already been too much pain in her life, and this was simply something she couldn't handle.

Terrified Clint was going to catch up and stop her, she rushed past people in the lobby. Slamming out the front doors, she totally concentrated on getting a carriage and escaping. But before she could call the doorman, who was helping a lady from a coach, a large hand clamped over her mouth and she was jerked back into the shrubbery, kicking and struggling to get free.

Chapter Twenty-four

Furious with herself for forgetting the danger of Oakes, Lacey struggled in his arms, but he was even bigger and stronger than she had thought. Before she had a chance to scream, he tied a handkerchief around her mouth to gag her, then hoisted her over a shoulder as easily as he might have a feather. Even though she beat on his back and kicked out as best she could, it seemed not to bother him in the least.

He stayed in the shadows of the hotel, then ran for the cover of the square. Once there he stayed off the paths, keeping to the darkness of the trees and shrubs. With a firm grip on Lacey, he ran to a side street where he had left an enclosed carriage. He tossed her inside, then pulled off his belt and bound her hands behind her. Slamming the door shut, he stepped up to the driver's seat and urged the horses forward.

Lacey struggled to sit up, unable to see much in the darkness. Desperately trying to free her hands, it seemed impossible in the wildly careening coach. Suddenly, she heard a groan near her and looked around. Rand! Shivering, she worked even harder at her bonds but realized she wasn't going to be able to get free.

Trying to keep her balance, she turned her back

to the door and moved toward it. If she could get the door open, she would throw herself out the moving carriage as soon as it slowed. She might get hurt, but anything was better than being held prisoner.

After several tries, she finally released the catch and pushed the door slightly open. Turning around, she looked downward. The ground was moving by in a blur and she realized for the first time just how fast Oakes was driving them. She didn't think she could survive that type of fall, but he had to slow down to take a corner and that was when she would jump out. Waiting, she heard another groan. Why hadn't Oakes taken Rand to a doctor, especially since he had to be losing a lot of blood?

Finally, the coach slowed abruptly. Lacey was thrown forward, and by the time she righted herself, the vehicle was pulling to a stop. There was no time to lose. She jumped and tried to roll, felt one foot take the brunt of her fall, then lay still. Free. Glancing around, she saw Oakes had driven them to the river. He was probably planning to take Rand and escape by sea. She had to get away fast.

Rising, she stepped away, felt pain shoot up her right leg, almost fell, then bent down, breathing evenly as she tried to control the pain. But she was still wearing the corset and deep breaths were impossible. When she escaped, she would never wear a corset again. This time when she rose, she put her weight on her left foot and began quietly limping toward the shadows of a nearby building.

Suddenly, she heard the carriage stop, a door slam, then footsteps run in her direction. She had no doubt Oakes had discovered her escape, and Lacey had no place to hide. Hobbling as fast as she could, she felt a hand clamp down on her shoulder.

"You're trouble," Oakes said, then tossed her over his shoulder again.

Full of frustration and fear, she looked up at the sky, hoping for a storm. If it got bad enough quickly enough, they wouldn't be able to put out to sea and perhaps Clint could find her. When she thought of him she wanted to cry. A Yankee! Yet she wanted his arms around her right now more then anything else in the world, even though she didn't know how she could betray her family, her heritage in such a way.

She reminded herself that he was a Yankee, that he had betrayed her. She couldn't depend on a Northerner for anything. And yet no one else knew about Rand and Oakes, or that she had disappeared. Suddenly, she realized how foolish she had been because she had been so sure that good would triumph over evil. She should have known better. Randolph's Raiders had burned and looted and murdered, and nobody had been able to stop them until she and Clint had come along. But their luck must have run out.

She was alone, wounded, and held captive by men who had no mercy. Yankees. And then she thought of Clint. It was very difficult to classify him the same as Randolph. Difficult? It was impossible. Could there be more than one kind of Yankee? Could Clint have been telling the truth that he and his government were trying to catch Rand? It did seem to be true, but at the moment she was so distraught she didn't know if she could trust her own thoughts, much less anyone else in her life.

Oakes took her on board a tugboat, dropped her to the deck, and tied her feet with a length of rope. As the wind rose, the boat pitched harder, and lightning flashed closer and closer, followed by loud bursts of thunder. She watched the storm, knowing it was the only thing that could keep her from being taken from Mobile. She wanted it to arrive fast, but it seemed to be setting its own pace, which for her was much too slow.

She watched Oakes as he lifted Rand from the carriage, then sent the horses clattering away from the dock. She had to give the man credit, for he seemed to be efficient as well as resourceful. Where had he found a carriage and a boat in the short time she was in the room with Clint? But that time hadn't been as short as she'd intended, then again maybe Rand and Oakes had already planned to leave that night by boat.

Once more she tried to get free, thinking that if it would only rain, she might be able to unbind her hands and feet. Several large drops hit her face, then nothing more. Frustrated, she struggled, but it did no more good than it had before. Her ankle throbbed, but she didn't think she'd broken anything when she jumped.

Oakes strode on board, carrying Rand. He didn't waste even a glance at Lacey. Instead, he went below deck and came back a moment later without the outlaw leader. He untied her feet, then pushed her toward the stairs leading downward. She stumbled, and he shoved her forward. Tumbling down into darkness, she hit her head, shook it, saw flashes of light, then was jerked to her feet by Oakes.

He half carried her into what appeared to be the captain's quarters. A lantern hanging from the ceiling had been lit and it swayed with the rocking of the boat. Rand had been laid on the single bunk against one wall of the small area.

"Fix Randolph." Oakes untied her hands and took off the handkerchief.

"What do you mean?" She played dumb.

He pinned her with a hard stare. "On riverboat you fixed McCullough."

"But he wasn't hurt badly." Now she knew Oakes had been standing in the shadows watching everything.

"You doctor people. Fix Randolph."

"Really, I don't—"

"No choice."

"I don't have my bag. Besides, he'll probably need a hospital and—"

Oakes grabbed her shoulders and lifted her feet off the floor. "Listen good, woman. You hurt Rand. You fix or you die."

"But without my bag—"

He sat her down, went to a nearby table, and came back with her medicine bag. Thrusting it into her hands, he frowned.

"How did you get this?" She couldn't stop her hands from shaking even as she held the bag against her breasts.

"Rand planned to take you with him tonight, no matter what. Got you some clothes, too."

Even though it was hot and muggy in the small cabin, she felt chilled. She had vastly underestimated her opponent, and now she was paying for it.

"You fix Rand."

"Let me look him over and I'll decide if he needs to go to a hospital."

"No hospital." He turned around, left the room, and closed and locked the door.

Oakes wasn't going to let her out or near a hospital. He'd said her life depended on saving Rand, but could she do it without help?

Glancing at Rand's still body on the bunk, then back at the door, she made a quick decision. She tried the door, but it didn't open. Furious, she beat upon it, then cried out, calling for help over and over, hoping somebody might be in the area and hear her. Then she heard Oakes start the steam engines. They were loud. Nobody would hear her now.

Frustrated, she turned back into the room. Her

301

ankle still throbbed, but she could walk on it better. Looking at Rand, she decided there was nothing else to do but try to save the life of the man she hated more than anybody in the world.

Pulling off the emerald ring and the gloves, she tucked the ring inside one, then pushed the gloves into a pocket, hoping nobody would notice her birthmark. She sat down on the edge of the bunk as she felt the tugboat pull away from the dock. As the pitch of the boat increased, thunder rumbled and finally rain began to fall in loud, heavy drops as it hit the boat. But that wasn't going to help her now.

The light wasn't very good, especially with it swaying to the pitch of the boat, but she was determined to do her best anyway. When she pulled Rand's jacket open, she was surprised to see her blue silk shawl wrapped around his middle. It had soaked up a lot of blood, which wasn't a good sign. Carefully pulling at it, she raised him slightly and slid it free. Dropping the shawl to the floor, she turned back to him.

He'd started bleeding again, but she could tell the derringer shot hadn't hit any vital organs. The bullet had gone to the side, pushing through muscle, fat, and perhaps nicking a rib. But she had to know if it had lodged or gone out the other side. She wished desperately for better light, a stable working situation, and a hospital. But that was more useless wishing, just like she wished to be free, and it did no good.

Turning Rand on his side, she felt the wound. The bullet hadn't gone through. If she didn't remove it, he would die of infection. She needed to cut, to explore, to find the bullet, then pull it out. She expected to find it lodged next to a rib. It was a difficult injury, but not bad in comparison to what she'd seen in the war when men had walked in drag-

302

ging legs that had festered until there was no hope of saving the limbs and maybe not the men themselves.

But that was the war and this was now. The wound was fresh. There'd been no time for infection. And he was unconscious. Those were all positive conditions. On the bad side, he'd lost blood, and she had poor lighting, a rocking surface, limited equipment, and no help.

She inhaled sharply and glanced down at her bloody hands. She needed water, hot water. Or whiskey. She packed the shawl back onto the wound to staunch the flow of blood. Standing, she almost lost her balance due to the pitch of the boat, then walked over to a built-in cabinet. Checking several drawers, she finally found a nearly full bottle of whiskey, and she gave silent thanks to the unknown captain.

Looking down at her violet gown, she shook her head at its sad shape, knowing it would never be the same again. But then so much would never be the same again. Clint. No, there was no point in thinking about him. Somehow, she had to get herself out of the mess she was in. She believed she could save Rand, and if he still wanted her, he would keep her alive. Eventually, they would put into port somewhere, then she could plan her escape.

But for now she had a job to do, a life depending on her. She sat down beside Rand. He groaned, moved slightly, then fell silent. She pulled away the shawl, then poured whiskey over the wound and her instruments. Finally, following the line of the bullet, she cut, enlarging the hole, seeking the bullet near a rib. Luck was with her, for she didn't have to search long, and bracing herself against the pitch of the boat and Rand's involuntary movements, she got it out.

The bullet looked deceptively small and innocent lying in the palm of her hand, but she knew better. Putting it in her bag, she decided to attempt a few stitches. It wouldn't be a neat job, but anything was better than nothing. Again she cleaned the wound with whiskey, then bracing herself, she sewed it closed, holding Rand still when he groaned and tried to rise.

Finally, she was able to apply a healing salve, then wrap the area with a thick bandage. Moisture dripped from her forehead as she cleaned her instruments with whiskey, then put them away. She also washed her hands with the liquor, then folded up the shawl Sarah had given her and tucked it in her medicine bag. Closing her bag, she stood up and carried it back to the table. She sat down, feeling drained and exhausted. She had no idea how much time had elapsed, but the room was stifling and smelled of blood.

She wanted desperately to get away. Thunder crashed outside and rain lashed the boat, and soon she wondered if they could survive the storm.

After a time, Rand groaned, coughed, and tried to sit up. Too weak and disoriented to move, he lay back down but turned his head to look about the cabin. "What happened?"

"I took the bullet out of you. You should be in a hospital, but Oakes is taking us somewhere in this tugboat."

"Storm?" He coughed once, then held the spasms as pain wracked his body.

"Yes. I hope we make it to land."

"Oakes is good." He panted. "Where's the whiskey? I can smell it."

"It'll help dull the pain, but I don't know if it's good for you right now."

"Damn it, bring me the bottle." He took several shallow breaths. "And don't think I've forgotten

304

what you did, woman."

"I haven't forgotten your crimes, either."

"Shut up and bring that bottle."

She was quite aware he couldn't do anything to her in his condition, but she also didn't want him or Oakes any madder than they already were. Carrying the whiskey over to him, she thrust it at him. "Here."

His hand shook as he reached for it, but he got a good grip around the bottle anyway. Tipping it to his mouth, he upended the whiskey, letting the liquid flow through his lips and down his chin. After a long moment, he lowered the bottle, cradled it against his chest, and sighed.

Moving back to the chair, she began to think about escape again. Perhaps she could overpower Oakes when he returned. No, that'd never work. Maybe she could hit him over the head from behind. But he was so tall she wasn't sure she could reach up that high. Besides, Rand might warn him. Then she heard snores coming from the bunk and decided Rand might not be a problem after all.

The storm raged around them and she clung to the table, wondering if Oakes would make for land in Mobile Bay or risk taking them out into the Gulf. There was no way to know from inside the tiny cabin, but the longer they traveled the more she feared their fate.

Finally, she felt the tugboat shudder as Oakes docked it, then cut off the engines. Now was her chance. She quickly searched the area for a weapon but found nothing. She would have to use whatever was at hand.

As she heard Oakes unlocking the door to the cabin, she knocked out the light and grabbed the chair. As he opened the door, he was silhouetted by lightning streaks across the sky. Then all was darkness again.

"Don't play games." He stepped into the room and shut the door behind him.

She crept up and hit him over the back with the chair. He bent under the impact, but as she fled for the door, he grabbed her arm and jerked her back. Slapping her across the face, he knocked her against a wall. She slid downward, stunned.

He opened the door, letting in the flash of lightning, glanced at her, then picked up Rand. Closing and locking the door behind him, he left her behind.

After a time, she shook her head, heard a ringing in her ears, and felt a constant pounding. She stood up uneasily, knowing she had to escape. But the boat rocked on its moorings and she suddenly realized Oakes might have left her there to die at the will of the storm. She tried the door, couldn't open it, then pounded on it with her fists.

It was jerked open and Oakes stood there, lightning flashing and thunder booming around him. She stepped back, but he grabbed her arm. Holding on to her, he picked up her medicine bag, then dragged her up the stairs.

The storm was fierce. She could hardly see anything for the hard-hitting rain, the debris stirred up by the wind, and if not for Oakes holding her steady, she would have been blown off her feet. She thought he must have somehow found his way to an island in the Gulf, but she couldn't tell for sure.

He pulled her past trees bent low in the wind, the rain drenching them, the thunder shaking the ground, while the lightning illuminated a cottage up ahead. When Oakes thrust her inside, shutting and locking the door behind them, she stood still, her head still ringing from the slap and the sound of the storm.

Glancing around, she tried to pull her wits together. They were obviously in someone's vacant summer cottage. Rand lay quiet and still on a day bed in one corner. Oakes shook the water from his hair and clothes, then leveled a fierce look at her.

"See to Rand. So long as he lives, you live." He began prowling the place.

There was no point in arguing, so she pushed her wet hair away from her face, rearranged the clips holding it back, then looked down at her gown. It was completely ruined and heavy with water. No longer concerned with modesty, she quickly slipped off two petticoats and dropped them in a corner. Now, although still wet, at least she could move around better.

She checked Rand and he seemed to be doing fine. In the kitchen area, she found dry cloths and used them to wipe off his face, head, and the bandages covering his wound. But she detested touching him.

Suddenly, he woke, shook his head, and grabbed her wrist. "Whiskey."

"Did you bring it?" She looked at Oakes.

He nodded, then picked up the bottle from a pile of clothing and other things he had brought in and dumped near the door. He handed the whiskey to her.

She gave it to Rand.

Taking a long draw, he leaned back, watching her with narrowed eyes. "So you're still with me."

"Oakes thinks it's a good idea."

"Right."

"You're better, then?"

"Yes." He glanced at Oakes, then back at her. "Get those pillows behind my back."

As she made him more comfortable, allowing him to sit up with his legs stretched out on the day bed, he judged her with cold, black eyes.

And again she wished for Clint. He had come South to capture and stop Randolph and his

Raiders, while Rand was determined to continue killing. Even though Clint was a Yankee and had betrayed her trust, she realized she still loved him, for he was her soul mate, the man she had visions of in danger just as her mother had foretold. She was sad and happy at the same time, but above all she was afraid she'd never live to see Clint again.

Suddenly, Rand grabbed her left wrist and pulled her hand to his face. Horrified, she closed her hand, realizing she had forgotten to put her gloves back on. He tried prying her fingers open but she resisted.

"Oakes, I want to see her palm."

It took the big man only a moment to open all her fingers, and there lay the spidery birthmark for all to see.

Rand screamed in rage and flung her hand away. "A Whitmore! I thought I got all of you back at your cottage. But somehow you survived and followed me. Now I know why you asked about the ring."

"It is my birthright," she replied calmly, knowing it was secure in her glove inside her pocket.

"Birthright!" He staggered to his feet and pointed at her. "You're going to die like your kin, but it's going to be slow and painful." He glanced over his shoulder at Oakes. "Tie her up."

"Why do you hate the Whitmores? What did my family ever do to you?"

"I hate all the doctors who helped the Confederates, because they prolonged the war. Your cottage was the worst, giving Rebels hope and a place to recover. Without people like you, the war'd have been won by the Union in months and some of my kin would have been left alive." Drained of his energy, he abruptly sat down, clutching his wound.

Oakes grabbed her and began tying her up.

Once more she struggled, even though she knew

it would do little good in the end.

"I made all you dirty Rebels pay." Rand's eyes were wild as he remembered. "I got your money and I burned Whitmore cottage. Now you'll suffer, too."

She raised her chin in defiance as she stared Rand straight in the eyes. He would never win, for there were plenty of safe houses left, plenty of Southerners who would help the wounded, returning former Confederates making their way home. But she would take that knowledge with her to the grave, if necessary. "You've lost, Randolph, even if you don't know it."

Rand grinned. "Go ahead, defy me, but I promise to break you before I let you find your peace in death."

And Oakes threw her to the floor.

Chapter Twenty-five

Clint stood on the prow of a tugboat, battered by the storm. He could see little in front of him except crashing waves, stinging rain, and wild lightning. Thunder crashed and rumbled all around. He held on tightly, determined not to give up till he'd found Lacey.

He was still shaken by the vision he'd had of her pulled off a tugboat onto an island and forced inside a small house. In his mind he continued to hear her screams of pain, only now they weren't as real as they had been in the sudden, overwhelming vision he'd had on Mobile's docks when he was searching for her. Even now he found it hard to believe he'd been touched by the Whitmore legacy, but he couldn't think of any other reason for the sudden vision of Lacey in danger unless it was simply his own terrible fear for her.

Still cursing himself for not catching up with her in time, he thought back to when he'd seen Oakes grab her. He'd almost caught up with them in the square, but Oakes had surprised him by having a carriage nearby. Left standing with no way to follow, he'd run down the street until he'd found a horse. Stealing it, he'd started off, sure he could catch up with them. But the animal had thrown a shoe and he'd had to run the final distance to the docks.

Feeling the rain sting his face, he didn't even bother to protect himself as he thought about how he'd been unable to find Oakes's carriage. He'd asked up and down the docks, finding a few hardy souls staying with their boats through the storm. Finally, he'd found a captain who'd seen a tug put out to sea just ahead of the storm.

Something about that news must have triggered the Whitmore legacy in him, for afterwards he'd felt sure Lacey had been on that tug. Now the vision was all he had to go on, and he had an overwhelming fear that if he didn't reach her, soon she would be dead.

But nobody on the docks had wanted to go chasing out into the storm and he'd almost given up hope, when a crusty old sea captain had agreed after taking a hefty bribe. When he'd described the island and the house he'd seen in his vision, the captain believed it was Dauphin Island just off Mobile Bay in the Mississippi Sound.

Now Clint could only hope the captain was right, for there wasn't time to be wrong. As they sailed out of Mobile Bay, the storm began to abate and he breathed a sigh of relief. Now he would be able to watch for the island and the boat he'd seen in his dream. As the rain ceased, he searched the area, but the mouth of Mobile Bay wasn't the right place.

As he scanned the ocean for islands, he continued to hope the sea captain knew his way around the waters as he'd said he did. But either way Clint had to trust the older man's knowledge, for at this point there was no other choice. Yet if he were wrong, he didn't think he'd ever see Lacey alive again. And that thought was unacceptable.

Suddenly, he saw a large island ahead with a string of smaller ones running toward Mississippi Sound. Glancing back, he saw the captain nod and point at the island they were fast approaching. Dauphin Island. He scanned the coastline for the image he had seen in the dream, but nothing looked familiar. Perhaps they were too far away. But he felt his heartbeat increase and he clenched his fists, wanting the boat to go faster.

Soon the captain pulled closer to the island, then swung around toward the smaller islands nearby. Suddenly, Clint saw the scene from his vision, and he gave thanks to the Whitmore legacy or whatever had inspired his vision. Just ahead lay the tug moored on a low beach and the house was right up the sand from it. Lacey! He turned back toward the captain and pointed out the boat. But the captain had already seen it and was heading inward.

Not long afterward, the captain cut the steam engines and let his tug drift quietly on in to shore.

Clint hurried back to him. "I'm going in alone. Have you got weapons?"

"I've fought pirates and I've fought Yankees." He scratched his wiry beard. "I never go no place without a gun."

"The men in that house are Yankees and wanted by the law. I'm going in to get them. If they come out alone, will you stop them and take them in?"

"Figure you could use some help. I can go with you."

"They've got my fiancée. I'd rather have you here in case I don't make it."

He frowned. "Damn bluebellies. Sure, I'll get them. But the law ain't the same no more."

"Tell them it's Randolph and a Raider."

Clint didn't wait to see the expression on the captain's face, but as he walked away, he heard a string of imaginative cussing that put anything he'd ever used to shame. Swinging over the side of the boat, he waded through water to the shore. Pulling out the pistol he'd been carrying when Lacey ran away, he crept up to the house.

And heard her scream just like in his vision. There was no time now to try sneaking in to take them unawares. He had to stop whatever they were doing to her no matter the danger to himself. The beast in him took over. He shot the lock off the door and kicked it open. Holding his pistol before him, he stepped over the threshold to one side. And was filled with terrible rage at the sight before him.

Lacey stood in the middle of the room, her hands held behind her back by Oakes. Randolph, a bloody bandage tied around his stomach, was taunting her with a large knife. The bodice of her violet gown had been ripped to the waist, exposing her bare flesh above the corset. Bleeding cuts and scratches covered her breasts and arms, and her face was swollen and bruised on one side. Her dark golden hair was in a wild tangle down her back.

For a moment the tableau was frozen, for everyone was caught by surprise. But Rand broke the stillness when he suddenly whirled around to see who had busted through the front door. Oakes looked up, ready to pounce on the intruder. Clint wanted to shoot Rand, but the outlaw leader stood so close to Lacey he didn't dare for fear of hitting her.

Lacey took advantage of her captors' distraction and kicked back at Oakes. Grunting in surprise and pain, he released her and went for his rifle nearby. As Oakes raised his gun, Rand grabbed Lacey and put his knife to her throat.

Clint aimed at Oakes and fired. The bullet struck the man in the chest. Blood spurted outward as Oakes stumbled, then raised his rifle. Clint fired a second shot, again striking Oakes in the chest. Still trying to aim, Oakes went down on one knee then the other, blood spilling from his wounds. Finally, he fell over on his face, still grasping the rifle, and lay still.

"Throw down your gun," Rand commanded.

Clint decided Oakes was dead and turned his attention to the other outlaw. But he didn't let go of his pistol. He had three shots left.

"Go ahead, shoot her," Rand taunted, pressing his knife to Lacey's throat, "or throw down your pistol. I'm getting out of this stinking Rebel hellhole. And I'm going out alone."

Cornered, unable to see Lacey hurt any more, Clint dropped his gun to the floor, then waited for his chance to jump Rand.

"Your wounds," Lacey whispered, hardly daring to speak as the blade cut into her flesh. But she knew she had to distract Rand so she could somehow disarm him.

"You patched me up fine." Rand watched Clint. "I've got plenty of food and money on the boat." He took a quick breath as sweat beaded his forehead. "Maybe I'll build me a kingdom on one of these islands." The knife slipped in his hand, then he quickly pulled it back against Lacey's neck and drops of blood began to form. "The only people down here who know me are you two, and you'll be dead."

"You're not well. You need a doctor." Clint was afraid Rand would slit Lacey's throat before he could save her. "Take Lacey with you. She won't talk. You can't make it alone."

"Liars!" Rand panted. "I'll be free and you'll be fly food."

"You need help. Your wound is bad." Even though her words were true, Lacey was stalling so she or Clint would have a chance to overpower him. Then she felt Rand's body tremble, and she knew she had to take advantage of his weakness before he got Clint's gun and killed them both.

"Shut up!" Rand's breath was coming fast. "Kick

314

that pistol over here."

Clint did as he was told, watching the knife at Lacey's throat and nothing else. He didn't want to endanger her further, but he had to do something soon or it'd be too late.

"Okay, *Miss* Lacey, you're going to bend down with me so I can get that gun." Sweat ran down Rand's face. "Try anything funny and you're dead."

With blood trickling down her throat, Lacey knelt slowly, keeping pace with him. When he leaned forward, slightly off balance to pick up the pistol, she tilted her body so that he faltered and began to fall. She grabbed his hand holding the knife and jerked it away from her throat. They struggled for possession of the sharp blade, and he held on, pulling her with him when he fell.

For her, it was like the struggle over the derringer, and she didn't know who would win this time. But she couldn't stop, even though the cuts on her body had weakened her. They rolled back and forth, and his blood smeared her bare flesh. He was weakening, but so was she. She had to win. Suddenly, visions of Whitmore cottage burning, of her dead parents, of her murdered friends, filled her head, and renewed vigor and determination flowed through her.

Screaming, she rolled him over onto his back and, knowing just where his heart lay beating, wrested the knife from his hands and shoved it with all her might deep into his heart. And it beat no more.

Exhausted, she sat back on her heels and looked at Rand's still body. Tears stung her eyes. She'd killed him. Glancing down at the bloody knife in her hand, she began to cry.

Having retrieved the pistol, Clint tucked it into the front of his trousers, then gently raised Lacey to her feet. Pushing her hair back from her face, he kissed the bruise on her cheek, then took off his shirt and helped her into it. Blood from her wounds quickly soaked the fabric, but at least she was covered. Later he would burn the violet gown, for he never wanted to see it again.

"I killed him." Tears spilled down Lacey's cheeks as reality set in.

He pulled her close. "It's all right. You had no choice."

"But I'm supposed to save lives, not take them."

He set her slightly back so he could look into her eyes. "Lacey, listen to me. You can't blame yourself. Randolph killed hundreds of people. He killed your parents, your friends. He would have murdered you, me. You did the right thing."

"But I didn't want to hurt anybody."

"Sometimes we're forced to hurt others to save ourselves, but it doesn't make us guilty."

She bit her lower lip, then looked down at Rand's still body. After a long moment, she nodded, then raised her chin. "I suppose you're right." She wiped away the tears. "It's just that I believe it's wrong to kill."

"This killing was right, not wrong." He shook her slightly. "You must believe that or you can't go on." He squeezed her shoulders. "Do you hear me?"

"Yes." She looked down at herself. "They hurt me."

Clint crushed her to him. "Yes, they hurt you! Sometimes you're so innocent you're like a child. And they hurt many others, too. You did what you had to do and now they'll never hurt anybody again."

She nodded, looking better but still obviously stunned by the violence she'd endured.

He knew how she felt. Early in the war, brave young soldiers had worn that look after their first hand-to-hand battle. Killing a man from a distance was vastly different from killing him with your bare hands. But did it have to make you a beast? He'd thought it had, but looking at Lacey, he could only see beauty, pure, untouched, no matter what she'd just done.

Suddenly, he realized she'd always be a beauty, but perhaps he didn't have to be a beast, except when he needed to protect those he loved. That he could understand and accept. Beauty and her beast.

"Lacey, go outside and wait for me. I'm going to cover these bodies, then later I'll see the United States Army cleans up this mess."

"Please get my medicine bag." She put a hand on his arm. "It's all over, isn't it?"

"Yes. You're safe. Now wait outside."

Without looking back, she stepped from the cottage. The air was fresh and clean. She could smell flowers. The storm had passed. Although the sky was still gray, the clouds were moving away and it would be a beautiful day.

But Clint had just now been so brusque with her. Did he hate her for causing him so much trouble? Was he going back home now that his job was done? Was this the end of it all for them? Could the Whitmore legacy have been wrong?

Rubbing the birthmark on her left palm, she walked away from the cottage as she tried to outdistance the questions. She felt as if the woman who had vowed to get revenge for her parents was a lifetime away. But she'd done what she had set out to do and it wasn't pretty. In the process, she had been changed. There was no doubt in her mind now that there were good and bad Northerners, just as there were good and bad of all types of people.

Still, she had fallen in love with a Yankee. Her parents would have been shocked. But her mother would have told her to follow her destiny, to cling to her soul mate. Yet, what if that weren't possible?

Clint was a military man. He didn't need her. He had a job, another life.

Walking slowly down the beach, she felt weaker and weaker. She didn't want to go on without Clint, her Yankee love. Still, she was a Southerner, a former Rebel and Confederate. Thinking back to the initial glory of the Confederate States of America, she realized she was descended from romantics, people who were willing to give all for a cause, a belief, a way of life. A love. Could she suddenly do any less?

Smiling, she looked back as Clint walked out the door of the cottage. He was her man and she was going to fight for him. She walked quickly to him and flung her arms around his neck, then she kissed him long and deep and with no reservations.

When she raised her head, he looked at her in surprise. "I thought you hated me."

"Well, I never said you weren't a damnyankee. I just decided maybe you were worth keeping around." And she fluttered her eyelashes in a perfect imitation of a Southern Belle. "That is, if that Union Army doesn't own you body and soul."

Clint laughed, lifted her in the air, spun her around, then set her in front of him. "If you're not the damnedest woman I've ever known." He grinned. "But don't think those Southern Belle wiles will work on me. Remember, I know at heart you're an Iron Magnolia."

Glancing up at him from under her eyelashes, she said, "What did you say didn't work on you?"

He shook his head. "It won't be easy, but I can get stationed down here." He put an arm around her shoulders and drew her close. "I want to be part of rebuilding the South. Besides, my kin's in Alabama."

"I think you could help us all."

He gently touched the bruise on her cheek.

"There's a reward for Randolph and his Raiders. It'll be enough to rebuild Whitmore cottage, if you want."

She smiled. "Thanks. But right now I don't know. The South needs so many things. Perhaps a small hospital." She looked into the distance as if seeing the future, then suddenly she glanced back at him. "Are you always going to be part of the army?"

"No. I won't reenlist. I want to spend my days with you in the life we'll build." He took her hand, turned it over, and kissed the spidery birthmark. "Will you marry me, Lacey?"

Beaming, she clasped his hand. "Yes. But I was about to ask you since you were so slow."

"My Iron Magnolia. We'll build our own place, and we'll always be here for each other. . . ."

"In times of danger and in times of happiness, too."

"Yes. You know, that's how I found you. I had a vision."

"Oh, Clint! Now I know we're the truest of soul mates." She took the Whitmore heirloom ring out of her pocket and handed it to him.

And as he slipped the emerald ring onto the third finger of her left hand, the sun broke through the clouds and bathed them in pure golden light.